Praise for

Pack Discipline

'The Duty of a Beta' starts off with a sensual bang...an excellent read. I highly recommend it. ~ *Whipped Cream*

...admire how realistic Kim Dare had drawn this character to make me so mad at him, as if he were a real person... Kim Dare took the preconceptions about duty and love, and which partner in a D/s relationship is the one who stands up for the pairing, and turned them upside down ~ *Queer Magazine Online*

5 out of 5!... Kim Dare does an awesome job...has amazing characters whose flaws are actually their strengths. Kim Dare's Pack Discipline Series is definitely a series not to be missed.
~ *Dark Diva Reviews*

If you enjoy a good shape-shifter with hints of BDSM, then this well written and plotted story is for you. Read and enjoy.
~ *Literary Nymphs Reviews*

PACK DISCIPLINE
Volume Two

The Duty of a Beta

The Love of a Mate

KIM DARE

Pack Discipline Volume Two
ISBN # 978-0-85715-730-0
©Copyright Kim Dare 2011
Cover Art by April Martinez ©Copyright 2011
Interior text design by Claire Siemaszkiewicz
Total-E-Bound Publishing

Published in 2011 by Total-E-Bound Publishing, Think Tank, Ruston Way, Lincoln, LN6 7FL, United Kingdom.

THE DUTY
OF A BETA

Dedication

To falling in love with the right person,
even when you don't realise how
right they are at the time.

Chapter One

Gunnar registered the sound of running water just a moment too late. Steam swirled around the hot, humid little space as he pushed open the door and walked into the bathroom he was temporarily sharing with several other members of the pack. He was just about to take a pace back, close the door behind him and wait for the other wolf to finish his shower when he realised who was standing under the spray.

There was no step back. Gunnar froze as he ran his gaze over the slim frame that had been drawing his attention ever since he joined the pack.

Talbot blinked rapidly, no doubt in an effort to clear the water from his big, blue eyes. Bubbles from the soap he'd been lathering himself with continued to conceal parts of his torso for a few seconds, but they quickly slipped away under the force of the water. The omega was left entirely exposed to Gunnar's inspection.

Damn, but he was stunning. And, somehow, while he stood in the shower, he looked far more naked than he ever had at those times when he'd just switched back into his human form and hadn't had time to get dressed. He seemed far more naked than the beta was himself.

Gunnar looked down for a moment, eager to see if the little wolf had been doing more than washing under the hot spray.

No, Talbot wasn't even hard. Gunnar tried not to wish he'd taken an even longer route on his run and arrived just a few minutes later, when perhaps the omega would have been in the middle of something more interesting.

Dragging his gaze back up Talbot's body, Gunnar met the smaller wolf's eyes. Talbot immediately dropped his attention to the shower room floor, quick to show all due respect for their respective ranks within the pack.

That was exactly what he should do. It was precisely what Gunnar should *want* him to do. Still, he couldn't help but think that a few moments in which he could admire the younger man's eyes wouldn't have been such a terrible thing.

Shaking his head and forcing himself to snap back into the real world, where there were far more important things for a beta to think about than pretty blue eyes, Gunnar reached for the door handle. He stopped with his fingers wrapped tightly around it as the omega stepped towards him.

"You can..." Talbot waved a hand towards the shower. "I'll wait until after you've finished."

Gunnar remained motionless for several long seconds as the steam rushed past him out of the room. He should leave. It was far too tempting for him to linger in the naked omega's presence. Gunnar knew that. Yet, somehow, he still found himself stepping into the bathroom and closing the door behind him, sealing them in the small space with the heat and vapour from the shower completely surrounding them.

Talbot swallowed rapidly as Gunnar silently stalked towards him. It was hard to believe that he wasn't already regretting inviting his pack mate to take his place. As Gunnar moved past Talbot and stepped under the shower, the little wolf retreated several paces, putting himself well out of range of the cascading water.

Folding his arms across his chest, the omega seemed to do his best to blend into the stark white tiles that covered every wall of the wet room. As if there was any chance they could share any space without Gunnar being acutely aware of exactly where the smaller wolf was!

Gunnar tilted his head back and let the water run through his hair. After all the rain that had fallen over the last few days, his run had left him streaked with dirt. The water turned muddy as it ran down his body and swirled around his feet. The warmth of the hot spray quickly sank into muscles that ached after so much exertion out in the cold, and sent a shiver of pleasure running down his spine.

As he reached for the shampoo, Gunnar glanced towards Talbot. He was just in time to see a far less enjoyable shudder run through the smaller man's body. Gunnar's eyes narrowed.

"Talbot."

Maybe it was the displeasure in his tone, or maybe it was just his voice in general, but the omega damn near jumped out of his skin at the sound of his own name.

Gunnar bit back a curse. Anyone would think he'd threatened to hang, draw and quarter the guy on a regular basis — that he hadn't actually gone out of his way to be kind to the omega ever since he joined the pack.

Nervous blue eyes blinked up at him from beneath a damp, blond fringe, but the little omega didn't say a word.

"Come here," Gunnar ordered.

Talbot slowly did as he was told, closing the gap between them with all the enthusiasm of a man who really did think he was heading for a noose.

Finally he stopped in front of Gunnar, just out of range of the spray.

"There was something you wanted?" Talbot asked, as the silence finally seemed to become too much for him to bear.

You!

Gunnar managed to bite the word back, but having to keep the truth inside his head did little for his temper. A growl emerged in its place.

He wanted Talbot. He wanted him facing the wall, with his hands braced on the pure white tiles, his legs spread and his back arched as he eagerly offered his arse to his more dominant mate.

Gunnar's hand tightened into a fist at his side. Well, he wasn't going to bloody well get what he wanted, so there was no point daydreaming about it.

Catching hold of the smaller man's shoulder, he dragged him under the shower. The little wolf gasped. He stumbled. Reaching out, he instinctively sought to brace himself against the tiles as he struggled to keep his footing. His hands skidded against the slippery surface.

Gunnar lurched forward. His arms quickly slid around the smaller man's body, holding him upright, instinctively seeking to keep him safe.

Talbot looked up over his shoulder and at him in confusion.

Be careful what you wish for, some sarcastic little part of Gunnar's brain piped up. *You just might get it!*

He had the omega against the tiles, exactly where he'd said he wanted him. But he couldn't do a single bloody thing with him now that he had him there.

"I wanted you to get back under the water before you froze to death," Gunnar snapped, as he snatched his hands away from the other man's skin and took half a step back. "What did you think I wanted?"

Talbot swallowed again, his Adam's apple bobbing rapidly with his obvious nerves. "I thought, maybe…"

He took his hands away from the wall. Either obedience or an instinct to prevent hypothermia made him move to stand properly under the hot water.

"You thought?" Gunnar prompted as he glared down at the omega.

A blush rose to Talbot's cheeks as the hot water slicked the pale blond strands of hair back from his face.

"Answer the question," Gunnar ordered.

"I thought perhaps there was something you wanted me to…" Talbot whispered. "I know in some packs…" He wrapped his arms around his body again, and there was no way in hell it could have been because he was still cold.

Gunnar's eyes narrowed once more. "What do you think happens in 'some packs'?"

Talbot shrugged.

Gunnar folded his arms across his chest. It couldn't have been a more different gesture from the way Talbot habitually hugged himself. Planting his feet firmly on the floor and stationing himself blatantly between the lower ranking wolf and the door, Gunnar didn't have to say a word to make it completely clear that they would stay exactly where they were until he got his answer.

"I…" Talbot cleared his throat and tried again. "I know that an unmated omega is sometimes considered to be…useful to the other unmated wolves in the pack," he stuttered.

Gunnar opened his mouth. He closed his mouth. No words emerged. If Talbot hadn't kept his gaze so firmly on the floor, he'd have seen his beta do a bloody good impersonation of a goldfish.

As he fought for the right words, Gunnar strove to push down his anger at the accusation. Talbot really thought he would…it would be little better than…

Gunnar lowered his gaze slightly as he ground his teeth together and struggled to keep his temper in check. The thoughts racing around his head suddenly froze solid.

The other wolf hadn't been hard when Gunnar first walked into the room. He had no doubt about that. The omega had been entirely soft while he stood shivering on the other side of the room, too. But now, Talbot wasn't getting scared by the idea of the big nasty beta pouncing on him and forcing him to submit to whatever he wanted to do with a man too small and too weak to fight back. He was getting turned on.

Gunnar's frown deepened as he looked back up to the omega's face and met his eyes. Talbot tried to look respectfully away, but, before Gunnar could even think about what he was doing, he had a tight hold of the younger man's chin. "Look at me!"

Confusion flashed across the omega's face as he looked everywhere but at Gunnar. "I don't understand, I—"

"Do as you're told," Gunnar bit out. "I won't take it as a challenge."

Talbot slowly obeyed the command. Scared blue eyes met Gunnar's. For the first time, Talbot held his gaze as several silent seconds passed. His jaw moved under Gunnar's touch as he swallowed rapidly, as if his nerves were close to getting the better of him.

Still not at all inclined to relent, Gunnar kept him there, making him keep his eyes up, until he was sure he had the best possible read on what the other wolf was thinking.

There was fear in him, but it didn't seem to be anything more dramatic than the base level mild panic that the other wolf seemed to spend his whole life paddling about in.

"You told me once before that omegas like to be useful."

Talbot nodded.

Suddenly, Gunnar couldn't help but wonder if the omega had been talking about the duties each member of the pack was assigned after all.

Reaching for the shelf, set in easy reach of the shower, Gunnar picked up a bottle of shower gel and pushed it into the smaller man's hands. "Make yourself useful."

Talbot looked from him, to the bottle, and back again, as if he really couldn't work out what the hell was going on or what he should do next.

His attention went to the bottle once more. Apparently working as much from muscle memory as anything else, he flicked open the lid and poured a small amount of the gel onto his palm. His hands were shaking. As Talbot reached out and put his fingers on Gunnar's shoulder, the beta could feel the younger wolf's touch trembling against his skin.

He made no mention of that fact as Talbot careful caressed his way down the outside of his arm, slowly working the shower gel into his skin.

It had been a long run, and he hadn't bothered to stick to the cleaner paths. There was still plenty of mud clinging to him, even after he'd been under the spray off and on for several minutes. Talbot frowned slightly as he rubbed at Gunnar's skin a little harder.

His tongue flicked out against his bottom lip as he seemed to focus in on the task he'd been assigned and forget everything else, even his own anxieties.

Gunnar glared down at him, more than a little bit enchanted by the simple submission in the smaller wolf's every movement. He had an easy, natural way about him, now that he seemed to be doing something other than panicking.

When Talbot's hand suddenly left Gunnar's body without his permission, the beta's first instinct was to catch hold of Talbot's wrist and pull him back where he belonged. He only just managed to keep that desire in check. His restraint was quickly rewarded when Talbot failed to retreat any further than the shelf where he'd left the shower gel. Pouring some more onto his hand, he worked it into a lather between his palms.

Talbot glanced back up at Gunnar, as if asking for permission to resume his task.

The beta nodded.

Reaching up, the smaller wolf set both his hands on Gunnar's shoulders and slowly massaged the lather down his chest. His movements seemed to grow more confident simply because no criticism was offered. Within minutes, he appeared to be enjoying himself a great deal.

Talbot never once looked up, but right then Gunnar wasn't sure if that was because he was submissive as hell or if the omega was just appreciating the view just as much as Gunnar was enjoying studying the other wolf's naked body in return.

He really was gorgeous. As Talbot's hands wandered over him, Gunnar had no way of hiding how his body responded to the other man's touch. His shaft was soon just as hard as the omega's cock, and curving back towards his stomach just as enthusiastically.

Talbot blinked rapidly as he seemed to notice that for the first time. His tongue flicked out to lick his lips.

Alfred.

Some annoying little part of Gunnar's brain repeated the name over and over inside his head, screaming that he should be looking at Alfred that way, that he should be sharing the shower with Alfred and he should be wondering what Alfred would do if he stepped forward, pinned him to the tiles and claimed him with a kiss.

Gunnar took a deep breath. He tilted his head back, letting the hot spray run over his face in the vain hope it might wash through his mind, too, and somehow clear the persistent fantasies of the omega out of his head.

The hot water failed to cool his lust in the least.

As Gunnar looked back at the omega, he found Talbot staring up at him with something dangerously close to hero worship in his eyes and what couldn't be anything but desire in his scent. Even the torrent pouring down over them couldn't disguise a wolf's scent that much.

Helpless to resist him a moment longer, Gunnar took half a step forward. He only just had time to catch a brief glimpse of the surprise that flashed across the omega's face before he brought their lips together.

Hot and strong and perfect—and so much better than anything Talbot had been able to imagine when he lay alone in his bed and tried to guess what it might be like to feel the beta's mouth against his.

As Gunnar's tongue swept past Talbot's lips and demanded entry to his mouth, the omega's hands grappled at the other wolf's shoulders. Gunnar was so much taller than him, he'd had to dip his head into what had to be a very uncomfortable angle to kiss him. Talbot quickly stretched up onto his toes in order to make their mouths meet more easily.

Suddenly the larger man stepped forwards and Talbot found his back pressed against the cold, wet tiles. It wasn't just their mouths that touched then. Gunnar's body pressed against him everywhere.

Talbot's cock rubbed against the other wolf's bare skin again and again as the beta pinned him against the wall with his whole body. A whimper echoed around the bathroom, a soft, pleasure filled, needy little sound that could never have come from Gunnar.

Another whimper escaped from the back of Talbot's throat. He'd never even realised he could sound like that before, but now that the ability had been unearthed, it was impossible for him to keep the little whimpers and moans back from the wider world.

The beta's tongue danced against his, seeming to purposely coax more and more desperate sounds out of him with each second that passed. The beta even encouraged Talbot to kiss him back, but he never went so far as to give up the lead to him.

Talbot had no doubt that Gunnar had scooped up every ounce of control that existed and claimed possession of each and every bit of it for himself the moment their lips met, and he couldn't have been happier about that.

Talbot's hands fumbled against the other man's shoulders, clumsily trying to pull him closer, to get more of anything and everything the other wolf was willing to offer him before the beta had a chance to change his mind.

Suddenly Gunnar growled against his lips. The next second, strong hands were wrapped around Talbot's wrists. His fingers were jerked away from the beta's skin so quickly shock ricocheted through Talbot's body. He gasped as Gunnar pressed his wrists against the tiles on either side of his head.

The beta's growl turned to a pleased, triumphant little noise as Talbot instinctively tried to move his arms, failed, and quickly fell still. A shot of pure bliss raced through Talbot's veins as he realised that he'd somehow stumbled onto an action Gunnar approved of.

The larger man took another half a pace forward, but Talbot's back was already to the wall. There was no way he could retreat. All he could do was spread his legs slightly and make room for the other man's feet between his.

The new arrangement once more brought his cock into intimate contact with the beta's thigh. Talbot moaned his pleasure as the water-slicked skin teased the tip of his erection.

"Please," he whispered, as Gunnar briefly broke the kiss.

The request was greeted by a new growl, but Talbot couldn't look down and display his submission the way he usually would. He couldn't have turned his lips away from the possibility of another kiss if his life had depended on it.

After so many months of watching the beta, and of hating himself for hoping that Gunnar might glance in his direction rather than Alfred's, he wasn't capable of turning away from anything the older man was willing to offer him.

Gunnar rocked his hips slightly, twitching his leg between Talbot's thighs and teasing his shaft. Talbot's hands clenched into fists above the beta's hold on his wrists. He whimpered and squirmed against the tiles, desperately trying to work out how to complement the other man's movements as bliss rushed into his body and his moans mingled with the sound of the shower still pouring down around them.

Instincts that Talbot had never explored slowly made their way to the surface. His body began to move in perfect counterpoint to Gunnar's. Water ran over him, teasing his skin wherever it wasn't pressed tightly against the other wolf's larger frame. Every inch of him sung out in pleasure as the more dominant wolf deftly took possession of his whole body, and with it a little part of his soul.

Whimpering into a new kiss, Talbot frantically tried to hold back as he felt himself rushing towards his orgasm. It was impossible to stop his ascent towards pleasure. He needed to come so badly and the pressure built quickly inside him, doubling over and over again.

Pulling at Gunnar's grip on his wrist, he tried to free his hands, to slow them down just enough for him to be able to scrape up a little bit of control.

The beta would be angry with him if he came before they could even mate properly. And he didn't want Gunnar to be angry with him. Talbot needed Gunnar to be pleased with him so badly he could barely breathe through his desperation. He needed the wolf he—

Talbot didn't even have time to finish the thought. Gunnar's grip tightened around his wrists, his growl vibrated against his lips and he casually threw Talbot over the edge he'd barely managed to scramble back from a few seconds earlier.

Pleasure tore through the omega, deeper and hotter than anything he'd ever felt while experimenting with his own hand. Suddenly he found himself trapped in a cascade of ecstasy that was capable of searing its way through his mind and branding the deepest part of his mind.

Gunnar swallowed Talbot's howl, muffling the sound with his lips. Then, just a second after Talbot fell still, the beta broke the kiss. Gunnar tossed his own head back, but he remained completely silent as he came. The beta was just as in control of himself as he was of Talbot—maybe even more so.

Talbot had to blink water out of his eyes, and even then his vision seemed muzzy with afterglow, but there was no denying that the beta was glorious. Talbot stared up at him, completely entranced.

Gunnar's muscles tensed, his hips thrust forward again, rubbing his cock against Talbot's hip. Cum splashed against him as Gunnar came, but the water quickly washed it away. With his hands still trapped against the tiles, there was nothing Talbot could do but helplessly watch it disappear under the force of the spray.

Gunnar didn't disappear though, the beta was still there and his body was still pressed against Talbot, holding him against the wall.

When Gunnar looked down he caught Talbot staring up at his face. For a few seconds, his expression was unreadable. Then, without any warning, Gunnar pulled away. Talbot thought he caught a fleeting change of expression, before a wall seemed to go up behind the older man's eyes.

Talbot looked down. He'd been right to try to hold back, and so very wrong to give in to the temptation of his own release. The other man was angry with him, so obviously disappointed in his lack of control. He'd had one chance to impress the other man and show the beta he could please him, and he'd ruined it.

The breath caught in Talbot's throat as regrets rushed through him fast enough to make his head spin. There was no way Gunnar would want him to be available to him again now. He wondered for a second if admitting his complete lack of experience would convince the other wolf to give him another chance, or if it would be another black mark against him in Gunnar's book.

A movement out of the corner of his eye caught Talbot's attention. The beta was reaching for the shower gel again. Talbot watched as the older man poured some onto his own hand before silently offering the bottle to him.

Talbot automatically followed the more dominant man's lead and copied the other wolf's actions.

Gunnar worked the gel into a lather between his palms. Talbot did the same.

Part of him had hoped that perhaps he'd feel the beta's hands on him, and that he'd be allowed to finish washing the other man too, but when Gunnar turned his attention to his own body Talbot didn't have the courage to do anything but do the same thing himself.

They showered next to each other, sharing the spray without exchanging another touch or a single word. When Gunnar was finished, he quickly moved out of range of the water and snatched up a towel. Talbot lingered under the heat for a little while longer, not sure what the beta would prefer him to do.

The older man briskly dried his body, rubbing the rough towelling against his skin and his hair as if nothing at all unusual had happened while he was in the shower.

Talbot couldn't help but stare, couldn't do anything other than glory in every glimpse he was permitted of the other man's body in a moment that seemed curiously intimate and private.

He was so scared of doing the wrong thing, the omega did nothing, until Gunnar finally tossed his towel into the hamper and strode out of the room, shutting the door behind him without ever looking back at him.

Talbot closed his eyes as he found himself alone once more. He stood there perfectly still and silent for several long seconds before he was able to convince himself to reach out and turn off the taps.

The silence that filled the room after the last few drops of water fell was almost deafening. Talbot reached out and touched the wall behind the shower, stroking his fingers across the tiles Gunnar had held him against as they...

A blush rose to Talbot's cheeks as he lowered his gaze.

Turning away from the wall, he swiftly dried himself off and hurried back to his bedroom to get dressed. Just as he suspected, he'd spent too long daydreaming after the beta left. He was the last wolf to arrive at the breakfast table and it was impossible for him to take his place without his tardiness being noticed.

Bennett frowned slightly as he spotted him sneaking in late, and Talbot was well aware that the alpha's attention was still on him when he rose from the table at the end of the meal.

"Talbot."

Stopping halfway across the room, en route to leaving his plate by the sink, the omega turned to face his alpha.

"Is everything okay?" Bennett asked as he reached his side.

Talbot nodded.

Bennett didn't look at all convinced.

Talbot scraped up a half-smile to go with another nod. "I just ran late," he whispered.

The alpha smiled then, as if he understood what was going on. Reaching out, he ruffled Talbot's hair as he walked past him with his own plate. "Well, don't worry about that. There's no harm done, is there?"

Talbot shook his head.

"Go on," Bennett allowed with another smile. "See to your duties."

Leaving his plate next to the others on the counter ready for whichever wolf was on kitchen duty that day to attend to, Talbot quickly made his way upstairs as most of the other wolves left the house to take care of that morning's tasks outdoors.

The laundry hampers in the bathrooms were all heavy and cumbersome, and most of them were full to the brim. Decanting some of the contents of the first one into a smaller, more manageable basket, Talbot gradually took the first few loads of washing down to the old pantry, off the kitchen.

Working methodically and almost entirely by rote while his thoughts persistently strayed back to his time in the shower, Talbot began to sort the clothes into various piles and load the first batch into the machine.

The sound of the whirling motor soon took over the room. The contraption was old. It tended to sound as if it would explode at any second, but that day, Talbot barely spared it a glance before he picked up his basket and went to fetch more laundry from the upstairs rooms.

He was halfway through retrieving the contents of the various hampers when the first load finished. Pulling it all out of the machine, Talbot dumped it in another basket. The weight of the water made the clothes much heavier than they had been when they were dry. Talbot's shoulders protested as he heaved the wicker carrier towards the door.

A glance into the kitchen showed Steffan was still at the sink, just finishing with the first of his chores that day. The larger wolf quickly dried his hands and strode across to take the basket from Talbot when he spotted him.

Giving it up without a fight, Talbot meekly followed Steffan out into the garden at the back of the farm house. The sun was shining. It wouldn't take long for the clothes to dry, but Talbot couldn't spare much thought for the weather. He wasn't even sure he'd have noticed if the rain was pouring down around them.

He looked in every direction and peered around every corner they passed, but Gunnar was nowhere to be seen.

"Are you okay, Tal?"

Talbot jumped as he spun around to face Steffan. The bigger wolf was standing patiently at one end of the washing line, holding the basket for him.

Rushing to catch up, Talbot quickly picked up the topmost item of clothing, snatched two wooden pegs from the bag attached to the basket and hung it up. "I'm fine."

"Are you sure?" The gamma pushed, very gently.

Talbot nodded.

"Do you want me to finish up with this while you take a break?" Steffan offered.

Talbot shook his head slightly.

"Maybe—" Steffan began.

"Is Francis okay?" Talbot rushed out, eager to distract the other wolf before he somehow guessed that he was thinking about having sex with their beta. If there was one thing that was always guaranteed to do that, it was his mate.

True to form, Steffan smiled at the very mention of Francis. "He's fine. He's gone into town with Caden to fetch some supplies. Gunnar said it would do us both some good to stop living in each other's pockets every second of the damn day."

Talbot felt the heat rush to his checks at the sound of the beta's name. Keeping his head down, he took another garment from the basket of wet clothes and reached up to hang it a little further down the line.

"Are you sure you feel okay? You look like you might be coming down with something." Steffan set down the basket and pressed the backs of his fingers to Talbot's forehead. "You don't feel too hot… "

"It just gets warm sometimes, lugging all the baskets and things around," Talbot hedged.

"Do you want me to speak to Gunnar about assigning a lighter set of duties to you?"

"No!" Talbot's eyes opened very wide at the idea of anyone speaking to Gunnar about him. He cleared his throat as he rushed across to pick up another shirt from the pile in the basket. "I…thank you, but you don't need to do that. I'm fine. I don't have any problem with any of duties I've been assigned."

Steffan retrieved the basket from the ground and held it for him, so he wouldn't have to bend down to pick up each item. He was silent for a few moments, and Talbot almost started to believe that he had lost interest in the subject.

"How are you getting on with Gunnar?"

Talbot held back a sigh and stared very hard at the next shirt as he hung it out. "Fine," he whispered, not entirely sure who he was trying to convince. "We're getting on fine."

His cheeks immediately went hot again. He was pretty sure it was only his new-found interest in hiding his face behind the wet clothes he was pegging out that stopped Steffan trying to take his temperature again.

Chapter Two

Gunnar strode through the kitchen. His head was bowed and all his attention was on the notebook in his hand as he set off to check up on the gammas he'd ordered to begin work on the fencing around the far field. With any luck, Alfred would be in one of his less bratty moods and he'd actually have done some work rather than skived off or wound up the wolves he was supposed to have been working alongside.

Halfway across the room, Gunnar glanced up. He stopped short as he spotted Steffan standing in front of the duty roster he'd pinned to one of the cabinet doors. Apparently unaware he was being observed, the hulking great gamma reached for the pen hanging from the length of string tacked up next to the roster.

"Do you remember what happened last time you tried messing around with the duties I assigned to the wolves in this pack?" Gunnar asked.

Steffan looked over his shoulder. There was far less guilt in his eyes than Gunnar would have expected. The beta leant slightly to one side in an effort to peer past the larger wolf's shoulder and see what Steffan was trying to reassign Francis to this time.

He frowned as he realised that Francis' wasn't the name the pen had come to rest alongside.

"Talbot?" Suddenly, Gunnar found himself across the room, glaring at the gamma from just an inch or two away from the end of the other man's nose. "Why are you so interested in him?"

Steffan blinked. "What?"

"I know what it means when you start trying to move someone to different duties!" Gunnar bit out. "You did exactly the same thing with Francis. And I'm still waiting for an answer — what is your interest in Talbot?"

Steffan looked from him to the duty roster and back again. "Francis is my mate... " he said slowly, as if trying to work out what the hell was going on and failing miserably.

Yes, you've got the mate you wanted. Stop sniffing around mine. Gunnar growled as he pushed the words down. "That's not an answer."

Steffan turned completely away from the cabinet to face him properly. "I wasn't changing anything. I was checking what Talbot's duties are for the rest of the day. He seemed out of sorts this morning. If he's coming down with something then Francis and I could —"

"Then it's still not your place to counteract the orders I give any of the wolves in this pack," Gunnar snapped. "If you have concerns about the work I assign someone, you bring them to me, no one else."

Especially if it's about Talbot. He barely kept those last words back either, but even if he hadn't said them aloud, they were true. At least part of him found it impossible to believe anyone else had a right to look after the omega.

When their eyes met, Steffan quickly lowered his gaze, but Gunnar still had time to see his confusion.

The beta didn't know why that should surprise him. He was already well aware he was making a bloody fool out of himself. "Go," he barked.

Steffan turned to leave. He was at the door leading out into the courtyard when Gunnar called out to him again.

"Where's Talbot?"

"I think he's in the laundry room," Steffan said, turning to face him again. "I was just going to check on him when—" The gamma cut himself off, as he seemed to sense that Gunnar was willing to be damned before he'd give him leave to do any such thing.

Luck had already put him between the oversized gamma and the door leading towards Talbot. Gunnar folded his arms across his chest and let his body language speak for him until Steffan finally turned and left the kitchen without any further protest.

Gunnar didn't linger a moment longer than was necessary to see Steffan safely out of sight. All thought of checking up on Alfred and the other gammas abandoned, he strode towards the utility room door and threw it open.

The little wolf jumped as the door banged into the work bench behind it. The sheets he'd been putting into the machine fell in a messy heap at his feet. He turned his head and looked towards Gunnar. The blood actually seemed to drain from his face right before the beta's eyes.

"Steffan said you were ill," Gunnar informed him, as he closed the door, in an effort to give them some semblance of privacy.

Talbot shook his head. Unfurling himself from where he'd been crouched down in front of the washer, he straightened up to his full height, such as it was, but he didn't lift his gaze from the piles of fabric that seemed to litter the entire floor. Stepping over the confusion of laundry, Gunnar moved to stand directly before him.

The omega looked as if he might hyperventilate at any moment. Gunnar tightened his hand into a fist at his side, trying to resist the temptation to reach out and touch Talbot. He had no business touching him—not then, and not when they'd shared a shower either.

Alfred—that's who he should be concentrating on. Gunnar knew that as surely as he knew his place in his pack and what his alphas expected their newly acquired beta to do.

Except, Alfred wasn't Talbot and... Gunnar bit back a frustrated growl as it threatened to escape from the back of his throat.

"I can do better," the omega suddenly blurted out.

Gunnar frowned down at the smaller wolf. "Better?"

Talbot glanced up at him for just one brief moment. All Gunnar caught was a tiny glimpse of big blue eyes before Talbot's lashes dipped back down and hid them away again. "In the shower this morning... " he whispered.

"What about it?" Gunnar demanded.

The omega flicked out his tongue and moistened his lips, making it near impossible for Gunnar not to wonder what it would feel like if the little wolf was lapping at his cock instead of his own mouth.

"If...if you did want us to... I could do better next time."

Better... Gunnar stared down at the smaller man in silence for a long time, trying to wrap his mind around what Talbot seemed to be trying to tell him, what he appeared to be attempting to offer him.

"If you'll tell me what you like, then maybe..." Another brief sight of those pretty blue eyes was offered to Gunnar.

Brief wasn't enough. Gunnar tucked a knuckle under Talbot's chin and forced him to tilt back his head and look him properly in the eye.

"I know," Talbot whispered. "I know that when you're mated to Alfred, it'll be different, that we couldn't... But maybe until then..."

Heat rushed to Talbot's cheeks, making him look far healthier than he had when Gunnar first walked into the room and far more innocent than a wolf who was offering himself to another man that way should ever be able to appear.

"That's what you want?" Gunnar asked, his tone far harsher than he intended.

"I..."

That tongue was so wasted on caressing Talbot's lips, no matter how dry with nerves they might be. The beta bit back the urge to howl his frustration.

And in that moment, when he had no choice but to face the fact that there was no way he'd be allowed to keep what he wanted permanently, it was impossible for Gunnar to do anything but lower his head and bring their mouths together while he still had the chance.

Talbot gasped his shock into the kiss, but he made no move to push him away. The little omega tilted back his head to give Gunnar the best possible access to his mouth. At the same time, Talbot's hands remained at his sides, leaving his body completely available should Gunnar want to reach out and touch any part of him he might desire.

He couldn't have formed himself into a more perfect little parcel of natural submission if he'd tied a damn bow around his neck. A frustrated growl rumbled through Gunnar. That wasn't what he was supposed to want. He was supposed to want a challenge, to relish having a brat to tame. He was supposed to want Alfred.

Talbot pulled back. A startled, little whimpering sound escaped from the back of his throat in response to the growl.

Gunnar's hands quickly wrapped around Talbot and stopped the smaller man's retreat. One palm settled on the back of the omega's head, fingers threading quickly into the short blond strands and taking a firm grip on them.

His other hand slid around Talbot's body and pressed against the small of his back, dragging him forwards, pulling their bodies firmly against each other. At the same time, Gunnar dipped his head and brought their lips back together in an instinctive effort to reassure.

The idea of Talbot being scared of him turned Gunnar's blood cold, even as it made his heart race painfully fast behind his ribs. Talbot should never be scared, or hurt, or worried about anything. Gunnar knew all of those things without even needing to think about it. The knowledge was there, right in the centre of his soul.

The depth and quality of Talbot's submission should be cherished and nurtured. It should be held tightly, and not by a gamma, but by a wolf who was dominant enough to really appreciate it.

Talbot's hands had moved too. Gunnar felt them come to rest against his shoulders, not pushing him away and not pulling him closer either. The omega's hands just lay against him, deepening the connection between them while still accepting whatever he should choose to do.

It took every scrap of self-control Gunnar possessed to pull away from the omega and break the kiss again. Lowering his head, he moved his lips to Talbot's ear.

"Whoever told you that your place was to be used and abused, to be screwed and cast aside by all the more dominant wolves in your pack was a fool." Gunnar's grip on Talbot tightened. A *fool* was the most charitable thing he could think of calling the sadistic little bastard. If he ever got his hands on the man who'd told him that...

Gunnar forced himself to temporarily push fantasies of revenge aside. There would be time enough for those when he didn't have a far more erotic reality in his arms.

Talbot made a soft whimpering sound as if he somehow sensed Gunnar's anger and had no idea that it wasn't directed at him. The omega moved slightly within Gunnar's hold. His body rubbed against the beta's larger frame with the motion, perhaps by accident, perhaps because something inside him thought that the best way to distract him from his fury was to redirect all his blood to his cock. It only took the slightest movement on the omega's part to have him hard and aching.

"Is that why you've looked so bloody afraid of me, ever since I joined the pack?" Gunnar demanded. "Were you afraid that I'd demand you let me screw you...?"

A moment of pure silence surrounded them. Talbot's chest stilled as he seemed to hold his breath in anticipation.

"Or were you afraid that I *wouldn't* demand that?"

"I..." Talbot murmured.

Gunnar pulled back, just far enough to look down into the other wolf's eyes.

His scent screamed his desire. But there was fear there too, and it was impossible for Gunnar to work out what the other man was really feeling. Talbot blinked up at him, his expression as confused as the rest of him.

"I don't demand sex from wolves who aren't interested in providing it," Gunnar informed him.

"I...I'm interested," Talbot blurted out. His eyes opened very wide, as if he was shocked at his own daring in admitting such a thing.

Gunnar continued to glare down at the other wolf. "It could only last until things are settled between me and Alfred," he forced himself to say. There could be no misunderstandings on that point. Sooner or later, he'd have to do his duty.

Talbot dropped his gaze before he nodded.

"Not good enough," Gunnar snapped. There was no way in hell a nod of the head could be enough to settle things between them.

"I..." Talbot swallowed rapidly as he met Gunnar's gaze with obvious effort. "I understand. I know what I'm saying yes to."

Did he? Gunnar hoped like hell that he did, because the longer he stared down at him, the more impossible it was for Gunnar to imagine himself ever turning away from him.

Dipping his head once more, the beta brought their lips back together. At the same time, his other hand slid between them to cup the omega through his jeans. Barely nineteen, and as inexperienced as hell, it didn't really take a master technician to have Talbot rolling his hips and thrusting eagerly against another man's palm.

Breaking the kiss, Gunnar gazed down, thoroughly enchanted by the simple honesty in the omega's reactions.

Letting go of the smaller wolf's hair, Gunnar covered Talbot's mouth with his palm as he walked him back and pressed him against the white-washed wall.

The omega's eyes flew open. Astonishment filled his expression. His hips bucked. Just in time, Gunnar's hand created a tight seal over his mouth and muffled the sound of the younger man's howl.

A few precious moments stretched out into something that felt more like a lifetime as he watched pleasure and amazement fly across Talbot's face. Even when the omega finally stilled, collapsing back against the wall, Gunnar remained exactly where he was for an extra few seconds.

His hand remained over the smaller man's mouth. Talbot sucked against his palm. His tongue lapped against his skin, stealing a taste of him. Still, Gunnar only intended to give Talbot permission to talk when he wanted to permit it, not just when he had finished howling. It was important that the omega realised the difference right from the start.

It was impossible to tell if it was that knowledge or coming in his trousers that made Talbot blush again. Either way, it was a pretty reaction and Gunnar had every intention of keeping that colour in his cheeks as often as he could. If the best way to do that was to remind the smaller man that he was under another wolf's control, then all the better.

When he finally released Talbot, Gunnar took a step back. The omega stayed where he was. That wasn't a bad thing. Gunnar wasn't even sure Talbot would be able to support himself if he did try to step away from the wall.

The only things that moved were the younger man's eyes. He looked in every direction and at everything in the room bar the wolf standing directly in front of him.

"Is there…what can I do for…?" Talbot trailed off as their eyes finally met.

Gunnar glanced to his left. The step back he'd taken provided him with a view through the small, high window that looked out of the laundry room over the fields. The sun was high. The other wolves would soon be making their way back to the house after completing their morning duties.

What he wanted Talbot to do for him and what there was time for Talbot to do for him were two very different things. Gunnar held back a groan of pure frustration as his cock pleaded with him for release. There was barely even going to be time for what *needed* to be done with Talbot. He'd just have to wait.

Snatching a pair of Talbot's trousers off the top of one of the piles of freshly washed and dried clothes, Gunnar tossed them to the omega. The younger man wasn't so fuddled with afterglow that he couldn't catch. His brain however, seemed to be far more affected than his reaction times. He blinked at the garment in his hands as if he had no idea what to do with it.

"The others will be back soon. Get changed," Gunnar ordered.

Talbot lifted his gaze. He stared at the beta for several long seconds as the other man's words completely failed to register in his mind. Finally he managed to look back at the trousers.

Get changed. The order made perfect sense. The trousers he was wearing were already feeling more than a little sticky and uncomfortable. For some stupid reason, he still found himself standing there like an idiot, unable to move a single muscle.

"Talbot!" There was an impatient little snap to the beta's voice which kicked Talbot back into action.

Blushing more furiously than ever Talbot reached for his fly, but his hands didn't want to work. His fingers were clumsy. The top button wouldn't come undone.

Without any warning, bigger, stronger hands pushed Talbot's fingers aside. Gunnar made quick work of the fastening. Within moments, Talbot's trousers were down around his knees and Gunnar was holding onto his arm, helping him kick off his shoes so he could step out of the tangle of material.

Snatching his trousers off the floor, the beta tossed them onto one of the loads of clothes still left to be washed. It was the wrong colour pile. If they were left there, the dark blue denim would turn all the whites grey. Standing half naked in the middle of the room, Talbot decided he didn't need to point that out to the other man right then.

He glanced across at the sink in the corner of the room instead. "I should probably…"

Gunnar didn't seem to be listening. He didn't step back to let Talbot pass so he could clean himself up the way the omega expected he would. He moved forwards and put his hands on either side of Talbot's waist.

Talbot let out a startled little gasp as the larger man picked him up and sat him on the old work bench that ran along the wall opposite the washing machines. A large palm came to rest on Talbot's chest and nudged him to lie back on the bench, still naked from his waist down.

"What are you…?" Talbot trailed off as it quickly became obvious that the other man still wasn't listening to a word he said.

Lacking any way to influence what happened next, all Talbot could do was watch in silent fascination as Gunnar lowered his head. A dart of pink was his only warning before the beta's tongue licked its way along his softened shaft.

Talbot jerked at the first intimate touch of the other man's mouth. Gunnar's only response was to settle his hands more firmly on either side of Talbot's torso and pin him down more determinedly against the battered work top.

Talbot's hands rushed to the other man's shoulders in return. His fingers slid against Gunnar's shirt as he whimpered.

It was too soon for him to take any real pleasure from the attention being paid to his cock right then. His shaft was far too sensitive, the tip too tender. Talbot's head dropped back against the hard bench. His teeth bit into his bottom lip as he tried to hold back a moan and failed. He managed to lift his head and look down his body just as Gunnar glanced up.

The beta was just licking him clean, Talbot told himself, that was all. It shouldn't feel like the most amazing thing he'd ever experienced. It shouldn't be enough to make him really glad that he'd come in his jeans either.

Talbot was sure he should feel silly and embarrassed and a million other terrible things, but with Gunnar's grip on his hips so tight it was turning his skin white around his fingertips, it was impossible for him to feel anything except...

Talbot dropped his gaze, but the thought was still there in his head. It was impossible to feel anything except as if, for the first time in his life, he was right where he belonged—because he knew without any doubt that Gunnar wouldn't tolerate him being exactly where he wanted him.

Talbot whimpered again as the beta's tongue moved swiftly against him in agile, confident licks as it made its way over his crotch. The omega's hands fisted in Gunnar's shirt. The beta ignored that as much as he ignored his murmurs and moans. There was nothing Talbot could do but accept whatever attention the other man wanted to bestow upon him until the beta finally straightened up.

Even as he let out a breath he hadn't realised he'd been holding, Talbot found himself entirely unable to release his hold on the other wolf's shirt. He was dragged into a sitting position as the older man pulled away, but the beta made no complaint about that. He let Talbot keep hold of him as he picked up his clean pair of trousers and put them on him without a word.

By the time their eyes met, Talbot was once more neatly dressed. He was reasonably sure that he looked as if nothing out of the ordinary had just happened. Appearances could be so deceptive...

"You don't want...?" Talbot asked, with as much strength in his voice as he could muster.

"There's no time," Gunnar informed him.

Talbot looked down, trying to hide his regrets as best he could. It seemed more and more likely that the beta wasn't as interested in an omega lover as Talbot had hoped he might be.

"But there will be time, later," Gunnar added.

Talbot blinked up at him. Later... Later, he'd be allowed to... His breath caught in his throat.

Gunnar hooked a finger under Talbot's chin and demanded he look up. Their lips met. For the first time, Talbot tasted his own cum on another man's tongue. He leaned quickly into the kiss, eager for more. When Gunnar suddenly stepped back, he almost fell off the counter top.

The beta only remained close for long enough to make sure he didn't actually collapse in a messy heap on the floor before he half smiled and strode out of the utility room into the kitchen.

Stopping only to move his trousers to the appropriate pile and bury them in between enough other garments that he could be sure the cum stains wouldn't be noticed, Talbot hurried after him.

He entered the kitchen just in time to see the alphas walk in through the door leading in from the courtyard.

Marsdon had his arm around Bennett's shoulders. They were laughing with each other, leaning in to each other's touches.

That's what it was like, being mated to someone. Talbot had come to understand that as he watched the other wolves in his pack. It meant having someone who was the other half of you so thoroughly it was impossible to imagine being with anyone else. It was perfect and special, and it was silly for an omega to think that he was going to be chosen by a wolf like Gunnar to—

"Talbot?"

He looked up.

Marsdon beckoned him across to the counter and handed him the cutlery. He ruffled Talbot's hair as he stepped past to pick up one of the platters of food that had been laid out on the counter top. Talbot managed a smile as he tried not to regret the way the alpha had casually wiped away any lingering sensation of Gunnar's touch.

Stepping carefully in between the other wolves as everything was brought to the long pine table that filled the left hand side of the kitchen, Talbot let the noise and the fuss of a dozen men float over him. Laughter, teasing, bickering and everything else wasn't relevant. He only had room in his head for one wolf.

Finally taking his seat, Talbot found he'd been placed next to Caden that day. The pretty young wolf immediately looked from him to where Gunnar sat opposite them, and back again. Caden's eyes narrowed, as if there was a big flashing light above both their heads proclaiming exactly what they'd been getting up to that morning.

Gunnar's brother seemed to have lost all interest in his food. When Caden's attention moved to Alfred, Talbot felt the blood drain out of his face.

"Stop being a brat, Cade," Gunnar muttered, half under his breath, as he leant forwards in his seat so only Talbot and his brother would hear him.

"I didn't say anything," Caden pointed out, perfectly mildly.

"Keep it that way," Gunnar ordered, just a little louder.

"Play nicely, children," Bennett advised from further down the table. The hint of warning in his tone made it clear he'd caught those last few words. "If you start to squabble at the dining table, you'll end up going hungry."

All the pack fell silent as they turned their attention to the food, but Talbot was well aware that Caden and Gunnar hadn't actually stopped glaring at each other across the table. The brothers were good at relaying silent messages to each other — messages no other wolf in the pack could quite understand, even if they did manage to catch a fleeting glimpse of one of them.

Talbot could barely drag his gaze away from the staring match for long enough to take more than the occasional bite of his own food. His nerves were fraying by the time he heard one of his alphas clear his throat.

"Gunnar," Marsdon began.

Talbot's attention was already on the beta. He saw Gunnar give his brother one last glare, before turning his attention to his alpha. "Yes?"

"The dry stone wall bordering the north field. Bennett and I inspected it today. Can you rearrange the duty roster and free someone up to rebuild it as soon as possible?"

Gunnar nodded. Talbot continued to study the beta in fascination, his fork halfway to his mouth, as the older wolf stared down at his plate as if mentally running it all over in his head. The second Gunnar looked up, their eyes met.

"Talbot can do it."

Talbot blinked at him. He was vaguely aware that the whole table had once more fallen silent around them, but he was too busy trying to work out what the hell was going on to take a great deal of notice.

"I could do—" Steffan began from somewhere near the other end of the table.

He stopped abruptly when Gunnar turned his head in that direction, his expression making his feelings on the suggestion quite clear.

Once he seemed sure the gamma was appropriately cowed, Talbot saw the beta turn his face towards the alphas.

"Are you sure you've made the best choice?" Bennett asked him.

Lowering his gaze, Talbot quickly turned all his attention to pushing his food around his plate. He knew, just as all the other wolves in the pack had to know, that he wasn't the best choice—not for re-building a wall, and not for so many other things. Gunnar could have his pick of wolf for either.

Talbot closed his eyes for a moment. All he wanted to do was jump up and rush out of the room, to hide from the facts of his station in the pack in a way he'd never needed to before. Gunnar didn't need an omega for *anything*. The knowledge sliced deep into Talbot's chest, as if it really was trying to cut his heart out.

"He's the right choice."

Talbot's head jerked up. He stared, wide-eyed, at the beta for what felt like several consecutive eternities. He was sure he couldn't mean that, that there would be a 'but' added to the sentence at any moment.

"I'll take him out there and show him how to start re-building it tomorrow," Gunnar said. He seemed to look from one of his alphas to the other, then back again. "With your permission, of course?"

"What do you say, Talbot? Do you think you can do it?"

Talbot heard Marsdon's words, but he couldn't tear his eyes away from Gunnar.

The beta had picked him. He'd had his choice of all the wolves in the pack. They all knew that Marsdon and Bennett had given him free rein to assign the duties however he saw fit. There was no need for Gunnar to pick him, but he had.

And it simply wasn't in Talbot to let the other wolf down, no matter how strong his own doubts about his suitability for the task might be. His need to please Gunnar overruled everything right then, his alphas' concerns, the rest of his pack's obvious doubts—it even overruled reality.

"M...May I try?" Talbot managed to turn towards Marsdon. He met his alpha's eyes for a second before quickly dropping his gaze in due deference.

He looked back up just in time to see Marsdon and Bennett exchange a glance he had no way of interpreting. They were just as good at silent communication as the brothers were.

Talbot could only hold his breath and hope, as Marsdon raised an eyebrow at the other alpha. A second later, Bennett half smiled. He nodded his decision.

"If you want to try, you have our permission," Marsdon confirmed. "Gunnar can work on it with you tomorrow and decide if you want to take on the rest of the project tomorrow night."

Talbot nodded his understanding. He glanced at Gunnar just in time to see the beta do the same.

He was going to do the work Gunnar wanted him to do... He was going to spend tomorrow with the beta...

Talbot took a deep breath as he smiled down at his plate. He wasn't sure which fact pleased him more.

The idea of so many hours spent alone with the beta, in a part of the pack's lands that were far enough from the farm house to mean they'd have relative privacy. That alone had his heart racing so fast his hand shook as he tried to lift another forkful of food to his lips. The possibility of being able to prove to the other members of the pack that Gunnar had made the right decision when he chose him for the task made his stomach turn over with nerves.

There was a slightly odd atmosphere around the table as the meal continued. Conversations gradually started up around them once more, but Talbot could only bring himself to be half aware of that, and couldn't convince himself to worry about it at all.

"Have you finished your morning's duties, Talbot?" Bennett asked, as they all rose from the table and those on kitchen duty that afternoon began to clear the plates away.

"I'm halfway through what I'm supposed to do today," Talbot agreed, cautiously. "I'll make sure I've finished everything before tomorrow." There was no way in hell he was going to let anything stop him being there with Gunnar, not when the mere thought of it already had him half hard inside his newly-donned pair of jeans.

Bennett glanced around the room. "Francis." The other wolf strode across to where they were standing, near the utility room door. "Keep things ticking over until Talbot comes back," the alpha ordered with a nod to the laundry.

The gamma slipped through the door without a word. A second later, Talbot heard him emptying the machine of the load that had finished while they were eating.

"Follow me." Bennett walked out of the kitchen and into the courtyard. There didn't seem to be anything for Talbot to do but to trail along behind him as the alpha led the way to the wood pile at the back of the farm house.

Someone had obviously been working hard there earlier that day, but there were still several piles of logs laid out, waiting to be split. As Bennett took up the axe, Talbot automatically picked up one of the lengths of wood and set it on the chopping block, before stepping back out of the larger wolf's way.

One swing had the log cleaved neatly in two. Talbot quickly replaced it with another piece of wood and picked up the split halves, stacking them neatly with the others that were ready to be carried inside and set next to the hearth.

Several more pieces of kindling met the same fate before Bennett spoke.

"Have you ever tried your hand at dry stone walling?"

Talbot shook his head. He'd already put a log on the block, but Bennett didn't seem to have any interest in lifting the axe to chop it.

"I've never...the wolves who've assigned duties to me have never..." he dropped his gaze to stare at the length of unsplit wood some more. None of them had ever thought he could be capable of completing that sort of duty.

"No rank of wolf is born knowing exactly how to best fulfil his duties," Bennett told him. "The instinct may be there, but the brain sometimes takes a little while to catch up on the details. That's true for everyone. Marsdon and I had a few faltering moments too."

Panic clenched around Talbot's stomach. "If I'm doing something wrong..." he began, very softly.

Bennett shook his head. "You're doing fine. So is Gunnar," he added. "He's a good wolf—and he has the potential to be a good beta for our pack. But that doesn't mean every idea that comes into his head is a good one. He's still learning."

Talbot lifted his gaze for a moment and met his alpha's eyes.

"So, don't worry about tomorrow too much, okay?" Bennett said. "No one is going to be angry with you if it doesn't work out. The only thing that will happen is that Gunnar will move a little further along his learning curve as a beta. Next time, he'll make a better decision. No one will be disappointed in you, or him."

Talbot nodded his understanding. He loved both his alphas, he really did. But as the alpha's axe once more began to slice cleanly through every piece of wood in its path, he was sure he'd have felt a lot better hearing those reassurances from Gunnar rather than Bennett.

In that moment, he realised that the rest of the pack being pleased with him wouldn't mean a damn thing if the beta didn't feel the same way.

Chapter Three

"You can start here."

Talbot watched Gunnar pick up one of the big stones that lay strewn around on the grass surrounding the damaged section of dry stone wall. It had obviously been down for quite some time. Moss was starting to grow on some of the larger stones. Grass had sprung up around them and was hiding some of the smaller ones completely.

As much as he tried to concentrate on those chaste details, Talbot continually found his attention drifting back to the way the larger wolf's muscles moved beneath his shirt. Gunnar barely had to strain to lift the huge chunk of masonry. It was all Talbot could do to stop himself reaching out and tracing the lines of muscle with his fingertips as the other wolf strode past him.

"You'll need to clear the area first—it'll give you room to work, and let you see all your materials before you start trying to work out what stones you want to use where when you start rebuilding. For now, just set the larger stones here." Gunnar set the big stone down on the grass to the left of the damaged length of wall. "And put the smaller ones there." He tossed one of the smaller ones a little further away from the base of the wall to his right.

For several long seconds, Talbot could only stare helplessly at the task laid out before him. It was so far outside the experience he'd gained working on his usual duties, he didn't know where to start.

Gunnar raised an eyebrow at him. That prompted Talbot into action. The beta had just told him where to start. All he had to do was follow the other man's instructions. He could do that. Talbot quickly set about collecting up some of the smaller stones. He'd already moved most of them into the appropriate place when he realised that Gunnar had stopped working.

The other wolf was leaning against a section of the wall that was still standing firm a few yards away from that part that had fallen into disrepair.

Talbot glanced in the beta's direction. The larger man had his arms folded across his chest, his legs stretched out before him as he leant back against the stonework behind his hips. He looked so perfectly relaxed, so in control, and yet, at the same time —

"I didn't tell you to stop."

Talbot blinked and quickly looked away as he realised he'd been caught staring. He turned his attention to the ground around his feet. There were no small stones left to be moved. He looked uncertainly back at Gunnar.

"Try." It was nothing more nor less than an order, and the beta had been staring at one of the largest displaced stones as he said it.

Talbot considered the lump of rock very carefully. It was huge compared to the ones he'd just moved, but there didn't seem to be anything he could do but attempt to follow the command.

The edges of the nearly square block were just slightly weathered and rounded off. Talbot found he was able to get his fingertips beneath it. Doing his best to squirm his fingers further under, he attempted to rock it from side to side in an effort to get a better grip on it.

It weighed far more than any of the laundry baskets he'd carried around the house the day before. There was no way in hell he was going to be able to move it more than a few inches. And it was suddenly obvious that no one from the pack was going to turn up and provide him with a smaller stone the way they'd given him smaller, more manageable baskets the moment they saw him struggling.

Hauling against the solid weight of it, Talbot was determined to at least make sure that Gunnar saw that he'd tried to follow his order. If he had to disappoint the beta, he realised, he'd rather Gunnar hated him for being weak than for being disobedient.

The stone moved. Only an inch or two, but it did move. Talbot heaved again. Another tiny bit of progress was made. Taking a deep breath, Talbot put everything he had into his endeavour. Several inches of ground passed beneath the stone as Talbot finally managed to lift it completely off the ground and transport it what felt like a truly substantial distance closer to the place where Gunnar wanted it.

A feeling of success rushed through him as it suddenly seemed possible for him to please the other man. Taking off his coat, Talbot hung it over the wall and returned to his task with more determination than ever.

The stone wasn't very clean. By the time Talbot straightened up, having finally wrangled it close to where Gunnar had placed the other large stone, he was aware that both his clothes and his hands were liberally smeared with dirt from beneath the stone. The moss that had grown on the northwards side of it had been crushed against his body by his efforts, leaving green smears down his T-shirt.

But, when he looked across to Gunnar, the beta was...smiling?

Talbot held the other man's eyes for several long seconds. His breaths had been rushing into his lungs more and more quickly as he worked, but the next one he tried to take snagged in his throat. There was no doubt about it. The normally so serious beta was actually smiling at him, a real smile and not just that half twist of the lips he usually favoured the world with!

He continued to stare at Gunnar until the beta looked pointedly towards the other stones that needed to be moved. Talbot didn't even hesitate. Gunnar had smiled at him. The older wolf was pleased with him. Suddenly, fighting to move stones that were twice as heavy as anything any other wolf in the pack would have ordered him to tackle was the only thing Talbot could possibly want to do with his day.

Stealing occasional glances at Gunnar, and inevitably finding the beta watching over him with what felt suspiciously like ever-increasing approval, Talbot ignored the way his arms and his back began to ache. He paid no attention to the knocks and scrapes that flourished across his hands and forearms as he threw himself into his task with more enthusiasm by the moment.

The more work he did, the more pleased Gunnar would be with him and—

"That's enough."

Talbot set down the stone he'd been moving. "But I haven't finished..." he looked towards all the other stones that he still needed to transfer away from the base of the wall before he could start to rebuild it.

Gunnar shook his head. He reached into the backpack he'd brought with him and took out a bottle of water. Setting it on the ground by his feet, he nodded to the grass next to it. "Sit."

With one last, regretful glance at the remaining stones, Talbot did as he was told.

After digging around in his bag once more, Gunnar extracted another bottle of water and a large packet of neatly wrapped sandwiches that must have been provided by the wolf on kitchen duty that day. Sitting down next to Talbot, the beta silently unwrapped their lunch and handed him one of the sandwiches.

"Thank you," Talbot's words were more than a little hoarse. Quickly opening his bottle of water, he took several big mouthfuls of the refreshing liquid. After being left in the shadow of the wall all morning, it was gloriously cold as it slid down his throat, soothing and quenching him at the same time.

As he took the bottle away from his lips, Talbot leant back against the cold stone wall and turned to face Gunnar. He was just in time to see the beta take a long drink from his own bottle of water. His lips moved against the plastic. His Adam's apple bobbed as he swallowed it down.

All at once, Talbot was back in the middle of the thoughts that had kept him awake for most of the night. Only, in his fantasies, it was his mouth caressing the tip of the beta's cock. In his mind it was his throat moving over velvety soft skin, and it wasn't mere water he was swallowing down…

"You're stronger than any of them give you credit for," Gunnar suddenly announced. "You're not a pup. You're not an invalid. There's no reason for them to fuss over you the way they do, as if you'll break under the slightest pressure."

Talbot stared down at his sandwich for a moment, not sure he'd be able to look at the other man without coming in his jeans, let alone stare at him and think clearly at the same time. They weren't in the laundry room any more— he'd be stuck in his sticky jeans for the rest of the day unless he quickly learnt some control.

"You're better than that," Gunnar went on, apparently completely unaware of the thoughts running through Talbot's head. "Omegas aren't weak. They're submissive—there's a difference. It's time someone taught you that."

Talbot risked a glance at the older man out of the corner of his eye. Gunnar had pulled one knee up in front of him, and was resting his forearm on it. He was also staring back at Talbot very intently. It was the look in the beta's eyes as much as the way Gunnar's cock disturbed the denim covering his crotch that made Talbot sure he knew what was going to happen next.

His pulse began to race. He licked his lips as they went dry with nerves. Gunnar might not have realised what Talbot was thinking, but suddenly Talbot was completely sure the thoughts in the beta's head weren't all that different.

Gunnar was obviously capable of thinking about sex while talking about something else. The older man smiled slightly. Talbot had no idea why he should—unless, just maybe, Gunnar wanted him almost as much as he wanted the beta. Almost was as close as it would ever get, though. Talbot had no doubt it was impossible for someone to want an omega as much as he wanted Gunnar right then.

Water and half-eaten sandwiches quickly forgotten, the other wolf brought their lips together.

Talbot's eyes fell closed. His mind shut down. All that existed was the kiss as Gunnar's tongue slid past his lips and danced against his tongue. Talbot whimpered against the other man's mouth, desperately trying to keep up with the more experienced wolf's technique. It was impossible, but the attempt still sent pleasure racing around his body fast enough to make his head spin.

Gunnar's hands roved over Talbot's body, the beta apparently not the least bit concerned by the mud and dirt coating his clothes. Fireworks exploded beneath his skin wherever the older man caressed him, but all Talbot could do in return was cling helplessly to the larger wolf's shirt as he found himself rolled onto his back against the grass. Within seconds, he felt Gunnar's hand against his fly.

Yes!

Even as part of him whimpered with pleasure at the thought of imminent release, Talbot knew that he couldn't let that happen. Whatever else might occur between them in the shadow of the wall, it couldn't be that.

"No!" The word was half muffled by the kiss, almost unintelligible.

Talbot pressed his palms against the beta's shoulders, trying to push the larger man away from him. Gunnar's fingers continued to fumble against his crotch for several seconds, before he seemed to realise that Talbot was desperately trying to get his attention.

No?

It took far too long for the single syllable to sink into Gunnar's brain. Pulling back, he blinked down at Talbot, trying to make sense of the word.

The omega gasped for breath as he stared up at him, wide-eyed and gorgeous. Gunnar frowned as he pulled further back from the smaller man in an effort to make his brain think of something besides sex.

Gunnar shook his head at himself. He should know better than to pounce on someone as inexperienced as Talbot. The omega needed far more gentle handling than that.

He might be capable of doing heavier work than the other members of the pack were willing to give him, of being treated like a full-grown wolf rather than a pup, but that didn't mean he was suited to getting screwed at the drop of a more dominant wolf's hat.

All his knowledge of what it meant to be a good beta told him he'd be a fool to show any weakness to another wolf, but as he sat up, Gunnar knew the words couldn't be avoided. "I'm sorry. I shouldn't have—"

Talbot scrambled up from his prone position as if he couldn't bear to be in such a vulnerable position in front of a man who'd just betrayed his trust at the first opportunity. But he didn't beat a hasty retreat the way Gunnar expected him to. He…came closer?

The omega's somewhat grubby hand came to rest on his arm. "I didn't mean…"

Gunnar scowled at the younger man, looking from Talbot's hand to his face and back again. "No isn't a word that's easy to misunderstand."

As soon as the words left his lips, Gunnar knew his tone was all wrong. He'd meant it to be reassurance or maybe a simple statement of fact. But it sounded far more like an accusation—as if he didn't think that Talbot had the right to say no to him, to anyone he didn't want to have sex with. Gunnar mentally cursed himself. That was the last idea he needed to put into Talbot's head.

"I just meant…"

Gunnar forced himself to stay silent, to wait as patiently as he could as Talbot struggled to find whatever words he wanted to say to him.

"I always...I mean...Last time you didn't even... Isn't there something I can do for you instead?" the omega finally stuttered out.

Gunnar studied the younger man in silence for several long seconds. "Such as?"

Talbot looked down. He blushed, but apparently, it wasn't just an omega's natural inclination to drop his gaze that took his attention to Gunnar's crotch. Talbot licked his lips, in that way that seemed to have become his favourite habit of late.

A moment after that, the younger man lifted one slightly muddy and stone-battered hand and brought his fingertips to his lips.

"You're offering to suck me off," Gunnar said, determined there wasn't going to be any room left between them for misunderstandings.

Talbot's blush deepened, but he managed to nod. "If you...do you like...?"

Gunnar didn't laugh, but only because it was so obviously an honest question. Talbot really seemed to think it was possible that he wouldn't want the omega's mouth wrapped around his cock, that he wasn't desperate to feel his tongue lick delicately against his shaft and see his eyes looking up at him as Talbot dipped his head over his crotch and—

"Yes," Gunnar said, a little more roughly than he intended. "I like it."

"With me?" Talbot checked.

He was such a sweet little thing, so wary, and so uncertain of everything. Gunnar reached out and stroked his knuckles down his cheek. "Yes, with you."

He couldn't think of anyone he'd rather be with. And that was the problem, wasn't it? He should be doing this with Alfred. Except, as Gunnar's fingers wandered to Talbot's lips, it was barely even possible for him to remember that there was such thing as a wolf other than Talbot.

The omega instantly opened his mouth in acceptance. Gunnar stroked across Talbot's bottom lip with his thumb, sliding the digit a little way into his mouth. The omega's lips instinctively closed around it. His tongue licked against the tip of his thumb. His cheeks hollowed slightly as he began to suckle. Gunnar clenched his other hand into a fist as he fought against the desire to tear his fly open and tug Talbot down towards his shaft.

It had to be Talbot's choice. Gunnar had no right to let things be any other way. Taking his hand away from Talbot's face, Gunnar dropped it to the ground at his side and forced himself to keep it there no matter how desperate he was to feel the other man's skin beneath his fingertips.

Talbot blinked at him as his eyes slowly opened. His breaths were still unsteady as his attention dropped straight to Gunnar's fly. Talbot reached out. He gently traced the line of Gunnar's shaft through the denim with his fingertips, leaving a smudge of mud in their wake.

Gunnar didn't move. He barely dared to breathe. Talbot lifted his gaze. Their eyes met, but there was no challenge in the younger man's expression, no reason for Gunnar to want him to lower his eyes in due respect to his rank within the pack.

Talbot's touch grew bolder as he seemed to sense Gunnar's acceptance, both of his touch and his submission. The heat from his palm soon seeped through the fabric. There was no room behind the garment for Gunnar to harden any further.

The younger man seemed to realise the same thing just a second later. His fingers went to the button at the top of Gunnar's fly. He fumbled a little, but he finally managed to push the metal through the fabric. The zip was drawn carefully down.

Talbot's focus was all on what he was doing, but Gunnar's attention stayed on the other wolf's face. He saw the way the omega swallowed down his nerves as he felt Talbot carefully free him from the fabric.

His hands were small, his touch very cautious, very tender. Gunnar's larger fists wrapped around the blades of grass on either side of him as he did his duty by the less experienced wolf and let him move forward at his own speed, no matter how loudly part of him howled its frustration and demanded to be allowed to tell him to hurry the hell up.

The fragile blades of grass were crushed within his grip as Talbot finally bowed his head over Gunnar's lap.

The little wolf's tongue flicked out to tentatively taste the head. Pre cum had already gathered there in expectation. The omega whimpered his pleasure. The vibrations from the sound caressed the tip of Gunnar's cock.

Quickly rechanneling all his self-control to his hips, Gunnar somehow managed not to thrust forwards and bury his shaft deep inside Talbot's mouth, but he couldn't keep his hands at his sides as well.

The best he could manage was to settle his hand on the omega's shoulder rather than on the back of his head. Somehow, he found himself able to keep his touch gentle, too. He didn't grip the smaller man's shoulder. His palm and fingers rested flat against Talbot's back as he caressed his way down the smaller wolf's spine. The front of the omega's T-shirt might have been smeared and battered by the stones he'd moved but the back of it was still pure and white.

The younger man dipped his head a little further, taking the tip of Gunnar's cock into his mouth for the first time. As Gunnar's hand reached the waist band of Talbot's trousers he tugged at his shirt and freed it from the denim. Quickly sliding his hand underneath the fabric, Gunnar stroked his bare skin, eager to deepen the connection between them.

At almost exactly the same moment, Talbot wrapped his fingers delicately around Gunnar's shaft, holding it steady as he suckled ever so gently around the head. His tongue was clumsy, his technique nonexistent. But his enthusiasm was undeniable, and that alone seemed able to make it feel better than anything Gunnar had ever felt while wasting his time with higher ranking wolves.

Minutes passed in a blur of bliss. A little confidence seemed to seep into Talbot's attentions to his cock, but it didn't bring with it any apparent attempt to take control of anything that happened between them. The desire for that simply didn't seem to exist inside the younger wolf.

There was no hint of a challenge from him. Gunnar took a deep breath as he leaned more comfortably against the old stone wall. For the first time he felt the spring that had been coiled tightly inside him ever since he joined the pack as their new beta relax.

There was no need to keep his guard up with Talbot. With that knowledge came a deep-seated pleasure that grew inside him with every single lick and kiss the smaller wolf lavished on his cock. There were no ulterior motives with Talbot, no need to try to work out if there was a test behind his actions. It was just pure, perfect submission.

Talbot dipped his head further, trying to take more and more of Gunnar's shaft into his mouth, as if desperate to be completely filled with him. The glans touched the back of his throat. Talbot pulled back very quickly, spluttering and wiping his lips.

His eyes flashed up towards Gunnar. He looked so scared, so worried that he had failed.

Gunnar quickly lifted his hand from the ground to his left. Broken blades of grass fell from his fingers as he stroked his fingers through the omega's hair.

"I'd have been bloody surprised if you'd taken that in your stride," he said. His voice was rough, but he had no idea if Talbot was experienced enough to know that it was deep and hoarse with desire rather than anger. "Just take your time," he ordered. "There's no rush."

No rush…

Gunnar pushed the thought away as quickly as he could. He wasn't going to think about time. Not when they had so bloody little of it before he'd have to turn his attention back to his duties.

He stroked his fingers very gently through the omega's hair again, while he still had the chance. Gunnar had no doubt that Talbot would need to have a fuss made of him now. He was bound to need to be reassured and have his feelings coddled before he was inclined to make an attempt at finishing what he'd started.

He blinked down in surprise as the omega immediately lowered his lips back to his task. Gunnar's hand still rested on the back of his head, but the younger wolf didn't seem to be the least bit scared by the way his fingers remained nestled snugly in the short blond strands of hair.

Such complete trust…such perfect submission. Gunnar moaned his pleasure, at Talbot's instincts as much as his actions.

The beta's head dropped back to rest against the wall. His grip on Talbot's shirt turned white-knuckled as he forced himself to keep the other hand gentle against his hair. Pleasure rushed through him faster and faster as Talbot sucked and licked around him.

As if he could sense his lover getting closer to the edge, Talbot bobbed his head more quickly. His attention focussed in on the most sensitive part of Gunnar's cock, right where the head met the shaft.

Gunnar's hips rocked forwards. Talbot didn't seem the least concerned by that. As the beta stared down at him, it was hard for him to imagine that anything could faze the inexperienced young wolf right then. The omega was completely lost in his newly emerging instincts, and he was glorious.

All Talbot's attention was on his lover, but as Gunnar's fist released the other man's shirt and he slid his palm down to rest on Talbot's arse, he realised that the omega's hips were rocking too.

The omega's body was concerned with his own orgasm, even if his mind wasn't. He pushed his arse excitedly back against Gunnar's hand, squirming and pressing against his palm.

If his mind had realised what his body was getting up to while its focus was on other things, Gunnar knew the other man would have blushed bright red. As it was, his instincts had free rein, and his arse wanted Gunnar.

Another lick to that sweet spot right near the head of his cock, and Gunnar's orgasm suddenly roared through him, catching him completely off guard. He didn't even have a chance to warn Talbot before he jerked and came rapidly into his mouth.

A howl threatened to escape from him, but Gunnar clamped his throat down around it. A howl might bring the other members of the pack to their quiet little corner of their territory. Gunnar couldn't allow himself that pleasure right then.

The omega spluttered again, but this time he only pulled back far enough to ensure Gunnar's cum would land on his tongue. Keeping his lips wrapped around the tip, he swallowed rapidly, apparently determined to take every drop Gunnar could give him.

But he hadn't learnt how to do that properly yet. No one had taught him how. No one had been granted the *opportunity* to teach him anything at all, because he was sweet, and innocent, and perfect. As Gunnar's orgasm faded away and the beta collapsed, completely sated, against the wall behind him, he couldn't help but relish the simple fact that he was the first wolf Talbot would ever taste that way.

The younger man continued to suckle contently around his cock as he began to soften in the omega's mouth. His hips continued to rock as he squirmed against Gunnar's hand, too.

His movements all slow and sleepy with afterglow, Gunnar reached beneath the smaller wolf and deftly drew down the zip on his fly. Talbot started to pull back, but Gunnar quickly killed that idea by simply refusing to lift his hand from where it rested on the back of his head.

There was no struggle for control. As soon as Talbot seemed to register his lover's desire, he conceded to it. Gunnar's other hand deftly freed the omega's shaft from behind his fly and wrapped his fingers around it as soon as it was clear who was in charge.

Talbot's eyes opened very wide as he glanced up at him from the corner of his eye. He gasped around Gunnar's softening cock, his tongue flicking rapidly against the tip as he tried to look down beneath his own body. Gunnar smiled slightly. There was no way for Talbot to see what was happening. His position was as effective as any blindfold could have been.

The sucking action around the tip of his cock increased rapidly as Talbot squirmed, thrusting his hips and frantically trying to pump his cock against Gunnar's hand.

Allowing his smile to broaden a little, Gunnar stilled his fist. He let Talbot take over and do all the work himself, while he merely sat back and admired the performance the normally self conscious little omega was putting on for him.

Every bit of pleasure Talbot's wriggling gained was passed straight to his lover via his mouth. Every whimper and every moan vibrated around Gunnar's shaft. There was no way in hell the other wolf could get him hard again right then, but he certainly seemed to be doing his damndest to try.

Pleasure caressed and encased Gunnar's cock again and again as Talbot fought for his own release. That was good. It was about time someone taught the other wolf to fight for what he wanted. A submissive was one thing — every pack needed a good omega in its ranks. No pack needed to include a petrified doormat in its numbers.

"That's right," he murmured under his breath.

Tilting his head to one side, Gunnar watched the omega's shaft slide against his palm again and again, slicking it with pre cum with every motion. Tightening his grip slightly, Gunnar rhythmically massaged the omega's cock as he teased the head.

A muffled howl surrounded Gunnar's shaft as the other man finally bucked his hips and spilled on the grass beneath him in long white ropes. Talbot's body jerked again and again as his muscles seemed to escape his control and find all those reserves of strength that the little wolf had never been encouraged to explore before.

Finally falling still, the omega half collapsed forwards, taking Gunnar's cock deeper into his mouth in the process. There seemed to be no fear in that for him now. With his head resting on the beta's lap and his whole body limp and trembling with satisfaction, Talbot was glorious, and Gunnar wanted nothing more than to drag him up onto his lap, wrap his arms around him, and keep him there forever.

Gunnar closed his eyes for a moment, making sure that the sight of Talbot like that was burned deep into his mind, just in case he never got the chance to see him like that again.

He let the younger man rest for a few minutes. Then, unable to hide his reluctance, he very slowly took his hands from Talbot's body.

"We both have duties to attend to," he reminded Talbot as he looked towards the broken section of wall. He'd never known any words to taste so bitter in his mouth.

Chapter Four

Duty...

The word echoed through Gunnar's head as his paws raced faster and faster over the forest floor. He growled at the world in general, but it was just a brief, harsh little sound. Gunnar kept the rest of his breath in order to race more rapidly across the uneven ground.

The wind whipped through his fur as he threw himself between the trees, putting every ounce of anger and frustration he possessed into simply moving all four of his paws as quickly as he could. Right to the edge of the boundary of the pack's land, then around the far field towards the north of their territory and back through the forest, Gunnar pushed himself to keep running no matter how hard his lungs screamed or his muscles protested.

All he had to do was keep running and everything would be simple. It was staying still that was the problem. Staying *here* that was the problem. Staying and doing his duty to his new pack...

Gunnar had never realised that the very thing he'd built his life around as he'd grown up and realised what being part of a pack really meant, could hurt him so much. But the idea of having to set aside his feelings for Talbot, of being required to live next to him as part of the same pack, yet still to go to his bed each night with another wolf...

Physical pain mingled with the mental anguish as his pushed his body harder than ever and joints and bones protested at such rough treatment, but Gunnar couldn't stop.

He had to run. He had to pick up Talbot and run as fast as he could carry him, out of the pack's lands and—

Gunnar's only warning was a brief blur of fur to his right. Then, he was on his back.

The momentum of the attack sent both Gunnar and his attacker tumbling uncontrollably down the slope leading towards the river that cut through the forest. Their tangled mess of limbs stopped rolling just short of the fast-flowing water's edge. Gunnar's back landed heavily on the rocky river bank.

Who was it? Gunnar tried to focus as his head spun. Who had found out?

Marsdon? Bennett? Had the alphas discovered what had happened between him and Talbot that morning? Had one of them realised that he'd disobeyed their wishes, disregarded the very reason they'd brought him and Caden into the pack, without the slightest hesitation?

Or maybe Steffan—had the idea that he needed to protect the little omega from the big nasty beta finally convinced the huge oaf to grow a pair? Or was it Francis, trying to fight above his weight?

As thoughts raced through Gunnar's head he twisted around, his paws scrabbling at the muddy rocks as he made to launch himself at his attacker and saw...Caden?

The pretty little wolf stilled when their eyes met. Within seconds, the other wolf had morphed back into an equally pretty young man. Leaf litter clung to his floppy blond hair as the wind blew it back from his face, like he was the star of a bloody shampoo commercial.

His skin was streaked with mud, but even that failed to make him look anything less than perfect. Somehow Gunnar's brother made it look like something a spa would lather on him rather than what anyone could find on the forest floor. But what Gunnar noticed above everything else was that his brother's eyes were full of entirely unaccustomed anger.

"What the hell's got into you?" Gunnar's words were more growled than spoken, his voice box barely having had time to transform back into its human form.

Caden snarled back at him. His muscles tensed as if he was barely restraining himself from throwing himself at him again.

"If we end up in that river, I'll throttle you, you stupid little sod," Gunnar warned, sparing a brief glance at the near-freezing water.

It took several minutes before Caden's inclination to attack appeared to subside. Even then it seemed to be more due to a realisation that he had no chance of winning against his older brother now that he was on his guard.

Still, Gunnar continued to watch him with a wariness that he was sure would have surprised the other members of their pack if he'd ever let them see it. Caden in a temper was a bloody sight more dangerous than he looked. Gunnar had seen more than enough wolves learn that the hard way. "Any particular reason why you've lost your mind?" Gunnar finally asked.

"As if you don't know!" Caden snapped, holding his eyes as he said it.

Gunnar's eyes narrowed in response. "Show some respect!" he ordered, as his hackles rose.

"Don't pull the big tough beta act with me," Caden spat. "That bull's not going to work on someone who can remember you when you were still carrying around that moth eaten bloody teddy bear!"

"Why are you attacking a member of your own pack?" Gunnar ground out, somehow managing to ignore the taunt and keep his own anger in check.

"Why are you screwing around with the pack's omega?" the younger wolf tossed back at him. "Do you have a death wish!"

Gunnar growled as he pushed his hand through his hair and shook away the worst of the forest floor that still clung to his skin. "That's nothing to do with you."

"The hell it's not," Caden shouted.

Gunnar glared down at the shorter man as they both sprung to their feet. He was probably right, in his way. They had joined the pack together. His actions would no doubt affect his brother's relationship with the pack. But still... "I'm not bound to Alfred yet."

Caden shook his head as if he couldn't believe how stupid he was being, but Gunnar pushed forward regardless. "Talbot's not mated either. We're just two wolves who are free to do whatever we want until —"

"And does Talbot know that?" Caden demanded, still determinedly holding his gaze. "Does he know you're just amusing yourself at his expense until you finally grow up and do what's expected of you?"

"Talbot knows exactly how things are," Gunnar growled. "Do you really think I'd lie to him about that — about anything?"

He stalked forward. The smaller wolf resolutely held his ground.

"Is that what you think of me?" Gunnar demanded.

"I think you're quite capable of being a complete bastard any time it suits you," Caden threw at him. "It's practically a beta's job, isn't it? And we all know how good a beta you are."

Gunnar growled, low and deep in the back of his throat as he ground his teeth together. Despite his best efforts, it wasn't the kind of noise a man made when he was squabbling with an annoying younger sibling. It was more like the sound of a wolf's last bit of patience being torn from his grasp.

"Don't do this, Gun?" Suddenly, Caden's voice was different. The anger drained away so abruptly it was hard to remember it ever being there.

The soft little lilt he was so good at employing with others when it suited him to smile and flatter and get his own way in that manner was absent too. For once, Caden sounded perfectly serious.

It was a simple request. Unless Caden was a better actor than even Gunnar realised, it was also an honest and heartfelt one. And it came from the one wolf who Gunnar would have said could have asked anything of him. *Anything*. Gunnar held Caden's gaze for several long minutes.

At least part of him knew his brother was right. He was acting like a fool, risking both their places in the pack to screw around where he had no business. But still, the words he should have said lodged in his throat.

Promising to walk away from Talbot was the sensible thing to do, but his voice box didn't seem to want to be sensible right then. A growl emerged instead, and even Gunnar had no idea who he was snarling at.

"You know who the alphas want you to be mated to," Caden reminded him.

Gunnar pushed a hand through his hair. "Of course I do." Every wolf in the pack bloody well knew it.

"Since when do you avoid doing your duty?" his little brother pushed.

Since I met Talbot.

Gunnar glanced at his brother.

I love him, Cade. I'm in love with our omega, and I don't know what to do.

Gunnar cleared his throat. That wasn't the kind of thing a beta said out loud. A beta didn't ask for advice from a gamma. He didn't admit to weakness or uncertainty.

"Remember our places in this pack," he advised the younger wolf. "You've no right to—"

"Bollocks! You're the one with a fetish for the established bloody hierarchy, not me."

Gunnar squared his shoulders. No, the last thing he could do was let Caden see him wishing he could act in any way other than that which would best please the alphas of the pack. An example had to be set—both for gammas and brothers.

"The others won't realise you don't mean it, if they hear you talking that way," Gunnar said, his voice sounding strangely dead. "They won't understand that you—"

"Will they understand why you're screwing their omega?" Caden cut in.

No, Gunnar doubted they would. Hell, he didn't understand it either. Turning away from his brother, Gunnar slowly made his way back up the slope, away from the river.

A bitter wind blew through the forest. Without his lupine fur to protect him, Gunnar soon felt it sink into his bones and chill him to the core. Even so, he stayed in his human form for the walk back towards the farm house.

A wolf's body might be more suited to the cold, but its mind was far less suited to unravelling the confusing mess of thoughts that tangled themselves in his head.

* * * *

Gunnar kept his eyes fixed firmly on the fireplace as Francis and Steffan finally levered themselves up from the sofa opposite him and made their way up the stairs to their bedroom. All the other members of the pack had already drifted away from the blaze. Soon after Alfred had left, even Caden had stomped off, with a glare in Gunnar's direction and a warning glance towards their omega as a parting shot.

The only wolf who still lingered in the main hall with him was Talbot.

Gunnar could feel the younger wolf watching him, studying him. It was all too easy to sense that Talbot was looking for any signal that might let him know how he could best please his more dominant mate right then.

Except he'd never be the omega's mate, dominant or otherwise.

Even knowing that, even having lectured himself on that very fact all the way back to the farm house earlier that day, Gunnar found himself helpless to do anything but turn his head and meet the smaller wolf's gaze. Their eyes locked. A hundred different emotions swirled inside the other man's expression.

The only thing Gunnar didn't see there was a challenge.

The beta closed his eyes for a second. "It's time you were in your bed." Against all Gunnar's expectations, his words came out as strong and as steady as any he had ever uttered. As he pushed himself up from his seat on the far end of one of the sofas, there was no audible hint of the pain saying them had caused him.

Talbot hadn't moved to occupy a more comfortable seat as the other wolves had left and the sofas became free. He still sat on the floor by the fire, his knees pulled up in front of him, his arms wrapped around his legs as if he were trying to hold himself together when he might easily crumble.

Gunnar knew he should walk away without another word, but somehow he found himself walking across to the fire and damping it down himself rather than leaving the task for the other man to attend to. As the fire died, a chill quickly crept into the room.

He couldn't leave Talbot there. It was too easy to imagine him remaining exactly where he was, getting colder by the moment, unless a more dominant force ordered him to do otherwise.

Gunnar held out a hand. The little omega blinked up at him as if he had never seen him before, but he also reached out and offered his fingers to Gunnar's palm, quick to put himself in another man's hands as soon as the opportunity was offered.

It was easy for the beta to pull the smaller man to his feet—too easy. Talbot damn near left the floor as Gunnar forgot to keep both his anger and his strength in check for a moment.

Unable to find his footing, Talbot tumbled against Gunnar's chest. His hand skidded against Gunnar's shirt. His fingers tightened around a fistful of fabric as he fought to steady himself.

Gunnar froze. Every instinct he'd ever possessed told him to wrap his arms around the smaller man, but as soon as Talbot had steadied himself, Gunnar forced himself to take a step back. Caden, annoying little sod that he was, had been right.

Talbot looked up at him in confusion. He probably didn't have the slightest clue how tempting that made him look, how in need of leadership and protection he appeared. Putting his hands on the younger man's shoulders, Gunnar determinedly moved Talbot away from him.

Turning him towards the stairs, he gave Talbot a nudge forward. With one hand remaining on the smaller man's shoulder, he did his best to make sure the omega didn't turn to look at him as they made their way out of the hall. If their eyes met again, Gunnar knew there was far too much of a chance that he'd forget why he was making the right decision in directing each of them to their *separate* beds that night.

Talbot didn't say a word as Gunnar damn near frog-marched him up to his room. Opening the door for him, Gunnar gave Talbot a gentle shove into his room before reaching in to close the door behind him.

That was a mistake.

Talbot turned to look at Gunnar, just as the beta's hand wrapped around the handle. The little wolf looked so lost, so confused. But he didn't utter one word of complaint. Gunnar held back both a growl and a sigh. He'd probably have felt like less of a bastard for closing the door between them if the other man had screamed and cursed at him.

The other wolves in the pack might think they were helping Talbot by cosseting him so much, but it had never been more obvious to Gunnar that all they'd succeeded in doing was making the omega think himself weak and worthless. He didn't even think he deserved better than to have his lover walk away without a word.

In spite of everything, Gunnar somehow managed to shut the door. And he only let himself stare at the woodwork for the briefest possible moment before he made his way towards his own bedroom. He was halfway down the hall, when he stopped, unable to take another step.

Gunnar closed his eyes for a second, digging into reserves of strength and determination until he reached the very bottom of the barrel, then digging through the thick wooden base in a desperate search for more. When he opened his eyes, he was half surprised that there wasn't actually a thick metal chain wrapped around his waist and leading back towards the omega's room. There might as well have been.

Suddenly, it was obvious that it wasn't just Talbot getting attached to him that he should have been worried about. The omega was exactly where he belonged, alone in his own room. Gunnar glanced towards his own bedroom door for a moment, but putting Talbot in the right place had taken everything he had to give. There was no control left, only desire. Muttering curses at his own weakness, under his breath, Gunnar stormed back down the corridor and pushed open the door leading into Talbot's room.

The other wolf was still standing in the middle of his bedroom. His arms were wrapped around his torso again. They remained there as Talbot lifted his head and met Gunnar's gaze.

He was far too small, far too vulnerable to be left to sleep on his own. An omega needed a stronger wolf in his bed to hold him close and let him know that he was safe. No matter what nice, logical, dutiful thoughts Gunnar tried to push into his head, those were still the facts of the matter.

Talbot could be made stronger and more confident over time, but he'd always need that. Gunnar stepped inside the room. He closed the door firmly behind him, shutting out Caden, the pack, and every other inconvenient reminder of reality. Talbot remained perfectly still as Gunnar strode towards him. The only tiny movement the omega made was to tilt his head back in invitation as Gunnar's hand threaded into his hair and brought their lips together.

Never losing any hint of his momentum, Gunnar kept striding forward, giving Talbot no choice but to walk backward until they tumbled onto his bed together. It wasn't a large room. It wasn't a large bed, either. The whole space might have been perfectly proportioned for Talbot's small frame, but it wasn't designed to accommodate a beta wolf nearly twice his size.

Gunnar's elbow slammed into the wall as he tried to stop his weight crushing the smaller man. He cursed into the kiss, but if he was risking everything, it was pointless to try to hold back. It would have been a crime to join the other man in his bed and not take to everything he could — not to *give* everything he could.

Talbot squirmed beneath him. His hands moved frantically against Gunnar's body, as if he really was as desperate as Gunnar to touch every inch of his lover all at the same time. A second later, the omega let out a scared little whimper, obviously unable to do everything at once, or to choose what to do first.

Gunnar quickly caught hold of Talbot's wrists and deftly pinned them against the mattress on either side of his head, taking both the decision and the problem away from him. "Stay still." Leaning over the smaller man, he tightened his grip on him, making sure he knew exactly who was in control of him right then.

Talbot's Adam's apple bobbed. His lips parted as he drew a deep breath into his lungs. Gunnar hadn't switched on the light when he deposited the omega in his room, or when he returned to it. The only illumination came from the moon outside Talbot's window, but it was still more than enough for a wolf to see by.

Gunnar took in every detail as Talbot stopped trying to work out what he should do and simply handed over control of all those decisions to the other man. His arms relaxed against the blankets. He fell still but for his rapid breaths.

"Is this what you want?" the beta demanded, keeping his voice low, as if they might be overheard and dragged apart at any moment.

Talbot nodded.

Gunnar was reasonably sure Talbot would have offered up the same gesture if he'd asked the omega if he wanted to jump off a bridge with him. He was agreeing with *him*, not with what he said. Talbot was simply offering himself to Gunnar to do with as he wished.

It was all lupine submission, not human agreement. And, as Gunnar stared down at the other wolf, it was hard to believe Talbot could ever be any other way with a lover.

His reactions were too instinctive, too perfect to be anything other than the simple truth about who Talbot was. He was all omega, all desire to submit to a more dominant wolf. It would have been cruel to ask him to give a different answer, to ask him to pretend to be someone else on that night.

Gunnar lowered his head and brushed their mouths together very gently. Talbot instantly parted his lips in invitation and Gunnar tenderly licked his way into the omega's mouth.

Gunnar guided Talbot's hands, slowly and calmly, up towards the narrow headboard at the top of the bed. There were a series of wooden rails there. As Gunnar deepened the kiss, he carefully wrapped the smaller man's hands around two of them.

"Keep your hands there," he ordered, as he pulled back just the merest fraction of an inch, to whisper the words against the other man's lips.

Talbot looked up, as if he'd been so lost in the kiss he really hadn't noticed what was going on.

Gunnar slid his fingers into the omega's hair and tugged at the strands, demanding that Talbot bring his attention back to him. "Do you understand the order?"

Talbot nodded.

"Tell me then."

"I understand," Talbot whispered back.

"And you're going to keep your hands right there for me?" Gunnar prompted, keeping his voice as soft as he knew how.

Talbot nodded again. "I'm going to keep my hands there," he echoed.

Gunnar pulled slowly away. True to his word, Talbot stayed exactly where he had put him.

When they'd landed on the bed, Talbot's legs had been pushed conveniently apart by Gunnar's. Kneeling between his spread thighs, the beta ran his eyes over the smaller wolf's body. For several long seconds he just stared down at him, studying every line of him.

There were clothes in the way. That wasn't right. Anything that kept them apart right then was no less than a crime.

Gunnar caught hold of the hem of Talbot's thin, blue T-shirt. He yanked it up, exposing his torso. Quickly pushing the material further up, over the smaller wolf's head, Gunnar's gaze rose away from the pale skin and lean lines of muscle being put on display for him just in time to see Talbot's hands leave the headboard.

"No!"

Talbot froze exactly where he was, his hands hovering aimlessly above his pillow.

"What did I tell you?" Gunnar growled.

Talbot looked up, following Gunnar's gaze. His eyes opened very wide when he realised where his hands were. He immediately grabbed the rails. His fingers wrapped around them so tightly his knuckles turned white. He looked back to Gunnar. "I'm sorry, I…"

Gunnar put his hand over his mouth. No apologies. Maybe they were both doing something they should be apologising for, but right then, Gunnar couldn't listen to those words.

Talbot fell silent, but his lips didn't close. As he took a breath, he sucked against Gunnar's fingers, as if he was desperate to have them in his mouth.

Gunnar couldn't deny him. Pale pink lips soon stretched around two of his fingers as he settled them against Talbot's tongue.

The omega murmured around the digits, tipping his head back slightly, seemingly to instinctively try to give Gunnar the best possible angle for deeper penetration.

Thrusting his fingers further past his lips, studying and analysing Talbot's every reaction, Gunnar pulled another gorgeous groan of pleasure out of the younger man. Then, as if that wasn't already enough to prove just how much Talbot needed to feel another wolf deep inside him — when Gunnar finally took his hand away, Talbot arched up off the bed, desperately trying to keep his fingers in his mouth for as long as possible.

He leant up as far as he could, but he didn't let go of the rails again. His grip on them tightened instead. When it was obvious to them both he couldn't rise any further without dislocating his own shoulders, he collapsed back onto the mattress, his breath coming in gasps.

Gunnar didn't waste another second before he reached for the fly on Talbot's jeans. His fingers were still damp as his knuckles brushed against the omega's stomach. The younger man's abs twitched. He squirmed against the bed, but he was also quick to lift his hips so Gunnar could pull his jeans down.

In mere seconds, Talbot was naked. Standing up, Gunnar left the bed. A whimper escaped from the omega in response, but Gunnar ignored it. Talbot would understand what his lover was doing soon enough.

He was just getting undressed. He wasn't actually leaving.

Talbot closed his eyes as he took a deep breath in an effort to calm himself. His senses were immediately filled with Gunnar's scent. He held his breath, trapping the air inside him, relishing the connection it gave him with the other wolf.

Gunnar smelt like pleasure and desire, like dominance and sex, and Talbot wanted nothing more than to be surrounded and filled by that scent forever. He hadn't realised quite how desperate he was for that until the beta had closed the door behind him, but having him walk back into his life so soon had confirmed it all to him.

He might never be Gunnar's mate as far as the rest of the pack was concerned, maybe not even as far as Gunnar was concerned, but Talbot knew in that moment, inside his own head, that was what he'd be for the rest of his life.

A soft rustle of fabric pulled him back to the present. Talbot blinked his eyes open just in time to see Gunnar toss his shirt onto the floor at his feet. Forcing himself to keep his fists wrapped very tightly around the wooden rails at the top of his bed, he watched, mesmerised, as Gunnar's body was slowly revealed to him.

He wasn't allowed to reach out and touch him right then. He might never be allowed to reach out to him that way. The omega bit down on his bottom lip as he fought for control of his own body, for the ability to obey the other wolf when all he wanted to do was catch hold of Gunnar and never let him go.

He'd have closed his eyes against the rude interruption of a reality he'd have much preferred to ignore, but Gunnar was right there, and he was naked now. Not simply naked the way a wolf was when he'd just changed forms or merely couldn't be bothered with inconvenient layers of fabric. Gunnar was naked because he wanted to have sex, and that was too glorious a sight to miss.

Pain shot through Talbot's bottom lip as he bit down harder. Naked because he wanted to have sex with *him*. A whimper escaped from the back of his throat as his eyes feasted on the length of the larger wolf's erection, from the glans all the way down to where the root nestled in short black curls.

The beta stepped forward. As he approached the edge of the bed, Gunnar reached out to him, bridging the gap between them that Talbot was forbidden from closing. Nothing could have pleased the omega more, but of all the things he had imagined Gunnar might do, catching hold of his bottom lip and pulling it away from his teeth wasn't even on the list.

"I'm the only one in this room who's allowed to do any biting," Gunnar informed him. His tone was still low, but it was obvious that he was perfectly serious, and that he fully expected to be obeyed.

Talbot nodded, effectively tugging at his own bottom lip as Gunnar kept a tight hold on it.

The beta lowered his head as he released the sensitive bit of skin. Talbot parted his lips further for the expected kiss, but Gunnar's mouth went to his chest instead. The other wolf's teeth nipped sharply at his nipple.

One wolf who was allowed to bite...

Pleasure and pain shot through Talbot, braided so tightly together they were almost inseparable. Talbot's hips rose off the bed, desperately thrusting forward as if begging the beta to move his mouth to his cock instead. Gunnar lifted his head a fraction. He smiled before he lowered it again, but there was little humour in his expression. The look in his eyes was pure...pure Gunnar. Talbot didn't know any other way to explain it.

It was possession and dominance and a somewhat grumpy inclination to be pissed off with ninety-nine percent of the world all mixed together. It was that same look that always made Talbot desperately want to be the one percent of the universe that somehow managed to please him.

Without any warning, Gunnar's lips sealed around Talbot's nipple and sucked around the little peak of nerve endings, introducing Talbot to another new possibility. He couldn't help but whimper his bliss as he wondered what other things he had never considered.

His hips rocked forwards again. His cock was already so hard it curved back towards his stomach. As he squirmed, it bobbed above him, desperate for stimulation but unable to achieve even the tiniest amount of friction against anything. Pre cum dripped onto Talbot's stomach as Gunnar lapped over and over again at the tender bud of nerve endings trapped in his mouth.

Closing his eyes, Talbot tossed his head against his pillow. His feet kicked at the bed. A sudden sharp pain in his other nipple made him open his eyes. Gunnar's thumb and forefinger had it in an unyielding grip, his nails pinching into the skin.

Sensations that Talbot had never experienced before flooded through his body, addling his mind, making it impossible to think. All he was capable of doing was wanting, needing—and he didn't even have the words to tell Gunnar that, to beg for his sanity before the last of it faded away.

Suddenly, the beta looked up as if sensing there was something Talbot wanted to say to him. Their eyes met. Gunnar's teeth caught hold of Talbot's nipple again. The older man's lips pulled back to allow Talbot to see the sensitive skin stretched by his teeth at his lover's demand as Gunnar lifted his head slowly away from his chest.

Talbot tried to breathe, but the air lodged in his throat. His head spun. Not one single word left his lips.

Gunnar smiled as he parted his teeth and released Talbot's nipple. He seemed amused when Talbot finally managed to draw a panting breath into his lungs. But his eyes quickly turned serious again as he dropped his attention to Talbot's cock.

The beta ran his thumb against the underside of his shaft. "Do you have anything we can use?" His voice was lower, rougher than Talbot ever remembered it being. The words were growled out, each syllable harsh and demanding, but there was no anger in the sound, only lust.

Talbot managed to tear his gaze away from the other wolf for just long enough to glance at his bedside drawer. Gunnar yanked it open so hard it slid off its rails. The beta made a pissed off sound in the back of his throat as half the contents spilled and clattered across the floor next to the bed.

For several long seconds, they both remained perfectly still, frozen in a statue that stared helplessly at the door. No footsteps sounded. No one burst in to see what all the noise was about. When Gunnar leant forward and placed the half empty drawer soundlessly on the floor, Talbot remembered how to breathe. Everything was going to be fine.

Rifling through the jumble on the bedside rug, Gunnar quickly found the unopened tube of lube that Talbot had blushingly bought when he'd been told he'd be joining a pack full of unmated wolves, just in case it would be needed.

Gunnar wasted no time yanking the cap off and smearing the lube over his fingers.

Swallowing down a sudden rush of nerves, Talbot shuffled his feet a little further apart on the mattress before pulling his knees back towards his chest in offering. The beta's fingers disappeared from his line of sight. A moment later, they brushed against his hole.

Talbot gasped at the first caress. The beta looked up and held his gaze as his fingers slowly circled Talbot's hole again and again, teasing him with the prospect of entering him until the omega was sure the tiny bit of his sanity that he still had left was going to vanish into the ether.

Unable to look away, not even in order to lower his eyes in respect for the other wolf's rank, all Talbot could do was wait and pray that Gunnar would have a little mercy on him and not tease him too much.

Finally, one of his fingers slid inside Talbot. Tightening his hold on the bed frame rails once more, Talbot did his best to use the leverage it offered him and thrust his whole body down onto the digit.

Suddenly, Gunnar's other hand connected firmly with his right buttock. It wasn't hard enough to really hurt, but the sharp stinging sensation burst through Talbot's senses so unexpectedly it made him gasp and clench down around Gunnar's finger in surprise as he lowered his legs.

"When I want you to ride any part of me, I'll order you to. Understand?"

Talbot nodded. "I…"

Gunnar smiled slightly, his lips twisting a little with the expression. "Enthusiasm isn't a bad thing—unless it ends up hurting you. That's not acceptable."

Talbot nodded again and he gave everything he had to staying still as Gunnar's finger finally began to move inside him, sending heat and hope racing through his body in equal measure. Several minutes passed in a blur of pleasure for Talbot, until another finger was added. He jerked and tensed as he was stretched open further, but more than half his attention was on the other wolf's cock rather than his fingers by the time a third digit joined those sliding in and out of his hole.

There was a drop of pre cum sliding down the beta's shaft. Talbot would have given almost anything to be allowed to lean forward and lap it up as Gunnar's fingers continued to dance inside him. Closing his eyes, he turned his head away from the sight, but the image of the other wolf's cock was still there in his head, still tempting him.

Suddenly, Gunnar's touch disappeared.

Talbot quickly turned back to him, but Gunnar had already moved away from where he'd been sitting on the edge of his bed.

"Don't go!" The words were out before Talbot could stop them, and they sounded more like an order than any he had uttered in his life.

Gunnar frowned down at him and Talbot knew he had said the worst possible thing. There was no way he'd stay now, not even if he might have been willing to a moment before. Nothing could have angered him more than someone expecting him to take orders from an omega.

Talbot had never been more shocked than when Gunnar reached for him again. The larger man's hands came to rest on Talbot's sides. A second later, Gunnar had rolled Talbot towards the wall.

"I'm not going anywhere." There was no hesitation in the beta's words. He obviously meant every one of them. There was a flash of something in his eyes, too, but Talbot couldn't work out what it was.

So much relief sang through Talbot's brain that there was no room for any sort of clear thought process in there. His eyes dropped closed. He gave little thought to the way Gunnar arranged them on the bed, the larger wolf spooning close behind him, except to relish the heat from the other man's body radiating against him from shoulder to heel.

It was only when a slicked shaft pressed against his hole that Talbot realised why they'd been rearranged that way.

Yes!

It was the only word that made it into his head, but Talbot was sure that was fine — it was the only word that needed to be there.

Gunnar calmly moved Talbot's hands to hold on to different rails, then, ones better suited to their new positions. Talbot still wasn't allowed to reach for the other wolf the way he longed to, but in that moment he found a strange kind of freedom in having his movements restricted.

There was no need for him to work out where to put his hands, or what Gunnar would like him to do with them. There was no requirement for him to know what he was doing at all. All he had to do was obey the beta in the very way that came so naturally to him, and everything would be fine. Gunnar would see to that.

Every instinct Talbot possessed screamed at him that he could trust the beta, more than he had ever trusted anyone else in his life, and with that instinct came a kind of peace Talbot had never even realised he'd been searching for. His mate would look after him.

The beta rocked his hips forward very slightly. The tip of his cock kissed against Talbot's well-slicked hole. Again and again, Gunnar let him feel the gentlest pressure against his arse, driving him near-mad with frustration.

Finally, when Talbot was almost ready to cry with pure need, the beta pushed forwards. The tip of Gunnar's cock slid past the tight ring of muscle. Talbot tensed at the unfamiliar sensation. The beta immediately stilled. His hand came to rest on Talbot's hip, holding him motionless, too, freeing him from any responsibility to hide that little moment of discomfort as he ordered him to simply wait it out.

Gunnar made a soft, soothing noise in the back of his throat, a sound so different from his normal growls it was almost impossible to believe it came from the same wolf. Except Talbot was sure no other wolf would ever feel so right against his skin, or so perfect inside him.

Gradually, as Talbot's body accept him more easily, Gunnar rocked his hips and buried his shaft further and further within him, until he was sheathed in him to the hilt. Stretched and full, Talbot squirmed, more desperate to come than ever, as every movement of the beta's erection pressed against his prostate and the sensation rushed to his cock.

There was nothing he could do, though. Gunnar would decide if he wanted to reach around and wrap his fingers around his shaft. The older wolf would decide if he wanted to let him push against his palm and come the same way he had out by the old stone wall. Gunnar would decide everything. As Talbot opened his mind up and accepted that fact into an even deeper part of his mind, fresh waves of perfection flooded him.

Just a moment later, as if the beta had somehow sensed his complete and willing surrender to his control, Talbot felt the other man began to move inside him. Slowly, almost tenderly at first, then with more strength and more dominance to his movements, he thrust deep into Talbot's arse again and again.

His lips caressed Talbot's neck. Teeth scraped against his skin. Gunnar's hands roved over his body with complete freedom, claiming more and more of Talbot as his own with every caress.

And through it all, the rhythm built between their bodies, calling to Talbot and pulling instincts he'd never realised he possessed to the surface. Pleasure built up inside him until it became bliss, then something beyond anything he'd ever known.

It was nothing like coming from a hand around his cock, from mere friction against his shaft. His orgasm seemed to tear through him as if it would rip him apart from the inside out. His whole body jerked. His muscles tensed around Gunnar's shaft as if he could somehow keep the beta trapped inside him that way and they would never be parted.

All control disappeared from Talbot's world as he spilled against his blankets. His body and his mind both belonged to ecstasy—they belonged to Gunnar. Talbot was barely even aware of the beta's hand covering his mouth, silencing his howl. Lights shone and fractured behind his lids as he closed his eyes very tightly and lost himself in a way he never could have done if he hadn't known Gunnar would be there to find him and put him back together again.

Gasping for breath, Talbot finally collapsed against the bed, exhausted, every scrap of energy drained from his body. A second passed, then another. Talbot managed to lift his head a fraction and look up towards the headboard. His hands were still around the rails. He hadn't let his mate down.

Another second passed, and Talbot felt Gunnar rock his hips, calling his attention back to the fact that he wasn't the only wolf in the bed who wanted to come that night. Talbot arched his back slightly, offering his arse to the other man as clearly as he knew how.

Riding him through his climax seemed to have taken Gunnar close to the edge of his own. It only took him a dozen extra deep, pounding thrusts to spill inside Talbot's body. His hips jerked rapidly, sending a different, milder kind of pleasure through Talbot's sated body, but Gunnar didn't make a single sound as he came. Talbot was the one who gasped out his pleasure at the other man's orgasm. The beta was still all control over the whole planet.

A moment later, regret crept into the edges of the omega's mind.

They'd both come...

It was over...

Gunnar pulled away a fraction, separating their bodies, as if he'd realised the same thing at the exact same moment.

Then, before Talbot could even protest his leaving, the beta moved back closer to him, so his chest was once more against Talbot's back. Gunnar's softened shaft pressed intimately against his buttocks as he relaxed alongside Talbot's body, his arms wrapping around him to hold him close.

"You're allowed to move your hands now," the beta whispered.

Talbot cautiously took advantage of the permission. One of his hands came to rest on the back of Gunnar's hand, where the beta had placed it on Talbot's stomach.

The larger wolf made no complaint about that. He made no comment about anything at all and it was impossible for anyone to tell what he might be thinking.

Talbot had no way of knowing if there were *two* wolves who wished that they could curl up in that bed forever and never let reality intrude upon the love he felt for the man at his side.

Chapter Five

"Alfred?" Gunnar stomped into the middle of the old barn and peered into the gloom, trying to spot the gamma among all the junk scattered around the dark, shadowy space.

There was no answer.

If Gunnar could have had the pleasure of seeking out Talbot rather than the gamma that the alphas were so keen to see him mated to, he could have taken the responding silence as proof that the wolf he was looking for wasn't within earshot. But, with Alfred...

Gunnar held back a sigh. It was bloody difficult to be sure of anything with Alfred. The annoying little sod was quite capable of keeping quiet and hiding away in some gloomy corner, just because it would amuse him to make someone go on a fruitless search for him all over the pack's lands.

Striding farther into the barn, Gunnar continued to look in all the unlikely as well as the likely places that the gamma might be.

Finally, Gunnar spotted a movement up in the hay loft. He tilted his head up. Leaping back, his reactions were only just quick enough to prevent him being showered by a mouldering old pile of hay.

He silently watched the last couple of pieces of damp, foul-smelling hay fall to the ground just in front of his feet before he looked up again. "Alfred…" he warned.

"Sorry, didn't see you there." The brat didn't sound even the slightest bit sorry.

"And I'll bet you're going to say that you didn't hear me either, right?" Gunnar demanded.

"Did you call me?" Alfred asked. He didn't have Talbot's skill for sounding naïve and innocent.

Gunnar counted to ten. It didn't make him feel the least bit calmer. "Get down here," he growled.

"Why?"

Because I bloody well told you to! Gunnar kept the words back somehow. "Alfred. Down here, now!"

For several long seconds, it actually looked like he'd have to go up there and carry the little bastard down, but finally, with a theatrical sigh, Alfred made his way towards the ladder.

Every step he took was insultingly slow.

Gunnar's hand tightened into a fist at his side.

"What do you want?" Alfred snapped as he jumped down the last step and glared across at him. He wasn't that much bigger than Talbot when considered from a logical perspective. As the lowest ranking gamma, his station in the pack wasn't really all that different to the omega's either.

Yet, somehow, the disparity between him and Alfred failed to affect Gunnar in the least. No hint of any protective or possessive feelings rose up inside him as he held Alfred's eyes.

It took far too long for the gamma to drop his gaze. Even when he did, it was a hardly a real acknowledgement of their respective ranks. It was far more like a reluctant acknowledgement that he wouldn't stand a chance of beating Gunnar in a fight. He was just as bratty as Caden had been out in the wood, but with none of the latter's charm.

"Come on." Gunnar turned his back on the other wolf and strode out of the barn.

"Where are we going?" Alfred asked, as he quickly caught up and fell into step beside him.

"For a walk," Gunnar ground out.

"Why?" Alfred asked, sceptically.

Gunnar marched on in silence.

Because it was his duty, he reminded himself. Because Alfred was the wolf he should be courting, not Talbot. Because betas were always considered to be good matches for trouble makers, not for sweet little omegas. Because if he had to spend time with the little brat it was far better to do it outside than be cooped up inside, where it was far too likely he'd give in to the temptation to throttle Alfred long before he could bring himself to want to do anything else with him.

Alfred easily kept pace with Gunnar without needing the beta to slow his stride the way Talbot might have. No matter how much Gunnar told himself it was unfair to blame the gamma for that, right then everything about him that reminded Gunnar that Alfred wasn't Talbot was something to hate him for. Nothing was said until they'd gone over a mile.

"The alphas were pleased with the work you did in the garage," Gunnar finally managed to mutter, as he stopped by a stout wooden fence and rested his elbows on it.

The vantage point took in several of the fields that made up the land to the west of the pack's sprawling farm house. It should have been beautiful and peaceful, the perfect place to steal a kiss. Gunnar kept his face turned towards the view.

As hard as he tried to force himself to at least attempt to see the gamma in a more positive light, Gunnar couldn't even stop himself comparing Alfred's reaction to his words with what would have been Talbot's likely response.

The omega would have blushed at the gentle compliment and glanced up at him, quick and shy, and the hope to have pleased another wolf would have been shining brightly in his eyes.

Alfred merely shrugged and stared out over the fields as if he didn't give a damn either way.

Gunnar clenched his jaw as he took a deep breath and reminded himself that Alfred wasn't the only one who should be making more of an effort.

"What's going on with you and —?" the gamma began.

"What?" Gunnar cut in, spinning around to face Alfred square on.

Stay away from him! If you lay one hand on my mate I'll...

It was only the growl that exploded from the back of Gunnar's throat that kept the words back.

Alfred shrugged again, as if it was no big deal. But, at the same time, his eyes narrowed. An ominous light came into his expression. His interest was well and truly caught.

Gunnar rattled off curses inside his head. There was no way he'd shake the little bastard off Talbot's trail now. Gunnar stepped forward, automatically seeking to remind

Alfred that there was no way in hell that he'd win any fight between them.

"It's so sad to see brothers falling out..." Alfred murmured. He dropped his gaze, but once more it was obvious that it had nothing to do with respect. He seemed to be averting his eyes simply so he could stare at nothing and suffer no distractions while he plotted.

But he was looking away, that was the important thing. There was no way Alfred could have seen his surprise.

Caden...? Alfred thought they were talking about Caden?

By the time the gamma looked up, Gunnar had schooled his expression into something more suitable for the occasion. "What is your interest in my brother?" he demanded.

Alfred's eyes were damn near sparkling. It had never been so obvious to Gunnar just how much the other wolf deserved his reputation as the pack's trouble maker.

"No interest at all," Alfred said, with another bloody awful attempt at innocence.

Gunnar folded his arms across his chest and stared down at the shorter man. "Alfred..." he warned.

The cheeky little sod actually seemed to bite back a smile as he plotted whatever the hell it was he intended to do to Caden.

That was one of the few things Gunnar couldn't hate him for right then, not without being a complete hypocrite. He was having enough trouble forcing back his own amusement. Talbot might not be any sort of match for the sadistic little brat, but Caden...

Gunnar knew full well that Caden had wrapped men who had twice Alfred's malice in them around his little finger with nothing more than a smile. The image of what he was capable of doing to Alfred if the other gamma got on his wrong side sprang up in his mind so fully formed, so perfect, Gunnar could barely keep back a howl of laughter.

If Alfred went after Caden—for a scrap, for a screw, or for anything else—it sure as hell wouldn't be the trouble maker who won. And Caden would no doubt handle it just as he did everything else—with a smile on his lips and without getting one strand of floppy blond hair out of place.

As he turned and walked away from Alfred without another word, Gunnar finally allowed his smile to creep out. He might as well have gift wrapped Alfred for his little brother!

And if Caden would be distracting Alfred, and Alfred would be distracting Caden...

Quickening his stride, Gunnar didn't bother to pretend, even inside his own head, that he was doing anything other than seeking out his favourite little wolf as he reached the farm house.

"Have you seen—?" he began, as he spotted Francis and Steffan out by the woodpile, apparently laughing with each other as much as they were chopping any of the wood.

"The alphas are both looking for you," Francis cut in.

Gunnar stopped short. "Did they say what for?"

Francis shook his head. "They're in their office."

Gunnar turned away from the other wolves and strode into the building without any further delay. He'd made damn sure his face remained expressionless, but behind the facade of a good beta who never worried about anything, his mind rushed forward.

Caden wouldn't have gone to the alphas. That wasn't his style. He liked to handle things on his own.

Alfred certainly would have gone to them, and really enjoyed landing two of his pack mates in it, but he obviously didn't know enough to be able to do that effectively.

Of course, Talbot could have gone to them himself, but…

Gunnar's steps sped up again. Talbot would only go to them if he was truly scared by what had happened between them the previous night.

Sneaking out of the younger wolf's room before the other members of the pack woke up hadn't left much room for gentle whispers and reassurance. There hadn't been the opportunity for him to speak with Talbot since he'd left the house to complete another day's work on the wall.

As possibilities rushed through his head, Gunnar's concern for the omega had him at the alphas' door in seconds. He only managed to remember to knock politely and wait to be invited into the room because he didn't want to scare Talbot by bursting in unexpectedly.

"Come in."

He opened the door with as much control as he could muster. There was no bang, barely even a creak of the hinges, and Talbot…wasn't there. Gunnar stared at the chair in front of the alphas' desk for a long time before that fact sank in.

"Gunnar?" Marsdon finally prompted.

"Francis said you wanted to speak to me," Gunnar managed to say, with something that sounded impressively like sanity.

"Yes, we've decided to start work on the old orchard in earnest. It'll mean you making some changes to the duties you've assigned the gammas."

Gunnar nodded. He stepped forwards and lowered himself into the seat before the alphas' desk. They just wanted to talk to him about his duties as the de facto foreman of the work parties. Nothing was wrong. Talbot was fine.

"It seems you have a good beta's instinct for which wolves are suited to which tasks," Bennett suddenly said, with obvious approval in his voice.

Gunnar met his gaze for a second.

"Talbot certainly seems to be enjoying his new task far more than either of us thought he would," the alpha went on.

Gunnar looked away. "Talbot is..." He paused for a moment to clear his throat. "He's far stronger than he looks. If he's assigned more challenging duties, I think he might gain some extra confidence about his place in the pack."

"Until now we've been very careful not to apply too much pressure to him," Marsdon prompted.

Gunnar stared at the desk for a few moments, trying to think of a way to explain Talbot to men who had known him for far longer than he had, without offering his alphas an insult. "If he isn't challenged, if all his skills and strengths aren't made use of, I think there's a risk he won't understand how valuable he is to the pack. It's important that he feels safe in the pack, but I believe he needs to feel worthy of it too."

Bennett nodded. "He certainly seems to have changed in the last few days. We're both very impressed with the way you're handling him."

Gunnar didn't say a word. He didn't even blink.

"Perhaps you're aware that his parental pack also kept him very close, very cloistered. He tends to be very wary of wolves he doesn't know very well. But you seem to have slipped past his defences. We're both very impressed," Marsdon added.

The beta kept his gaze on the paperwork covering the alphas' desk. "Thank you," he said, when it was obvious that he had to say something before the conversation could move on.

"It hasn't been quite so easy for us to read how well you and Alfred are getting along," Bennett mentioned, from the other side of the desk. He was as bad at pretending to be casual as Alfred was at pretending to be innocent.

Gunnar forced himself to look up and meet the alpha's gaze.

"Have you two been able to spend any time together?" Marsdon asked. He was leaning against the cabinet behind the desk, right behind his mate. Gunnar met his eyes, too.

"Alfred is a fine wolf," he said. He could have cursed himself as soon as the words left his mouth. Forget casualness and innocence, polite lies were obviously the weak point in his own verbal arsenal.

Marsdon's lips twisted into a knowing smile. "Let's say he has the *potential* to be a fine wolf. The right mate could be the making of him…"

Gunnar nodded his understanding. He could be the making of the gamma if he was mated to him. The pack would be stronger for it. And every wolf who belonged to a pack knew that everyone was expected to make sacrifices to make the pack stronger as a whole.

"Do you think the right mate could be the making of Talbot, too?" he blurted out before he could stop himself.

Bennett's attention had already strayed back to the paperwork on the orchard. He blinked as he seemed to struggle to change mental topic. Then he smiled. "We're not in a rush to find him a mate just yet."

"Oh," Gunnar said.

Marsdon chuckled as he stepped forward to pore over the plans with Bennett. "Finding a mate for an omega certainly isn't one of your duties, Gunnar. No wolf would ask a beta to do that!"

Gunnar knew he was supposed to chuckle along with them. He managed to scrape up a smile, but couldn't risk uttering a sound in case it came out as a low, heartfelt howl of anguish.

The conversation immediately moved on to the orchard.

Gunnar did his best to attend to his duties and pay attention to his alphas' words, but part of his mind was still very much on Talbot.

He shouldn't have mentioned the omega to them that way. Until he had, there had still been some vague hope inside him that they might reconsider which wolf he should be mated to.

As that hope died, it was damn near impossible for Gunnar to care about apple trees.

* * * *

Someone was watching him.

Talbot span around as the sensation sent a little shiver tingling down his spine. A smile was already rushing to his lips. He fully expected to see Gunnar standing there, arms folded across his chest and a frown gathering on his forehead as he assessed the work Talbot had already completed that morning.

Maybe if he was pleased with his progress, Gunnar would decide he should take a break and they could —

All those thoughts faded away as he saw a very different wolf standing in the exact spot where he'd expected to see Gunnar.

"Caden?"

"Were you expecting someone else?" the gamma asked, raising an eyebrow in a way that might have been more reminiscent of his brother if his brows were darker or his general expression more glowering.

He knows.

As their eyes met, Talbot had never been more certain of anything in his life. Caden knew about him and Gunnar. He didn't suspect, he knew, and there was no way in hell anyone would convince him that he was wrong. Talbot swallowed rapidly as the thought sank in. He should say something, Talbot was well aware of that, but he couldn't bring a single word to his lips.

The gamma slowly stepped forward and ran his fingertips over the edge of one of the stones Talbot had put in place. His touch was lighter and more delicate than his brother's would ever be, yet Talbot still found himself holding his breath as if the wall would crumble under his touch.

"Gunnar was brought here to be mated to Alfred."

Talbot shuffled his feet against the trampled-down grass near the half re-built wall. He waited for the gamma to continue, but when he glanced up he realised that Caden had no intention of doing that until he'd acknowledged the first fact that had been thrown at him.

"Yes," Talbot whispered, half-wondering in what other ways Caden was more like Gunnar than anyone realised. "I know."

"You could say that he's practically promised to Alfred," Caden pushed.

Talbot nodded. "Yes." Maybe he *could* have said that, but he'd have done everything he could have to avoid it.

"So how do you think Alfred would feel?" Caden went on. "Knowing that the wolf who is promised to him is running around behind his back, sneaking off to screw you whenever he gets the chance?"

Talbot closed his eyes, hiding from both the accusation and the truth behind it. "He doesn't know that—"

"And how long do you think that will last?" Caden cut in, a growl creeping into his voice. "Neither of you is half as good at subtlety as you'd apparently like to think you are. In fact—you both suck at it! I'd give you a couple of days at most before the whole damn pack knows what's going on under their noses."

"I..." Talbot had no idea what to say. He pushed his mud-streaked hands into his pockets, before pulling them back out and folding his arms across his chest. He glanced down at his body language for a moment. His posture had nothing of Gunnar's gruff determination about it. It was all weakness, all submission and a desire to protect himself as best he could as he hid from the less pleasant parts of the world around him.

"Put yourself in Alfred's place," Caden ordered. "Imagine how it would feel for everyone in the pack to know you'd been passed over in favour of another wolf, of a lower ranking wolf."

Talbot nibbled at his bottom lip. It was so easy to imagine the other man's pain. For just a few seconds, it distracted him from his own discomfort.

"You need to call a halt to it," Caden announced.

"Me?" Talbot's gaze rose to meet the gamma's as panic rushed through him. "I can't, I..."

"Not even for Gunnar's sake?"

Talbot could do no more than blink across at the pretty blond shifter.

"He's the one who'll get lynched for screwing you," Caden went on. "No one will be pissed off at you for doing whatever the hell you want with him, but how do you think they'll treat him when they realise he's been getting his rocks off corrupting the most innocent member of their pack?"

Talbot shook his head. "It's not like that!"

Caden took no notice. He stepped forwards until he and Talbot stood almost toe to toe. "If you care about my brother, even a little bit, you'll walk away and make sure Gunnar never lays a hand on you again."

Talbot tried to breathe, but the idea of even trying to do that stole all the oxygen from the air.

"If you don't give a damn about him, then..." Caden trailed off, but he didn't need to say anything else.

Talbot dropped his gaze. He was vaguely aware of the other wolf leaving him alone at the wall once more, but it wasn't Caden that filled his mind as he stood, alone and isolated at the edge of a field, as far from the farm house as he had ever been on his own.

Right then, it was impossible for him not to think about Gunnar's arms wrapped tightly around him as they had slept through the night together...to remember the feel of Gunnar's lips on his...of the other man's hands roving over his body, casually groping him in his sleep...Gunnar's cock sliding between his lips and spilling across his tongue when they'd worked together at the wall the day before and...

Talbot forced his eyes open. Caden was right. He had more than enough memories to wrap around his mind on cold nights now. It was greedy to want more than that from life. He had a good pack, he had his memories of Gunnar, and he even had the chance to remain on the edge of the beta's life and stay close to his mate for years to come.

An omega shouldn't demand anything more than that from his life. An omega was of most use to his pack when he learnt how to put himself last and everyone else first.

Talbot rubbed the back of his hand against his eyes as he tried to turn his body, if not his mind, back to the task at hand. Gunnar wanted him to finish re-building the wall. He couldn't do that if the stone work was going to go blurry all the time.

* * * *

"What's wrong?"

This time there was no way Talbot could be wrong about which wolf he'd find behind him. Gunnar's voice was unmistakeable, especially when he seemed completely pissed off with the world.

As Talbot turned to face him, the beta loomed out of the shadows in the orchard, seeming as large as any of the ragged old fruit trees growing around them.

"Nothing," Talbot rushed out. "Nothing's wrong, I just..."

After forcing himself to sit opposite the other wolf at the table that evening and not even glance in his direction, Talbot knew he had already drained all his reserves of self-control. It would have been asking for trouble to stay in the house, to remain close to the beta and still remember how important it was for him to keep his distance from the other man.

"Don't lie to me!" Gunnar stepped out from between the shadows. The stars provided the only light that fell on that part of the pack's lands, but it was more than bright enough for Talbot to see the older man's anger. Even if it hadn't been, the emotion seemed to extend out from the beta's body, tendrils of it curling through space and enveloping everything it touched.

"I think, maybe, it would be best if we didn't..." Talbot closed his eyes, lacking the strength to go any further.

"If we didn't what?" Gunnar demanded, a growl growing deeper in his voice.

"If you and I didn't..." Talbot faltered again. "Spend any more time together," he finally managed to stutter out.

"What?"

Talbot pushed his hands into his pockets in an effort not to reach out to him. "I think, maybe, we shouldn't be doing this."

"And this revelation occurred to you when?" Gunnar demanded, dipping his head to avoid a low-hanging branch as he stepped closer.

Talbot knew he should step back, but he still couldn't bring himself to put any more distance between them than was absolutely necessary. "You and Alfred —"

"Aren't mated yet," Gunnar cut in.

"I know, but you will be, and..." Talbot trailed off as their eyes met.

"Can you keep looking me in the eye while you tell me that you haven't wanted everything that's happened between us?"

"I wanted it."

As soon as the words were said, Talbot took refuge in staring at the floor, but Gunnar's growl soon had him raising his gaze.

Finally his body remembered how to move. He stepped back and almost tripped. Gunnar didn't reach out to catch him as he managed to steady himself, but Talbot had a horrible suspicion that was only because Gunnar had already known he'd somehow manage to keep his footing.

Gunnar knew everything. Gunnar could see straight into his soul and —

"I don't want to get you in trouble," Talbot blurted out, knowing the truth was the only avenue left open to him. He couldn't end things himself, he saw that now, but he could put the whole mess in his mate's hands and let Gunnar deal with it for him.

Gunnar's frown remained for several long seconds as he glared down at Talbot. Then, it started to fade away. A slight smile twisted Gunnar's lips. His hand reached out to stroke Talbot's cheek. "Is that what you're worried about, little one? That *I'll* get in trouble?"

Talbot swallowed. He tried to bring Caden's words back to the forefront of his mind, but Gunnar's fingertip caresses along his jaw line quickly took over his senses.

"I can look after myself," Gunnar informed him. He seemed to bite some extra words back then, but there was no doubting the honesty in those he'd said aloud. "You don't need to worry about me."

"But what if the alphas — ?"

One of Gunnar's hands stole any other words Talbot might have been able to say. His other hand came to rest on the back of Talbot's head, preventing him from pulling away from the very effective gag.

He held Talbot very still and completely silent as he stared down at him, his eyes seeming to shine in the half light as both dark stands of hair and even darker shadows fell across his face. "I don't want to hear another word about the alphas, or about any other wolf in this pack. Right here, right now, it's just you and me. Understand?"

Talbot closed his eyes. He wanted that to be the case so badly, but...

"Understand?" Gunnar pushed.

And, suddenly, there was no way to avoid the fact that he was completely incapable of disobeying the beta—not even for Gunnar's own good. Talbot tilted his head back, half to bare his neck and indicate his submission, half to offer his lips up to be kissed.

A whimper escaped from behind Gunnar's hand as something inside him got loose and did its best to beg the beta for his reassurance. A bare moment later, Gunnar's lips replaced his palm. His tongue thrust into Talbot's mouth, impatient and demanding, seemingly determined to remind the omega of exactly who was in charge.

Talbot's hands finally realised they weren't restrained. They weren't even bound to a headboard by the beta's will. Tearing them out of his pockets, he quickly moved them to Gunnar's back, pulling him closer, sliding his palms down to the older man's arse and caressing him through the fabric as he fought to touch as much of the older man as he could reach.

His brain stopped working as one kiss morphed into another, then another. If any part of Talbot remembered that he was supposed to be holding back and not kissing Gunnar, not even a tiny fragment of him remembered why.

Talbot's fists clenched in the beta's shirt until strong hands wrapped around his wrists and dragged his hands back behind him. Talbot whimpered in pleasure as the stronger wolf's demands rushed straight to his cock and he hardened rapidly behind his fly.

When Gunnar transferred both his wrists into the grip of one hand, Talbot suddenly found that the beta's other hand was free to play with him. It quickly went to Talbot's jeans and fumbled at the zip. For once, Gunnar seemed as desperate as Talbot felt. The older man's coordination wasn't as skilful as it usually was, his fingers seemed to shake slightly.

Then, before Talbot had a chance to wonder what was wrong and without any warning, Gunnar's hands were gone. And the beta's body was gone, too. Talbot stumbled as all the support he'd so quickly come to rely on was snatched away from him.

A confused sound left the back of Talbot's throat, but he was pretty sure he was the only one who heard it. The weak little noise was instantly drowned out by the shouting that swiftly surrounded them.

Talbot blinked as he stumbled and looked around him, trying to work out what the hell was going on. The orchard was full of wolves now. The whole pack seemed to be crowded in between the trees, in a mixture of human and lupine shapes. Turning from one man to the next, trying to gain some sort of understanding, Talbot's eyes finally fell on Gunnar—or at least on that small part of him that was currently within his line of sight.

The beta was more than half hidden from him, with Talbot's view of his lover blocked by both his alphas. Stepping forwards, Talbot instinctively tried to rush to Gunnar's side, but there was no way for him to get through the press of bodies.

He tried to work his way around the edge of the group and find an omega-sized opening. He tugged at men's sleeves trying to convince them to step just slightly to one side so he could squeeze through.

As desperation coursed through him, it was almost impossible for Talbot to focus on the actual words being said, but the anger in everyone's voices was unmistakeable. They were all furious with Gunnar, just the way Caden had warned him they would be. And it was all his fault.

If he'd been strong enough to say no, if he hadn't wanted Gunnar so badly, then everything would have been fine for the other wolf. If he hadn't been so weak, if he hadn't loved Gunnar so much, then—

Pushing his hands between two of the larger wolves that stood between him and the beta, Talbot put every scrap of strength he had into forcing them apart. Against all his expectations, the larger wolves stumbled to the side. Talbot clawed his way between them and stumbled into the centre of the circle of wolves.

Barely managing to keep his footing, Talbot somehow remained upright as he looked frantically around. Gunnar stood in front of him. Talbot's gaze went straight to his lover's eyes. The beta's expression was angry to start with—suddenly it turned furious.

The beta had tried to step towards him, but he hadn't gone one pace before Bennett grabbed the collar of Gunnar's shirt and yanked him back.

Talbot expected the beta to rail and struggle against the alpha's hold on him. And, for a second, it looked like he would. Then Gunnar fell completely still. His eyes went from Talbot to Marsdon and Bennett, then back again. His gaze became assessing. His posture changed, becoming far more overtly deferential to the alphas. His struggles subsided.

"I asked, if you have anything to say for yourself?" Marsdon demanded as he moved to stand directly in front of Gunnar, half blocking Talbot's view without a thought.

Stepping to one side, Talbot regained a clear line of sight just in time to see Gunnar hold the alpha's gaze for a second, as if searching for something in his expression. "I just want to say that there's only one wolf to blame in this."

Talbot's breath caught in his throat. Even though he knew it was true, to hear the other wolf say it still felt like someone was stabbing him in the heart over and over again, twisting the knife at every opportunity.

Marsdon took a step towards the beta, more anger filling his scent by the moment.

"Me," Gunnar finished.

Marsdon paused. His stance was still one that implied he was ready to attack at any moment, but Talbot saw the alpha's profile become assessing as his gaze narrowed. "Your actions could be taken as a direct challenge to the hierarchy of this pack," he said. "Wolves have been thrown into limbo for far less."

Talbot went pale.

Gunnar barely blinked. "I'm not asking for leniency."

"No!" It took Talbot a few seconds to realise that the word had come from him and not another wolf.

Marsdon and Bennett's attention turned to him for a second.

For the first time in his life, Talbot fought against the urge to lower his eyes and show them his complete respect and deference. "If...if someone should be put in limbo, it's me, not Gunnar," Talbot managed to stutter out.

"Tal?" Bennett asked.

"It's my fault, not his!" Just talking about limbo sent a shiver through him. It was all he could do to stop his teeth from chattering as he forced the words out.

Frowning, Marsdon looked from him to Gunnar and back again before he turned his attention to Bennett. Something silent passed between the two alphas.

"Back to the house," Marsdon ordered.

Talbot quickly stepped forward, desperate to walk back at Gunnar's side, hoping that perhaps he'd be able to whisper apologies for getting him into so much trouble, but Bennett kept hold of Gunnar's shirt collar and Marsdon caught hold of Talbot's shoulder.

The alpha maintained a firm hold on him and kept him right on the other side of the group as they all walked back to the farm house, some of the wolves still running at their heels in their lupine form.

Even though months had passed, without Gunnar at his side there was no way Talbot could keep his memories of the challenge circle out of his head. When Bennett had been standing in the circle, that had been bad enough, but to actually be the wolf in the centre of the ring, to have to fight every wolf in the pack...

The thought made his stomach twist and somersault inside him. But still, better him than Gunnar. The pack would probably go easier on him. And even if they didn't, Talbot had no doubt it would still be better him than Gunnar.

The moment they reached the farm house, Marsdon turned to the other members of the pack. "Go up to your rooms, or back to your duties. Either way, no one is to enter the main hall until we're finished in there."

The gammas all left in different directions, leaving Gunnar and Talbot alone in the main hall with the alphas. Bennett immediately marched Gunnar across to one of the big sofas flanking the fire and pushed him roughly down onto the leather-clad cushions. The beta tumbled back. His hands skidded against the fabric as he tried to steady himself. As soon as he regained his balance, Talbot saw him sit up straight, but he didn't attempt to rise.

Talbot tried to step forward, but Marsdon's hand was still on his shoulder and the alpha guided him, far more gently but no less determinedly than Bennett had moved Gunnar, to the opposite sofa. The alpha nudged him to take a seat. Talbot's legs were shaking so badly he couldn't protest. He landed heavily on the cushion.

"Are you hurt?" Marsdon gently touched Talbot's cheek, coaxing him to look away from Gunnar for a few seconds. "Are you hurt?" he repeated.

Talbot shook his head.

"We need you to tell us the truth, Tal," Marsdon said, very seriously. "No one's mad at you, and no one is *going* to be mad at you either. You're not in any trouble. Okay?"

Talbot swallowed. No one was mad at him. They were all mad at Gunnar—because Gunnar had told them all it was entirely his fault. "About being in limbo," he managed to whisper. "I—"

"There's no way in hell either of your alphas is going to put you in limbo," Marsdon cut in, just a touch of impatience creeping into his voice.

"I—"

"It's not going to happen," Marsdon told him.

Talbot looked down as he fought against every instinct and desperately tried to disagree with his alpha. He closed his eyes as he stared down at his clenched fists. He had to do something. If he was going to have any right to think about Gunnar as his mate, even inside his own head, he had to act.

"He lied." The words exploded from his lips

Marsdon's jaw clenched with obvious anger, but he nodded, and his tone was far more encouraging when he spoke again. "Tell us what he told you."

Talbot shook his head, his heart quietly breaking as he realised that all he was doing was making things worse. "You don't understand."

"We will if you'll tell us what happened. We'll believe whatever you say," Marsdon promised as he crouched down and brought himself closer to Talbot's height.

"It wasn't Gunnar's fault," Talbot said. "It was mine." He couldn't look his alpha in the eye when he said it. He said the words to his feet instead.

Gentle fingertips touched his cheek, encouraging him to look up. Finally, he managed to do as Marsdon wanted. The alpha frowned as their gazes met.

Talbot wanted, more than almost anything, to look away. But he resolutely forced himself to keep his attention up and on the other wolf's eyes.

It was his fault. Marsdon had to see that—both the alphas had to see it.

Talbot swallowed rapidly as he saw the expression in the other man's eyes gradually change. The other wolf pulled back from him. He turned to Gunnar.

"Do you have anything to say?" Marsdon asked, just a touch of genuine query mixing in with the demand.

"I was the one making the decisions," Gunnar said. His voice couldn't have been more different to the way Talbot's had sounded when he put his own case forward. Somehow, his lies sounded more like the truth than anything Talbot had said. "He doesn't know what he's talking about."

Marsdon's eyes narrowed. Bennett was still standing by the side of the sofa he'd pushed Gunnar down onto. He was glaring down at him too. Talbot could almost feel the alphas weighing up the different stories that were being offered to them.

Gunnar didn't even blink under their scrutiny. "How hard do you think it could be for anyone to convince an omega that something was his idea even if it wasn't?" he asked. "And how easy do you think it would be for someone to convince me of the same thing?"

Talbot shook his head, but no one was looking in his direction. The alphas were still focussed on the beta. The atmosphere changed around Talbot as he sensed anger building inside them. Reaching out, he tugged at Marsden's sleeve. The alpha didn't even seem to notice.

Talbot shifted forward on the sofa. "Marsden..."

"Shut up."

Talbot turned towards Gunnar as the beta's order hit the air.

"Mind your manners, Gunnar—you're in enough trouble as it is," Bennett snapped. He turned away from him then, as if dismissing him from his mind. "Tal—go ahead, have your say. You're under no obligation to obey his orders now."

"I...I wanted to...I wanted everything we did together," Talbot managed to stutter out. "I wanted—even before we...I've always wanted him, since the first day he joined our pack."

Marsden reached out and ruffled his hair with his fingertips. There was just a touch of sadness in his eyes when he looked down at him, but that didn't matter, because Talbot saw the beginnings of understanding and realisation there too.

"I was the one who decided what would happen between us," Gunnar cut in from the other side of the fire. "Talbot isn't responsible for any of this."

Marsden and Bennett both turned back to the other man, as if they were watching one of those strange human tennis matches and the truth was bouncing back and forth between Talbot and his lover as fast as any little yellow ball could.

It was only when the alphas looked away from them both that the atmosphere seemed to change once more. Bennett moved to sit on the arm of the sofa. "Meaning that if anyone is to be punished, it should be you and not Tal?" he asked.

Gunnar didn't even hesitate. "Yes."

"No!" Talbot burst out.

"Be quiet," Gunnar growled.

As their gazes met one more time, Talbot realised what was happening, why the beta was telling all those lies about whose idea things were. Before he knew what he was doing, and apparently before Marsdon had a chance to react and stop him, he was off the sofa, across the room and kneeling on the floor in front of the beta.

Unable to make his throat work, all he could do was shake his head. Gunnar couldn't do that.

Talbot felt a hand on his shoulder, tugging gently at him, ordering him to rise, but Marsdon's hand had little power over him right then, not when he was looking into Gunnar's eyes.

"Obey your alphas," Gunnar ordered, turning his gaze pointedly away.

"But, you —"

"Are not your concern," Gunnar finished for him.

Talbot shook his head again. Even if he was never going to feel the other man's hands on his skin again, or enjoy the way the beta's lips caressed his, Gunnar would always be his concern.

"You're in love with him, aren't you?" Bennett said from somewhere off to Talbot's right.

The omega could only nod.

Gunnar's hand came to rest on his cheek, trying to stop the gesture short. "Don't."

Even if Talbot could have obeyed every other order the beta might ever give him, he knew that one was beyond him. There was no way he could stop loving the other wolf. It simply wasn't in him not to belong to Gunnar and be his mate with his heart, soul and everything else at his disposal.

Talbot closed his eyes, knowing his answer wasn't the one the other man wanted to receive and not wanting to see the disappointment in Gunnar's eyes.

Chapter Six

Gunnar closed his eyes as Talbot bowed his head lower over his lap. Cupping the omega's other cheek in his other hand, he dipped his head to rest it against the younger man's temple.

"Everything will be fine," Gunnar whispered. "*You'll* be fine." That was the most important thing, after all.

Talbot tried to shake his head, but Gunnar tightened his hold on him and refused to give the younger man permission to disagree with him while he was the one who had the omega's best interests firmly at heart.

The beta had no doubt he could deal with the anger of the alphas and the rest of the pack. He was reasonably sure he could even deal with being sent away from the pack in disgrace. But Talbot had to be kept safe.

Gunnar let his lips brush very gently against the omega's temple one last time before he lifted his head and turned to face Marsdon and Bennett.

"He's not the only one, is he?" Marsdon asked.

Gunnar made sure no hint of emotion crossed his face. Dipping his eyes just once, to indicate that he had no interest in challenging the alpha's place in the pack's hierarchy, he quickly met Marsdon's gaze and held it.

The alpha looked away first, but there was no weakness in the move. He merely looked to his mate, as if to check that they were in agreement.

"Is there some reason why you didn't come to us and tell us that you found the idea of being mated to Alfred disagreeable?" Bennett asked as he moved to stand at his mate's side.

Gunnar held his gaze just as respectfully as he had Marsdon's, but he couldn't let the comment pass without answering it. "I haven't said I'm unwilling to be mated to him," Gunnar said. "I'm still not saying that."

"Oh?" Marsdon asked.

"I knew what you had planned for me when I joined your pack."

"So if we were to order the pack outside to observe a mating ceremony between you and Alfred, you wouldn't have any objection?" Bennett asked, sceptically.

"I'll respect my alphas' right to make that decision," Gunnar said, barely resisting the temptation to cover Talbot's ears so he wouldn't hear him say it.

The omega was barely nineteen. He couldn't be expected to understand why it was better for Gunnar to give in to their request rather than fight against it. He'd probably never even realise that his choice would be what mollified their leaders into accepting them both back into the fold without Talbot receiving any punishment at all. If it came to a choice between trying to get what he wanted and succeeding in keeping Talbot safe, there was no real choice to make.

Gunnar felt the smaller man flinch and hated himself all the more for screwing things up so badly. The fact that he had no doubt the omega would forgive him without the slightest hesitation was beside the point. That just made it worse.

"And if we order the pack outside to observe a mating ceremony between you and Talbot?" Bennett asked. The words seemed to come from very far away. Even then, Gunnar could barely bring himself to listen to them.

"Then I'll respect my alphas' right to..." Gunnar's lips kept moving, but the rest of the sentence faded away as the other wolf's actual words started to sink in. Looking up, he met Bennett's gaze.

"Gunnar?" Bennett prompted.

The beta looked from one alpha to the other and back again, trying to work out what the hell was going on. When he looked down and his gaze fell on Talbot, the little wolf looked so hopeful.

Gunnar swallowed. He dropped his hands away from Talbot's face. "May I speak to you both in private?"

Talbot's hand came to rest in the centre of Gunnar's chest. His fist tightened in his shirt, as if he thought there really was some way they would be able to hold on to each other.

"No," Marsdon said, after a second's consideration. "There's been more than enough sneaking around behind people's backs already. I think it'll do you both the world of good for each of you to say whatever it is you need to say in front of the other."

He was an alpha. It was his right to make that decision. But Gunnar couldn't help but wish he'd chosen to make a different one. "This isn't his fault," Gunnar forced himself to say, without once looking towards Talbot. "It isn't fair on him for you to make him think you'll give us your permission to be mated when—"

"Not even if we mean every word we say?" Bennett cut in. He smiled slightly when Gunnar looked up and met his gaze. "We're not so cruel that we'd dangle the prospect in front of you only to snatch it away at the last moment. If it's what you both want, then you'll need to be honest with us and tell us what the hell's been going on."

Gunnar turned back to Talbot. The omega nodded to him, but he didn't speak for himself. He just looked up at him as if he honestly believed that Gunnar had some magical power to make everything right for them both.

Stroking his fingers through Talbot's hair, Gunnar stared down at him in wonder. It was stupid to love another man having that kind of belief in him when it was so blatantly unfounded, but still...

Marsdon cleared his throat. There was a touch of humour in his expression when Gunnar and Talbot both turned their attention to him. "We're still here, and there will be conditions if we do give you our blessing," the alpha informed them.

"May I know what they are?" Gunnar asked, amazed at how calm his voice sounded.

"No more sneaking around. No more secrets from your pack," Bennett said, firmly. "And no more secrets from each other."

Gunnar nodded his understanding, although he felt as if he didn't understand a damn thing. He knew full well why he'd been brought to the pack, and...

"Alfred..." he began, only to find he didn't have anything to add to the word.

"Doesn't seem to have suited you as well as we first hoped," Bennett finished for him. He shrugged slightly. "We'll work something else out for him."

They were serious. As Gunnar looked from one alpha to the other and back again, that was suddenly obvious. They were seriously considering abandoning all their carefully laid out plans and allowing him to be mated to Talbot.

"You're in love with each other, aren't you?" Marsdon asked.

Gunnar's throat went dry. It closed up in a way it hadn't since he was a little kid. For once he knew without any doubt that if he tried to speak, all that would emerge was a pup-like little whimper. He nodded.

It was worth the struggle he'd gone through to find a way to reply when Talbot smiled up at him, almost as if he couldn't believe his luck.

"See how well things work when you're honest with each other about how you feel," Marsdon said.

Gunnar kept staring down at Talbot, wondering if it was really possible that it hadn't been obvious to the omega from the start. Had he really thought he'd neglect his duty, if there was anything he could have done to prevent himself from straying off the path higher ranking wolves had chosen for him?

"He's the reason why you've been so happy the last few days, isn't he?" Marsdon asked Talbot.

The omega turned to his alpha. He nodded. "Yes." The word was little more than a whisper.

Marsdon nodded his understanding. "Wait there, both of you."

Marsdon and Bennett strode across to the other side of the room. Gunnar watched them bow their heads together. It was impossible to hear what was being said between them from where he sat with Talbot.

Gunnar looked down at the younger wolf. The omega's fear that their leaders would refuse them permission to be together was clear in his eyes. Gunnar hesitated. He studied his lover more closely. No, he realised, it wasn't the alphas' decision he was so worried about. His attention was all on the wolf he wanted to be his mate. Talbot was worried about *his* reaction, not anyone else's.

"If you don't want—" Talbot began, but a shake of Gunnar's head silenced him.

"I've never doubted what I want," he informed the omega. "Or doubted *who* I want, either."

Talbot lowered his gaze for a second. The blush that crept to his cheeks really did suit him so well.

"We've made our decision," Bennett suddenly announced.

Gunnar slowly lifted his eyes away from Talbot and looked across the room at them. A fist seemed to clench around his heart, holding it still in his chest as he waited.

"If either of you had just stood back and let the other take the blame when you were obviously in this together from the start, you'd have deserved whatever punishment we saw fit. And, believe me, if we'd found out that anyone had been taken advantage of, all hell would have broken loose," Marsdon said.

Gunnar nodded his understanding.

"And you're wrong if you think you'll both get away scot free just because you're blatantly in love with each other and ready to jump into limbo to save each other's skins," Bennett added. "There will still be repercussions."

"Yes," Gunnar agreed.

"That said..." Marsdon looked from one of them to the other, then to where Bennett was leaning against the back of the other sofa.

Bennett smiled. "That said, we'd be hypocrites if we refused a love match just because you were both too bloody dense to ask for permission for one from the start."

"Come outside," Marsdon said, his face splitting into a grin. "There's a ceremony to be performed. Best do it now, before you two get yourself into even more trouble."

It took Gunnar several seconds to pull himself together as the announcement sank in. By that time, Talbot had already risen and was tugging very gently at his wrist, encouraging him to his feet.

Long before Gunnar pulled himself off the sofa, the alphas were shouting up the stairs and out through the back door into the courtyard, calling all the other wolves to follow them out to the spot on the edge of the forest where the mating ceremonies had been conducted since before Gunnar had joined the pack.

By the time they had walked halfway to the forest edge, it seemed to Gunnar that every other wolf had caught up with them. But if he was too distracted to notice that a few members were conspicuous by their absence, there were others who weren't.

"Where are Alfred and Caden?" Marsdon asked, a frown quickly growing between his brows. "Has anyone seen them?"

"We passed them by the wood pile," Francis said, from the other side of the Gunnar. "They were...busy."

"Too busy to attend a mating ceremony—?" Marsdon demanded. He broke off as Gunnar saw Bennett elbow him in the ribs.

"I think they mean Caden and Alfred are *busy*," Gunnar heard the other alpha say. Bennett's lips twisted into a small smile as he slipped his arm around Marsdon's waist.

Suddenly, Gunnar found both the alphas looking towards him for an explanation. For a few moments, he forced himself to think of someone besides Talbot.

"It would explain why Caden was so pissed off with me for not thinking Alfred was a bloody brilliant match," he realised. The cheeky little sod hadn't been worried about him hurting *Talbot* at all!

Marsdon looked back towards the house, as if he was thinking about rushing back to rescue Caden from some terrible fate. Gunnar couldn't help but chuckle at the idea. The alpha raised an eyebrow at him.

"Caden's wrapped far better wolves than Alfred around his little finger with nothing more than one of his pretty smiles. If he's set his sights on him, and if you decide you're in favour of allowing them to continue on that course, it's not Caden who might find himself out of his depth and needing to be rescued," Gunnar said.

A look passed between the alphas once more. Bennett was smiling at the idea. Marsdon seemed less sure of it, but he seemed willing to follow his mate's lead on that particular matter. He slipped his arm around Bennett in return as they resumed their journey.

Gunnar found his hand automatically going to the small of Talbot's back to steady the small wolf in much the same way Bennett reached for Marsdon, but there was no responding touch from the little omega.

Talbot didn't even look up from the grass underfoot until they stopped and Gunnar held out his hand, taking care to place it well within the younger man's line of sight. Talbot slowly reached out to him in return, settling his smaller hand neatly in Gunnar's palm.

His hand was cold. The beta strengthened his grip on it, holding him tighter, warmer, safer.

It seemed to do the trick. Talbot looked up, all big, blue, uncertain eyes, all hope.

Their alphas' palms covered their joined hands, increasing their grip over Gunnar's hold on Talbot, as if reassuring him that it was safe to hang on to him as tightly as he could ever want to, because once this was done, no one would ever be able to pull them apart.

"Alpha to both beta and omega, wolf to wolf, we offer you the chance to form a new life, a new bond, a new pairing within our pack."

Until the words were actually hanging in the air, part of Gunnar really believed that something would happen to stop it all in its tracks. A huge weight rose off his shoulders as he realised that the only people who could stop it now were him and Talbot, and there was no way in hell either of them would do that.

"An unmated wolf takes a mate and forms a bond with another unmated wolf from your pack," Gunnar said, making sure each word hit the air strong and clear. And maybe just a little bit of him couldn't help but use the words to remind any wolf within hearing that Talbot was his now, and anyone who messed with the wolf he loved would be messing with him, too. "A bond that can never be broken."

Talbot nibbled at his bottom lip as he listened to every syllable very carefully. He cleared his throat before he repeated them back to him. There was no dominance, no hint of ownership in those words. Gunnar was quite sure that he was the only wolf there who would ever guess that he'd been just as thoroughly claimed as Talbot had been, that he was just as owned as the younger man would ever be, and the omega barely had to raise his voice to do it.

As he reluctantly let go of Talbot's hand and turned to accept the congratulations of the other members of the pack, he immediately met Marsdon's eyes. And suddenly he was very sure that at least one other wolf knew that it was quite easy for a dominant wolf, even an alpha wolf, to be owned right down to the core.

"I think you're going to prove to be a very good match for each other," Marsdon said as they shook hands.

Gunnar nodded. He seemed to do a lot of nodding after that. By the time he finally closed his bedroom door behind them, sealing himself and Talbot away from the rest of the pack for a little while so they could strengthen their bond, he was damn near sure his head was going to fall off.

Reaching up, he rubbed at the back of his neck as he turned away from the door. Talbot stood in the middle of the room, much as he'd stood in the centre of another room not so long ago. And the omega was once again all nerves, now that they were alone together.

As much as part of Gunnar wanted to smile and make a fuss of him, as much as he longed to tell him everything would be fine, he bit back the inclination. He didn't need to *say* it was fine. He needed to make it fine. Saying it wouldn't mean a damn thing.

"Tell me what each of our ranks are in this pack, Talbot," he ordered, leaving over a yard of carpet between them as he folded his arms across his chest and stared down at the shorter man.

"You're a beta," Talbot said, cautiously. "And I'm an omega."

"That's right. But I think you forgot that earlier this evening, didn't you?"

The smaller wolf's Adam's apple bobbed as he swallowed rapidly. "I..."

Gunnar stepped forwards, closing the gap between them.

When Talbot would have looked down, Gunnar tucked a knuckle under his chin, demanding he keep his gaze up. "What were you thinking, stepping in like that, telling them it was your fault, saying that *you* should go into limbo?" he demanded.

A slight frown grew between Talbot's pale blond brows. That obviously hadn't been what the younger wolf had been expecting.

"If this mating is going to be a success—and make no mistake, Talbot, I fully intend it to be incredibly successful—it'll be because we remember who we are, because we work *with* our natures not against them."

The little wolf just continued to stare up at him, so lost, so confused, but without any doubt so submissive, too.

Somehow resisting the urge to ruffle the pup's hair or press a kiss to his temple, Gunnar kept his tone serious and his words strong. "You said you're an omega. Tell me what that means."

"I..." was all Talbot managed to say.

"Tell me what a beta is, then," Gunnar ordered.

Talbot cleared his throat. "Strong," he blurted out.

Gunnar nodded for him to continue.

"In charge. Confident." More words followed, tumbling out as Talbot seemed to scramble to fill the silence as quickly as possible.

Finally Gunnar reached out and put a fingertip to his lips. "That's enough. Now, I'll tell you what a good omega is like."

Talbot couldn't have looked more terrified if Gunnar had lifted a hand to strike him.

"Omegas are sweet, and gentle, and good. They prefer to follow rather than lead. They like to obey more dominant wolves. They like to be held and petted and fussed over. They like to be controlled—sometimes they like to be held down, or even tied up, and that's good too. They're inclined to forgive their mates for being bossy or demanding—just as they're inclined to make them feel protective and possessive as hell. Omegas are a perfect match for a certain kind of beta."

Talbot swallowed rapidly. A blush stained his cheeks a very pretty pink as he finally seemed to realise that there weren't going to be any insults thrown at him. Gunnar smiled as he stroked the heated flesh with his thumb. Over time he was going to come to realise that there was nothing to be ashamed of in his rank—he was going to realise that an omega was exactly what his mate wanted.

"There's only one wolf in this room who needs to step in front of his mate and keep him safe, only one wolf who needs to defend his mate," Gunnar said, very seriously. "What happened with the alphas today—you trying to rescue me—that doesn't happen again."

"I just—"

"Wanted to take the blame, to pretend you made all the decisions for us, to let me hide behind you?" Gunnar asked. "You think that's what I'd want you to do, that I'd let you get hurt so that I could get away scot free?"

Talbot shook his head.

"I love that you tried, angel," Gunnar told the omega, as gently as he could. "But don't try to be a beta for me. Because one thing you forgot to mention in your description is that betas are right bossy bastards. One of them is more than enough for any relationship."

Talbot's eyes opened very wide. He tried to bite back a smile, but he wasn't sure he did a very good job of it. He was pretty sure Gunnar had to have noticed that. When he saw the look in the beta's eyes he lost any doubts he might have had.

Gunnar smiled back at him. He stroked his fingers through his hair, tugging gently at the strands in the process. "Yes, I'm aware of my faults, little one. But that doesn't mean I want you to start trying to replicate them, understand?"

Talbot nodded.

"I want an omega," Gunnar whispered in his ear. "I've wanted an omega since the first day I joined this pack. I've loved an omega since not long after that, too. But all you did was act like you were terrified of me and run away every time I got close."

Talbot shook his head. "I didn't—"

"Don't argue," Gunnar cut in, as he pressed a finger against his lips once more. "It doesn't suit you, and you're not half so good at it as I am."

One of his hands was still on the back of Talbot's head. It guided Talbot forwards until his head came to rest on the beta's shoulder. He couldn't help but lean into Gunnar's body and snuggle slightly against the larger man's strength now that he suddenly felt welcome to do that.

"*This* suits you," Gunnar whispered to him.

The bare skin above the beta's shirt collar was right in front of Talbot's lips, far too tempting to resist, especially because it seemed just about possible that he was allowed to give in to his desires now. He licked at his neck.

Gunnar chuckled as he pressed his lips against the top of his head in return, making Talbot smile.

Once the beta coaxed him to look up, he transferred the kiss to his lips instead. And within seconds, every thought in Talbot's head had melted away like spring snow in the bright morning sunlight. He was barely even aware of what was happening until he toppled backwards onto the mattress.

Gunnar tumbled down onto the bed with him, but he seemed to hover in the air just above him rather than land with him in the tangle of limbs the omega would have expected. As the kiss ended, Talbot opened his eyes.

Gunnar loomed over him, his hands resting on the mattress to either side of Talbot's shoulders.

"Mine."

Talbot nodded.

"When I want you to stay silent, I'll gag you," Gunnar informed him. His lips twisted into a little smile.

Talbot stared at his lips, thoroughly enchanted. He'd hardly ever seen the habitually serious wolf smile that way at anyone, and now he was smiling like that at him. Now his *mate* was smiling at him...

"And if I want you to stay still, I'll hold you in place," the beta went on. "Or maybe just tie you up."

Talbot met his mate's gaze as the image of that possibility jumped into the front of his mind. It was so easy to picture it. He could almost swear that he could feel the bindings wrap around his wrists as they spoke.

Gunnar chuckled again, a full, rich sound, but somehow also a joyous one. "Do you like that idea, little one?"

Talbot swallowed.

"I meant what I said about gagging you, Tal. Speak up if you want to keep the ability to say another word during the rest of the evening."

Talbot tried to make words happen, but his lips didn't seem to want to move.

Gunnar pulled away. "Don't say I didn't warn you..."

Talbot jerked up into a half-sitting position. He reached out and caught hold of the edge of Gunnar's shirt, tugging at it, trying to get his attention.

"I like that idea," he finally managed to stutter out, as Gunnar glanced back at him.

The beta smiled over his shoulder at him.

Talbot blushed — there was no way anyone would have been able to doubt the honesty in his voice, or the enthusiasm in it.

"You're not tied up yet," Gunnar said. "And I want you naked."

It took Talbot a few seconds to put those two facts together and form them into an order. As soon as he did, he pulled his shirt over his head and tossed it aside. He reached for the buckle on his belt as soon as the thin cotton hit the floor.

Still sitting in the middle of the mattress, Talbot scrambled out of the rest of his clothes, as if they were burning his skin from tip to toe and his only chance of survival was to bare his skin before the other man — as if some part of him really thought that rubbing his skin against the beta's body would somehow put out the flames — or maybe allow the blaze to consume him completely. Either outcome seemed perfectly acceptable to Talbot right then.

Gunnar sat on the edge of the bed and watched him perfectly calmly. When everything that he could remove had been tossed off the bed, Talbot knelt in the centre of the blanket, his cock hard and his breath coming in shallow gasps.

"You too?" he asked, as his eyes ran over Gunnar's T-shirt and his jeans. As soon as the words left his mouth, he knew they were a mistake. Gunnar would think he was challenging him, trying to take control, and that was the one thing he knew a beta would never accept in a mate.

The only thing that stopped an apology leaving Talbot's lips was the way his throat closed up in panic. But, somehow, the frown he expected to flash across the beta's face didn't appear.

Gunnar smiled slightly as he stood up. "Have you ever challenged another wolf?"

Talbot shook his head.

"Then I'd be a fool to think you were going to start today, wouldn't I?"

Strong hands moved deftly as Gunnar quickly stripped himself down. Talbot watched, fascinated by and completely in love with every inch of his new mate in equal measure, and there was no need to lower his eyes for a single second. Part of Talbot started to understand that.

He was an omega and Gunnar was a beta. They both knew that. They both liked that. There was no need to make it obvious with his eyes.

Gunnar tossed every scrap of his clothing away, but as soon as he was stripped down to his bare skin, he picked up his belt again. The moment Talbot glanced at it, all thought of where he should keep his gaze became irrelevant. It was impossible for him to look away from the length of brown leather.

The larger wolf ran the belt through his fingers very slowly. Talbot swallowed. He didn't think. Instinct took over. He leant forward and pressed a kiss to the back of Gunnar's hand just where the leather was looped around his skin.

Gunnar brushed the leather across Talbot's cheek when he looked up at the beta.

"Do you like that?"

Talbot nodded, pressing another kiss against the other man's belt. He remembered the threat of the gag. "I like it," he whispered. And he was pretty sure it was something that it was very okay for a beta's mate to like a great deal.

Gunnar caught hold of his wrist without another word. He rubbed the leather across it, teasing Talbot with the prospect of it being secured against his skin.

Talbot glanced towards the headboard of Gunnar's bed. It was made in a different style than his own, smaller bed frame. There were no rails for the beta to tie his hands to. Talbot looked back to Gunnar for advice.

Gunnar didn't waste another moment. Tugging both of Talbot's hands behind his back, he quickly wrapped the leather around them.

Talbot looked over his shoulder, watching as well as he could as the older man's hands worked deftly to bind him to himself.

The next second, Talbot found himself falling forwards. All it took was a gentle push against his shoulders and he toppled helplessly away from the beta. He tugged at his bonds, but they held true. There was no way he could stop himself landing face first on the bed.

He closed his eyes, as if that might somehow help ease his landing, but halfway down he suddenly stopped, suspended in mid air. The belt tightened against his wrists, as if someone was holding it.

Talbot opened his eyes. The pressure against his wrists changed. The bed slowly rose up to meet him as he found himself being lowered gently to the mattress. His cock brushed against the bedding.

Gunnar laughed when Talbot whimpered at the sensation, but he continued his unhurried descent regardless. Gradually, every bit of Talbot's body came to rest on the soft blankets. Turning his head, he let his cheek come to rest on the bed, too.

A second later, he felt the mattress move beneath him as Gunnar rearranged himself on the bed with him. The beta's skin brushed against him as the larger man covered Talbot's body with his own.

Talbot flexed his fingers. They were trapped between their bodies now. He could feel Gunnar's skin against his palms, but there were no decisions for him to make. There was no choosing where his hands should go, where he wanted to touch the other man. The decision had been made for him, and Talbot couldn't have loved Gunnar more for that.

The older man rocked his hips and his cock rubbed against the cleft between Talbot's buttocks. He tried to spread his legs for the other man, but the beta's knees rested on the bed just outside his. He was trapped, unable to offer himself to his mate the way he desperately wanted to.

Talbot whimpered his frustration into the sheet as Gunnar kissed his neck, nipping gently at his skin. He wriggled beneath the larger man, but there was nothing he could do, nowhere he could go. All he could do was accept whatever his lover chose to give him. "Please?" Talbot whispered.

Gunnar's lips moved against his skin as he smiled.

Talbot automatically smiled into the blankets in response, pleased that he had pleased the other man in some way. If Gunnar wanted to hear him beg, Talbot was happy to oblige.

He opened his eyes and stared along the bedspread just in time to see Gunnar's hand slide under the pillow and extract a tube of lube. Apparently, begging wasn't necessary.

A second later, the beta's hands were slipping underneath him. Gunnar lifted Talbot's hips until he was able to get his knees back beneath him. It was impossible for Talbot to reach out and put his hands on the mattress to lift the front half of his body. His weight came to rest on his shoulders, arching his body up into a strange shape as his hands remained firmly bound behind his back.

There was no need to be embarrassed about having his arse up in the air in offering. He was arranged the way his mate wanted, and there was nothing that could have felt more natural to Talbot than that. And there was no need to struggle to make thoughts happen once Gunnar's slicked fingers began to work their way into his hole either. His mate was in control of the whole world. All Talbot could do was whimper and moan, and throw in the occasional begging murmur.

Gunnar didn't say a word. It was as if he knew any and every decision was his, and that Talbot wouldn't want it to be any other way. He had the complete confidence not even to need to ask Talbot his opinion on whatever was going to happen between them.

Talbot didn't need to scrape up a single syllable that made the slightest bit of sense before the tip of the beta's cock pressed against his hole and Gunnar pushed forward, sliding into him inch by inch. Talbot's hands clenched and unclenched behind his back, searching for more contact with the other wolf, hoping he might be able to find him before he tumbled helplessly into his orgasm.

He was so on edge he knew it would only take him seconds. A few thrusts and it would all be over. But, without any warning, Gunnar's hands moved to Talbot's shoulders. The beta jerked him up, so he was kneeling on the bed, leaning back against the larger wolf's chest.

Gunnar's arms wrapped around him as his shaft settled even deeper inside Talbot's arse. The larger wolf held him close and perfect. His whole body seemed to surround him, trapping Talbot's hands between them once more.

Each time Gunnar moved, their bodies rubbed together and it was impossible for Talbot to control even the tiniest detail of anything, all he could do was enjoy every moment as it happened.

His mate had no interest in following him—every movement Gunnar made was all about leading. Talbot groaned his pleasure again and again as he leant into the stronger man's hold and simply gloried in belonging to the beta in the most basic way a wolf could.

His orgasm thundered through him without any warning, and Talbot couldn't do anything except throw back his head and howl his ecstasy at it all.

Still untouched by anything but the brief caress of the blankets, Talbot's cock spilled across the bed in front of him. Gunnar's howl filled the air just a moment later, far louder than Talbot's, but still somehow blending perfectly with it.

And the beta's howl was all the more perfect simply because Talbot suddenly realised that, for the first time, Gunnar finally seemed to feel free to let go of any attempt to control himself. His howl was feral and heartfelt in equal measure and it seemed to seep into Talbot's very soul as it echoed through the room.

A moment later, they toppled forward onto the bed together, Talbot getting trapped snugly under his mate in the process. Every breath Gunnar took rubbed their skins together, sending just a little more pleasure vibrating through Talbot's body.

It was easy to forget that a world existed outside that bed, until a knock sounded on the door.

Gunnar let out an irritable growl against Talbot's shoulder before he lifted his head. "What?"

The wolf outside their door cleared his throat. "Marsdon says that it's still early. You're both to come downstairs and show your faces to the rest of the pack whether you want to or not. It's about time you stopped hiding yourselves away, and it won't kill you to get dressed for a few minutes."

Gunnar didn't seem impressed, but within a few seconds he'd pulled himself up from the bed and begun to follow his alphas' dictates. While Talbot remained clumsy with afterglow and his actions remained slow and sleepy, the older man simply took control, not just of dressing himself, but of dressing Talbot too. Buttons that were beyond Talbot's abilities right then were quickly fastened for him and, long before the omega was ready for it, Gunnar led him downstairs to face the pack.

As the beta made himself comfortable in the seat left unoccupied on the sofa, Talbot managed to pull a few brain cells together and realise that there wasn't room for him to sit next to his lover. Still high on endorphins and pure happiness, he couldn't bring himself to regret that for more than a moment. He'd be at Gunnar's side when they went to bed — that was the important thing.

Stepping past the sofa, Talbot moved forward to settle himself into his usual spot by the fireside but Gunnar's hand caught hold of his wrist.

A sharp tug had him stumbling back and toppling helplessly into Gunnar's lap. The beta caught him safely in his arms as if there was nothing at all unusual about him dragging his lover around that way.

Within a few seconds Talbot had been rearranged so he was settled perfectly comfortably, curled into the larger man's hold on him, more warm and snug than he'd ever have been sitting in front of the fire.

Through the whole process, Gunnar continued his conversation with Marsdon and Bennett as if it were all completely natural. When Talbot looked up, Marsdon and Bennett were smiling across at them, amusement dancing in both their expressions. They weren't quite sitting in each other's laps, but they were curled around each other as close as two wolves could get while they were still dressed.

Still not sure he should be squashing his mate, Talbot squirmed and tried to lift some of his weight off the beta.

Gunnar merely tightened his grip on him until Talbot realised that breathing and continuing to squirm weren't compatible. It was one or the other. He chose breathing.

As soon as he fell still, Gunnar's hands turned gentler. Once he stopped fighting and gave in to the other wolf's will the way he'd wanted to from the beginning, the beta pressed a kiss onto the top of his head in silent praise.

Talbot closed his eyes and snuggled a little more comfortably into his mate's body. That was what omegas were good at. They were good at being held. And betas were good at doing the holding.

It was the duty of the beta to look after him now. And, Talbot thought to himself, it was the duty of the omega to look after his beta in return.

Even if Gunnar probably didn't see that, as they snuggled on the sofa with the rest of the pack close around them, Talbot knew it. It was his duty as a beta's mate to make sure his lover knew there would always be someone he could smile at without worrying about anyone taking it as a sign of weakness, without inviting a challenge.

Talbot smiled against the other man's shoulder. He could do that. He was pretty sure that was something else that omegas would turn out to be very good at indeed.

THE LOVE
OF A MATE

Dedication

To Love.

Chapter One

Halfway through his shift from his lupine form into his human shape, Alfred sensed someone approaching from his left. His shoulders were barely formed when a blurry figure pushed against them, sending him staggering backwards.

"What the hell do you think you're—?" Alfred stopped abruptly as his back hit the wall alongside the woodpile. All the air rushed out of his lungs, stealing any other words he might have wanted to snarl at his attacker.

The rough bricks bit into his suddenly furless skin, his palms skidded against them as he tried to catch his balance on two legs instead of four. So soon after a shift, his movements were clumsy, his co-ordination non-existent. It was several moments before he could even make his eyes focus on the man standing before him and the blur morphed into—

"Caden?"

Alfred glared at the other wolf in disbelief as the pretty blond stepped forward, closing the gap between them.

It was bad enough having to put up with being pushed around by Gunnar. Alfred would be damned if he'd allow the beta's little brother to treat him the same way! A low growl building in the back of his throat, Alfred reached out to shove Caden away.

His hands quickly reached the place where the other shifter's shoulders should have been, but his claws only met empty air. There was no howl of pain as Caden stumbled and fell from the force of the blow.

A second passed slowly. One brain cell bumped gently into its neighbour inside Alfred's head. Werewolves didn't just disappear — they shifted. Alfred looked down, fully expecting to see a wolf looking back up at him, but Caden was still very much in his human form.

The gorgeous young wolf knelt prettily at Alfred's naked feet and retuned his gaze as if that were nothing out of the ordinary.

Bloody bizarre was what it was. Alfred frowned as his sluggish brain tried to make sense of it and failed. He lowered his hands, not above striking someone who was already on his knees.

Caden leant forward. Without any warning, a pair of perfect pink lips wrapped themselves around the tip of Alfred's cock. For several long seconds, Alfred waved his hands uselessly in the empty air, as they stalled halfway to their destination. A strangled noise escaped from the back of his throat, but not one single thought managed to work its way through his brain.

Hot wetness suckled firmly around the head of his cock as Alfred quickly began to harden under its ministrations. A wave of pure bliss swept through him when Caden swirled his tongue in a complex little manoeuvre that lapped away all his strength.

Alfred's knees threatened to buckle. If the wall hadn't been ready to support him, he'd have crumpled into a desperate heap right there next to the woodpile. The deep scratches the rough surface gouged into his back were a small price to pay for being able to keep his cock at the right height for Caden's mouth.

Delicate hands came to rest on Alfred's hips, steadying him further. Alfred tried to thrust forward as Caden dipped his head and took a little more of his cock into his mouth, but there suddenly seemed to be surprising strength hidden in the slim, artistic digits. His hips stayed firmly against the wall.

Growling his frustration, Alfred glared down at the other wolf. Their eyes met. For once, those stunning blue eyes seemed to be completely serious. Alfred was incapable of looking away. No matter what his place in the pack was supposed to be, he was helpless to do anything other than hold the other gamma's eyes and lose himself in the blue depths.

Caden looked away first, but it felt far less like a wolf offering another man his submission then a master technician dropping his eyes to pay better attention to the job at hand—or mouth, as the case may be. Gradually, Caden began to bob his head lower, taking more and more of the now-stiff shaft into his mouth.

His tongue danced along the underside of Alfred's cock each time he dipped his head. As he pulled back, he swirled his tongue around the glans, before rapidly taking the entire shaft back into his mouth, the tip sinking into his throat.

Without any warning, Caden looked up again. Caught off guard, Alfred could only whimper his admiration. The other wolf's lips were thinned out into a pale pink line, his cheeks slightly hollowed as he sucked, and somehow it all just made him more gorgeous than ever.

Alfred reached out, desperate to thread his fingers into the impossibly golden strands of hair and keep Caden exactly where he was forever. He was vaguely aware that one of the other wolf's hands had left his hip, but before Alfred had even had a chance to really notice that, Caden's fist was wrapped tightly around his wrist.

"What the—?" Alfred tried to say more, but words failed him as Caden's tongue lapped at the sensitive strip of skin where his foreskin joined his shaft.

As if nothing at all had happened to break his concentration, Caden calmly resumed bobbing his head over Alfred's crotch. At the same time, he guided Alfred to lean forward and rest his hand on his shoulder rather than in his hair. Alfred found his fingers clutching at the thin cotton shirt as he tossed back his head and howled his pleasure into the cold night air.

His hips bucked forward, and Caden was strong enough to stop him then. Alfred's vision blurred. The whole world condensed down into something more glorious than he could ever remember it being. Every fibre in his body whimpered its joy. Even his fingertips seemed to feel their share of his bliss as he came into his lover's mouth. Then, long before Alfred was ready to let go of it, the ecstasy faded away.

It could have been mere moments before he opened his eyes, it could have been hundreds of years. Alfred's brain wasn't working well enough to deal with complicated concepts like time. All he knew for sure was that Caden was still kneeling at his feet and suckling gently around his softening shaft when he finally managed to blink down at him.

Caden's eyes were peering back in return at him, apparently studying his every reaction very carefully. Seeming to realise Alfred was back with him, he leant back and delicately allowed Alfred's shaft to slip from between his slightly swollen lips.

Lifting a hand to his mouth, Caden ran his fingertips over his mouth, but not a single drop of cum had escaped his attention. Apparently satisfied he was as perfectly presented as ever, Caden smiled and rose gracefully to his full height.

More of Alfred's brain cells gradually remembered what they were supposed to be doing. He looked over Caden's shoulder. The very pissed-off wolves he expected to see heading their way didn't appear immediately.

"No one will have heard us," Caden said, his tone very soft and strangely intimate in the cool evening air. "They've all gone to the mating ceremony."

Alfred's forehead creased into a frown. "Gunnar and Talbot," he managed to remember through a haze of afterglow.

"Yes," Caden said, once more studying Alfred very carefully, as if waiting for his reaction.

Alfred's frown deepened. "Why the hell should I care?"

Caden's hand came to rest on Alfred's shoulder as if seeking to console him from some imagined hurt.

"At least now Gunnar won't be nipping at my tail every damn time I turn around," Alfred muttered. He tried to shake off Caden's touch, but the other wolf didn't seem to notice.

"I'm glad you feel that way," Caden murmured, leaning forward until his lips almost caressed Alfred's ear.

Struggling to turn his head and pull away far enough to see Caden's face, Alfred glared at him through narrowed eyes. "Why?"

"It wouldn't seem right for me to be mated to a wolf who had ever had real feelings for my brother."

"What!" Alfred damn near sent them both sprawling to the ground as he tried to jerk away from the other wolf.

Caden stubbornly refused to back away a single inch. "I said that it—"

"I heard what you said!" Alfred bit out. "I—You—What're you playing at?"

"I'm not playing," Caden said, with a sweet little smile and a flirtatious dip of his lashes. "I'm in love with you. I wouldn't joke about something like that."

Alfred couldn't bring a single word to his lips. All he could do was stare at the other wolf. Of course, he'd spent a fair amount of time staring at Gunnar's brother since the other two wolves had joined their pack—he was pretty sure everyone had. The guy was as hot as hell. But that was different. He'd just been staring at a sexy little parcel. Not even the damn alphas could have had a go at him for that.

Dropping his gaze, Alfred's attention fell on where his hand still rested on the other wolf's shoulder, tightly gripping his shirt in a white-knuckle hold. He couldn't have snatched his hand away from Caden faster if someone had actually put a flashing red warning light on his head and set off a damn siren. "You're not in love with me."

Caden's smile never faltered as he once more looked up at Alfred through his lashes. His other hand came to rest in the centre of Alfred's chest. As he spoke, Caden's fingers caressed up and down the centre line of his rib cage. "I know how I feel about you. I've known for a long time. And now that Gunnar has stepped aside, there's no reason why we—"

"There are plenty of reasons why we will *never* be mated," Alfred growled.

Caden blinked at him, a touch of hurt seeming to creep into his eyes. "You don't want me?"

"Of course I..." Alfred shook his head. Those teasing fingers were addling his brain. He caught hold of them in a tight grip and pointedly removed Caden's hand from his naked body.

Turning away, he squeezed past the other man. It was much easier to ignore the extra scratches the bricks had left on his shoulders than it was to avoid thinking about the erection he felt straining against Caden's jeans. It took all his resolve to keep walking away from him, making his way rapidly towards the house.

He'd be safe inside. Alfred wasn't entirely sure what he needed to be kept safe from, but that didn't slow his retreat towards the building.

The other wolves seemed to be making their way back home, too. Alfred pushed a hand through his hair as he spotted them approaching from the opposite direction. Caden had said something about a mating ceremony, hadn't he? Yes, of course, Gunnar and Talbot.

Well, good! Alfred thought to himself. He hadn't wanted the blasted beta anywhere near him anyway!

One faltering step was all it took. Suddenly, Caden had caught up and was walking at his side, for all the world as if Alfred had invited him along for a pleasant stroll.

Studiously ignoring the other wolf, Alfred made his way into the old farmhouse and towards the stairs on the far side of the room. Caden was still at his side as he began to climb the steep treads.

"Alfred. Where are you going?"

Looking over his shoulder, Alfred spotted Marsdon glaring up at him from the base of the stairs.

"To get dressed. I've been for a run," Alfred said, with as much composure as he could manage. Right then, that wasn't much. He was acutely aware of Caden right behind him and it was almost impossible to believe that there wasn't a sign over both their heads declaring exactly what they'd just done. Something touched his palm.

Alfred glanced down. Caden's fingers were twined with his. He tried to fling the other shifter's hand away from him but Caden might as well have smeared both their palms with superglue.

"Come straight back down when you're dressed," Marsdon ordered.

Alfred nodded.

"Caden?" he heard Marsdon call out behind him. "Where are you going? You're already dressed."

Finally managing to wrench his hand out of Caden's grip, Alfred made his escape while he had a chance.

"I'm going to help Alfred," Caden called out from somewhere behind him.

A moment later, Alfred heard light footfalls rushing to catch up.

The other gamma appeared just in time to deftly catch the bedroom door when Alfred attempted to slam it in his face. Closing it softly behind him, Caden sealed them both into Alfred's room as if it were something he did every day.

"I'm not a child."

Caden smiled as he calmly made himself comfortable on Alfred's bed.

Great, Alfred thought. The image of Caden all laid out there for him, ready and waiting, was all he needed while he was trying to get to sleep each night!

"I'd noticed."

Alfred frowned. "What?"

"I noticed that you're all grown up," Caden said, softly, his eyes dropping pointedly to rest on Alfred's crotch.

Feeling the blood rushing to his cheeks and his cock was a strange sensation. Alfred did his best to hide both reactions by turning towards the wardrobe in the corner of the room. He snatched up a clean pair of jeans and a fresh T-shirt.

"I'm quite capable of dressing myself," he growled. "I don't need your help."

"That's okay," Caden said cheerfully, as if he hadn't even noticed how pissed off Alfred was. "I'll just wait here, and admire the view."

The faster Alfred tried to scramble into his jeans, the more time the task seemed to take. The denim refused to co-operate. The buttons had a mind of their own.

Alfred snarled irritably as he finally pulled his T-shirt over his head, ripping the seam on the shoulder in the process. Not in any mood to bother with insignificant things like socks and trainers, he strode towards the door, only to hear Caden speak up at the last moment.

"I meant it when I said I'm in love with you."

Alfred glanced over his shoulder. "No, you didn't. I don't know what game you're trying to play with me, but it's not going to work. I'm no more interested in you than I was in your brother."

Caden pulled his legs up onto the bed in front of him and loosely looped his arms over his knees. He tilted his head slightly to one side as he studied him. "You really think you're that unlovable?"

Don't believe me? Ask any wolf in the pack, they'll tell you what a poor excuse for a mate I would be.

The words swirled inside Alfred's head, but he suddenly found himself completely incapable of bringing them to his tongue. He knew they were true. He was pretty sure every wolf in his pack knew it, too. But if Caden had somehow failed to get that memo when he joined them then…

Turning his back on Caden, he quickly made his way out of the room. It was pointless to waste time on what-ifs and maybes. Even if there was some way Caden could form some sort of interest in him, there was no way in hell Marsdon or Bennett would ever give them permission to be together and —

Alfred's mind went blank as he reached the bottom of the stairs and looked across the room. Every wolf in the pack was staring at him. He froze, his feet refusing to carry him another step.

What the hell are you all looking at? Alfred swallowed rapidly, but he couldn't make his throat work, not even to growl.

A gentle caress along the outside of his arm made him look over his shoulder. Caden stood on the tread directly behind him. A tender smile came to the other wolf's lips as their eyes met. Alfred watched, trapped by his own uncooperative limbs, as Caden's fingers slid further down his arm and their hands became entangled once more.

Caden made a point of dropping his gaze first. Alfred looked sweet with that rabbit-caught-in-the-headlights look on his face, but it wouldn't do to spend too long admiring his expression — not when his actions could be taken as a statement of dominance.

Stepping past his soon-to-be mate, Caden led them silently towards the sofas where the other wolves were already gathered. An uncomfortable shiver tingled down his spine, warning him that he wasn't the one who should be making the decisions for them or doing any sort of leading, but Caden pushed it away.

The other gamma tugged at Caden's fingers, apparently attempting to regain control of his hand. Caden tightened his grasp slightly in response, not so much that the other wolf would see it as a challenge, but maybe just enough to let Alfred know he really enjoyed holding his hand.

There wasn't room for both of them to sit on the sofa nearest the door. Caden had no doubt that was why Alfred had chosen to sit there. Not in the least bit daunted, the moment Alfred's backside hit the cushion, Caden climbed onto the sofa with him, to sit half next to him and half on his lap.

Still retaining possession of Alfred's hand, he rested his head on the other wolf's shoulder and gave a content little sigh as he rubbed his cheek against Alfred's T-shirt.

"Are you trying to get me killed?" Alfred snarled under his breath.

Caden lifted his head and looked up at him. "Why would I want to do that?" he asked, lacing his words with as much innocence and confusion as he could muster.

Alfred glared at him. He tried to squirm away but the only way he was going to be able to do that was by climbing over the arm of the chair in front of the whole pack.

"Caden?"

Turning to his alphas, Caden smile cheerfully across the room at them. "Yes?"

"Care to tell us what the hell is going on?" Marsdon asked.

Dipping his eyes with all due deference, Caden let his attention fall upon his and Alfred's joined hands. "When I realised that Alfred isn't as interested in my brother as I thought he was, I..." Caden paused for a moment to nibble at his bottom lip in a calculatedly pretty display of nerves. "I didn't mean any disrespect to my alphas or to the pack's hierarchy, but I had to tell him how I felt about him."

"And how do you feel about him?" Marsdon asked, in the same tone of voice a man might use if he was watching someone mix chemicals from unlabelled bottles, and he had no idea when any particular combination might go bang.

"I..." Caden looked to Alfred.

"He doesn't know what he's talking about," the other gamma snapped.

Caden was quick to agree. "Alfred's right. We should probably get to know each other a lot better before we ask for permission to court each other formally."

Alfred's eyes narrowed. Caden held his gaze, careful not to let any sign of guile or manipulation creep into his expression. Love, that was the only thing the other gamma needed to see there. Love and, maybe, just a hint of willingness to follow rather than lead, as and when the time was right.

"Is that correct, Alfred?"

Alfred turned away from Caden and moved his attention back to the alphas with obvious difficulty. "Um...yeah, I mean..." He cleared his throat, and glanced at Caden once more.

Nodding encouragingly, Caden squeezed the other gamma's hand. Apparently not sure what else to do, Alfred echoed his nod.

"That's..." Marsdon seemed to struggle to find the right word. "Good?" he hazarded, with a glance towards Bennett.

Caden smiled as if the alphas had given him the world on a stick, but he wasn't exactly heartbroken when one of the other wolves was sent to retrieve Gunnar and Talbot from upstairs and attention shifted away from himself and Alfred.

There was something very comforting about simply being able to curl in against his lover's side. Especially after the other gamma had seemed to get the hint that there was no escape and stopped squirming. His arm went hesitantly around Caden's shoulders as he tried to get comfortable.

Caden let his eyes drop closed, eager to let every wolf in the room know he felt completely safe and at ease with Alfred — and even more determined to make sure Alfred saw it too.

When he finally blinked his eyes open over half an hour later, Caden knew there was at least one wolf that wasn't buying any of it. Gunnar raised an eyebrow at him as their gazes met. Caden didn't bother to blink innocently at him. That act never worked on his brother. He held the other wolf's gaze instead, letting Gunnar see that he was serious about his new undertaking and wouldn't allow any other wolf to mess with it regardless of their respective ranks in the pack.

"I'm going to bed." Alfred jerked himself up from the sofa seat so suddenly, Caden almost toppled over.

Righting himself at the last minute, he saved himself from falling flat on his face. "That sounds like a good idea."

"What?" Alfred span around to face him.

"I'm sleepy," Caden said, with as much ingenuousness as he could squeeze into those three little syllables.

Alfred hesitated for so long Caden was able to rise to his feet, say his goodnights and stroll across to the bottom of the stairs ahead of him. He was already at his bedroom door by the time Alfred caught up.

A rough hand landed on his back as he pushed the door open. Caden didn't try to resist. He willingly stumbled through the doorway when the other man shoved him forward. Bracing himself for a hard landing, he did nothing to stop his fall.

At the last possible moment, Alfred snatched at his wrist and kept him on his feet. But Caden had no doubt that owed far more to accident than design. The hold the other wolf took on him was nothing to do with keeping him safe.

"What the hell are you playing at?" Alfred growled, jerking Caden around to face him, each word vibrating with fury.

Caden remained silent and dutifully allowed himself to be thrown around like a rag doll as Alfred slammed the bedroom door and pinned him against the woodwork.

"Answer me!" Alfred demanded.

Caden took a deep breath and tried to ignore both the ache in his cock and his instinctive desire to tilt back his head and bare his throat to a wolf he was quietly desperate to submit to. Swallowing rapidly, he forced himself to say the words Alfred need to hear rather than those he really wanted to utter. "I'm not ready for this."

"What?"

Caden dragged another breath into his lungs. He had to close his eyes for a moment before he could make himself go on. "I'd have to know I could trust a wolf before I'd feel safe agreeing to play rough with him. So, I'm not ready for us to play this way yet," he expanded.

Alfred snatched his hands away from Caden's skin as if he was hot enough to burn the flesh from the other man's bones. He took several paces back. "What are you talking about?"

Caden stepped carefully past him and took a seat on the room's only chair. He had to tilt his head back to look up at Alfred. It would be impossible for the other wolf not loom over him, not to feel bigger and stronger than him. "I don't mind if you want to be rough with me. I do like that," Caden promised. "But...not yet."

Alfred glared down at him as if he'd lost his mind. It was several minutes before he glanced at Caden's wrist and the way he was pointedly massaging it with the fingers of his other hand. His frown deepened. Suddenly appearing hesitant, he rocked back and forth on his heels. "Did I hurt you?"

Caden examined his wrist very carefully, turning it this way and that. No, he hadn't, but that wasn't because he was being careful with a less dominant wolf. It was only chance that he hadn't gripped the skin tightly enough to leave a vivid bruise in its wake, that he hadn't twisted the joint far enough to fracture the bones above it.

Alfred's grasp had been that of a brat having a temper tantrum rather than a dominant wolf taking a lover in hand, taking a more submissive mate under his protection. And it had to be dealt with now.

"My wrist will be fine," Caden finally said, with complete honesty.

Alfred pushed his hands into his pockets. "It's your fault anyway," he mumbled. "Acting like... Saying... " He took one hand out of his pocket and pushed it through his hair.

"All I did was tell you the truth," Caden said mildly, keeping his gaze down and his submission blatant. "I only acted the way I've wanted to act towards you since I first joined the pack."

Alfred paced towards the bedroom window, then back. He was on his third circuit when he suddenly stopped and span around to face him. "Did the alphas put you up to this?" His eyes narrowed. "Gunnar went off with Talbot, so you've been ordered to—"

"No!" Caden launched himself to his feet and hurriedly closed the gap between them, unable to stand hearing the pain in the other wolf's voice. "Gunnar's the one who always thought arranged matches were a good idea. He might have thought he wouldn't care who he spent the rest of his life with, but I've always known I care."

Alfred retreated rapidly, as if Caden was suddenly a damn sight more frightening than his big, scary beta of a brother could ever be. He only stopped when the backs of his legs hit the edge of Caden's bed. He sat down heavily on the edge of the mattress.

Caden didn't waste a second before dropping to his knees in front of him. "I want to be your mate. I want you to be my mate." Every lupine instinct he had screamed at Caden to stop there. It took every ounce of human stubbornness at his disposal to push on. "But—"

Alfred let out a burst of harsh laughter that obviously had nothing to do with amusement. "I should have known there would be a but—"

Caden lifted one hand and put his fingertips against the other wolf's lips. Alfred immediately grabbed hold of his wrist, but he'd barely had time to take hold of it before he checked his own show of strength. His hand remained wrapped around Caden's wrist, but he made no attempt to move his fingers away from his lips or to speak up from behind them.

"I just need you to prove that I'm right about you," Caden said. "Please?"

Alfred's frown deepened.

"I know you're a good wolf, and the only thing I want to do is put myself in your hands and be your mate. I want to submit to you and belong to you and... And I just need you to prove to me how right I am."

Caden stared up into the other wolf's eyes, begging Alfred to understand, to believe him. By the look on his face, Alfred had never had anyone say anything like that to him in his life. Caden had no doubt that if he had hurled insults at him or tried to order him around and control him, Alfred would have railed against him the way he so often seemed to chafe at the hierarchy in the pack, but suddenly being treated differently seemed to have brought his mind to a complete stop.

Taking his hand away from the other wolf's lips, Caden stroked the back of his fingers down Alfred's cheek.

The other gamma still didn't speak.

Dropping his hand back to his side, Caden bowed his head and simply rested it against Alfred's leg, making himself comfortable to wait patiently while the other wolf's brain caught up with events.

Within a second, Alfred had moved his hand to rest on the back of his head but, even as his fingers wound through the strands, Caden felt the other man tense.

"I don't mind," he said, leaving his head where it was and accepting Alfred's caress. "It's only when I'm going down on you that having your hand on the back of my head makes me nervous."

Alfred said nothing as his fingers carded gently through Caden's hair, no doubt making a hell of a mess of it. Caden smiled slightly at the thought of getting mussed up by the other wolf that way.

"I don't believe you," Alfred finally announced.

Caden could tell that Alfred was doing his best to regain his usual recalcitrant mood, but the tone of voice just wasn't there. The words were half scared and half gentle, and not the least bit bratty.

Turning his head, Caden pressed a kiss against his lover's jeans. "I don't mind," he whispered. "There's plenty of time. You'll realise I'm telling the truth soon enough."

"You're bloody sure of yourself," Alfred muttered.

"No, I'm sure of *us*," Caden corrected, very gently but no less firmly for that. Just because Gunnar was the only brother who shouted and stomped around, that didn't mean he was the only wolf from their parents' pack who was determined to get his own way in the end.

Chapter Two

"What do you think you're all looking at?" Alfred demanded as every wolf in the work party turned to stare at him at the same time. They'd obviously already been out there for some time, hard at work since first light.

Alfred didn't try to hold their gazes or stare anyone down, but he made a point of looking away from his pack mates rather than towards the ground. He was in no mood to display his submission towards anyone that morning.

Even after he'd left Caden's room in the early hours, he hadn't managed to sleep for more than a few minutes in a row. A night spent tossing and turning and trying to ignore both the ache in his cock and the pounding in his head hadn't helped his temper. But it was the uncomfortable feeling in the unexplored recesses of his mind that had his hand forming into a fist at his side.

There was something there, just out of sight, lurking in the deepest shadows. He could sense it creeping around, prowling in the darkness like a predator waiting for the perfect chance to pounce. If he dropped his guard for a moment, Alfred had no doubt it would launch itself into the front of his mind, then... And that was the problem. He had no idea what would happen then.

Alfred looked around the work party full of wolves once more, desperate to...to howl, to bite, to lash out at the whole world. He longed to sink his teeth into his nameless, faceless nemesis and shake it until it finally gave in and left him the hell alone.

He wanted nothing more than to land punch after punch on whatever the hell it was that made his whole body ache like the changing of a season that never actually came. He yearned for the chance to keep pummelling, clawing, biting until long after there was any way a reasonable wolf could expect anything to be achieved by hurting the world.

Alfred wanted...

He growled. Not knowing what he really wanted didn't make him feel any friendlier towards the universe.

Picking up the last shovel leaning against the tree nearest the river project, he threw himself into their work digging the new channel with more determination than all the previous days he'd been assigned there put together. Every ounce of anger and frustration streamed through his body and into his task as if he couldn't think of anything he'd enjoy more than helping his pack divert the course of the river running through their lands.

By the time he looked up, perspiration dripping into his eyes, the sun was high overhead. Right on cue, the alphas had arrived to inspect their work. Leaning on his shovel handle for a moment, Alfred wiped the sweat and the dirt from his face with his discarded shirt before tossing the grubby garment back onto the bank. Glancing over to where his leaders were speaking to Francis and Steffan, he noticed that the other gammas were smeared with dust and mud, too.

The alphas looked impossibly clean and fresh standing next to them, not to mention too bloody perfect by half. Lording it over the lower-ranking wolves as if they were something special, just because someone had looked at them when they were pups and decided they were going to be alphas when they grew up.

As if he could sense the angry glare burning into the back of his neck, Bennett suddenly looked over his shoulder. His eyes met Alfred's. Reluctantly lowering his gaze, Alfred forced himself to show due deference to the other wolf's rank in public, whatever his private feelings might be.

By the time he looked back up, the alpha was right in front of him. Bennett jumped easily down into the ditch alongside Alfred, handed him a cold bottle of water and casually took a seat on the muddy edge of the gouge being created in the landscape.

"Steffan tells us you've been working hard all morning."

Alfred shrugged well aware that no one really gave a damn what he said anyway. He glanced across at Steffan as he took a deep swig from the bottle of water. Perhaps if he'd been born that size, Alfred might have been the one whom the alphas had put in charge of the working party. Or perhaps if he'd been born growling, like Gunnar, he'd have been the one who had the beta role in the pack handed to him on a sodding plate.

If *he'd* been given that rank, he wouldn't have wasted it. He wouldn't have disobeyed his alphas and fallen for Talbot, of all people. Cold water spilled over Alfred's hand as his grip tightened and crushed the fragile plastic.

Very carefully, he eased his hold on it. The bottle sprang back into shape. The level of the water within receded. Would a wrist recover that easily?

"It seems Caden is proving to be a good influence on you."

Alfred jerked back his head and met his alpha's eyes.

Bennett smiled slightly. "Neither of us had realised that you had feelings for each other…"

"We don't. I mean, I don't…" Alfred frowned down at the bottle. It hadn't actually sprung back into shape as perfectly as he'd first believed. The damage was easily visible once a wolf thought to look for it.

A gentle, teasing chuckle brought his attention back to his alpha, but Alfred's mood didn't change.

"There's no rush to work out exactly how you feel," the other wolf reassured him, as if he was nothing more than a silly little pup to be humoured. "Such things take time."

Alfred said nothing. It was the only way he could be sure to keep back the growl that threatened to escape from the back of his throat.

"But, if you keep working like this, I'm sure you'll soon be a mate that Caden could be proud to call his own." Without waiting for a response, Bennett jumped easily onto the bank alongside the ditch. "In a few days I'll speak to Gunnar and see if we can arrange for you and Caden to share the same duties. That should let you spend some more time together."

Alfred shrugged, just to make it perfectly clear he couldn't care less one way or the other, but Bennett merely smiled all the more, as if he thought there was something amusing about that.

As Bennett re-joined Marsdon and Steffan, Alfred caught the other alpha's eyes. At least there was one wolf he was sure wouldn't be amused by the idea of him and Caden.

There was no way in hell Marsdon was ever going to do anything that involved smiling in Alfred's direction — that ship hadn't sailed so much as sunk without a trace a long time ago.

Quickly tossing back the rest of his water, Alfred flung the bottle aside and launched himself into his work with a fresh wave of anger to fuel him. There was no point in thinking anything was actually going to happen between him and Caden. Marsdon was never going to forgive him for causing trouble for Bennett all those months ago, and he sure as hell wasn't going to give his permission for him to be mated to a wolf like Caden.

Alfred's shovel cut deep into the earth. He wasn't sure who he was imagining tossing into the hole after he'd dug it so deep that they'd never be able to clamber up the steep sides, but he had the horrible feeling that, whatever he did, the only wolf who would end up at the bottom of it was him.

Hands that weren't used to being put to work with enthusiasm or for more than a few minutes at a time protested at the sudden onslaught against his palms, but Alfred wasn't in the mood to listen to them. There wasn't enough work in the world to allow him to vent all his anger right then.

* * * *

If he'd had the energy, Alfred would have sighed. Of all the times for him to actually be proved right about something, it had to be today, it had to be about this. Just as he'd suspected, there was no less fury burning through his veins as he slowly made his way back into the pack's old farmhouse that evening. The work hadn't eased his desire to lash out at the whole world one little bit, it had just added a hell of a lot of pain into the mix of feelings swirling through him.

His whole body ached. His feet were too heavy to lift off the ground. His steps were more a shuffle than a stride as he crossed the courtyard. His hands burned where the handle of the shovel had bitten back in revenge for the rough treatment Alfred had levelled upon both it and the ground that day.

Apparently, whoever said hard work never killed anyone was right—apparently, it just made you *wish* you were dead.

"You're back!"

"No shit, Sherlock," Alfred muttered, not even bothering to look over his shoulder as he made his way across the kitchen to the fridge and grabbed a bottle of cold milk. His hand screamed in protest as he tore the top off it, but the cool liquid soothed his dusty throat as he drank down big mouthfuls. It let him hope that his next words wouldn't sound so much like a death rattle.

Apparently as oblivious towards polite hints to piss off as his older brother had ever been, Caden joined him by the fridge. Turning pointedly away from him, Alfred left the half-empty bottle of milk on the counter and attempted a painful retreat towards the living room.

"I heard that you've made much more progress on the river works than Gunnar thought you would," Caden said, as if it was the most wonderful news he had ever heard in his life. "You guys are almost a day ahead now!"

"Yay," Alfred muttered. Another feather in Gunnar's cap. Bully for him. The idea of needing to go back out there and do another day of the same was almost enough to make him want to cry.

Without any warning, Caden reached up and stroked his fingers through his dusty hair.

Alfred waited impatiently for his own arm to swing up and push the other man's hand aside in annoyance, but somehow it stayed by his side. The energy for that kind of reaction simply wasn't there. He had little choice but to let the other gamma fuss over him and pet him any way he chose.

"You must be so sore after working hard all day," Caden cooed.

Alfred shrugged, and tried not to flinch as his shoulders promptly reminded him why a noncommittal noise would have been a much better option.

"Let me make you feel better?" Caden requested, his voice dropping into an intimate, flirtatious tone.

"And how do you intend to do that?" Alfred snapped.

He was pretty sure the only thing that was going to make him feel any less like he'd been run over was a whole body transplant, and while there were a hell of a lot of things he'd have been happy to do with Caden's body, complicated medical procedures weren't at the top of his list.

A smooth palm slid against Alfred's sore hand. Caden stepped back and tugged gently at his arm, encouraging Alfred to follow him up the stairs. Too curious to protest, too knackered to resist, Alfred let the pretty blond have his way, just this once.

He had no idea how he actually convinced his legs to carry him up the stairs, but within a few minutes he was standing in Caden's bedroom, facing the other wolf.

"Take off your clothes and jump in the shower," the other gamma ordered, with an enticing little smile. "When you're done, make yourself comfortable on the bed."

There was only one part of his body Alfred hadn't worked to exhaustion that day. Within a fraction of a second, his cock was hard and making an obvious outline in his jeans. Alfred automatically ran his gaze over the other wolf's frame. Perhaps there was a way Caden could make him feel better after all…

Peeling off his clothes, Alfred dropped them carelessly on the floor just outside the bathroom door. Stepping under the spray he quickly rinsed the worst of the earth and grit off his body.

His hands burned under the warm water. The soap ignited a full-blown blaze all along his palms. Alfred winced as he glared at the broken skin, but he didn't have time to worry about that. Did a little bit of pain really matter when Caden was waiting out there, ready and willing to make him all better?

Roughly towelling his skin dry, Alfred discarded the damp fabric on the floor and quickly made his way back into the bedroom. Halfway across the threshold, with one foot on the bedroom carpet and the other still lingering on the cold bathroom tiles, he came to an abrupt halt.

The curtains were closed. Tiny candles flickered on the bedside tables and along the top of the dresser. Alfred gazed at it all with something akin to horror, but as Caden stopped rooting around in a drawer on the far side of the room and glanced towards him, Alfred couldn't actually think of anything sarcastic to say.

"Jump on the bed and make yourself comfortable," Caden invited, that same smile still dancing around his lips.

He hadn't wasted all his time alone on silly romanticism. He'd also stripped off. Caden was bare-arse naked and, for once, Alfred found himself more than willing to do as another wolf commanded.

Shuffling towards the middle of the bed, he leant back against the headboard to watch as Caden finally rose to his feet and turned towards him. For a second Alfred's hand twitched, but he resisted the sudden wave of shyness and didn't rush to cover his erection with his hands.

Caden was stunning. Candle light danced over his skin, highlighting lines of lean muscle. It took Alfred a few seconds to realise the other wolf's lips were moving and words were coming out of his mouth. He only caught the tail end of the other man's sentence.

"...just roll over onto your stomach, and I'll get started."

Alfred frowned. "What?"

Caden held up a bottle of something. It didn't look like any brand of lube Alfred had ever set eyes on.

"Your massage," Caden reminded him.

Alfred looked from the other wolf's face to the bottle of oil and back again. He was serious. He was bloody serious! He'd actually invited him up there for a damn massage.

Turning hurriedly away, Alfred swung his legs over the side of the bed. He looked wildly around the room, but he couldn't remember where he'd tossed his clothes. Despite his humiliation, his cock wasn't the least bit daunted. His erection continued to flourish regardless. A drop of pre-cum slowly slid down his shaft as he leant forward and looked around the corner of the bed.

There! Finally, Alfred spotted his clothes. He pushed himself forward, but a strong hand landed on his shoulder and stopped him short before he could even stand up.

"If we try to do anything more than that straight away, it'll just hurt. You've had a hard day. Let me help you relax first?" Caden asked.

Alfred hesitated. "First?" he asked, suspiciously.

Caden smiled. Leaning forward, he brushed their lips together. "Massage first. Then..."

Completely thrown off balance, Alfred didn't have it in him to fight against the suggestion, or to demand that Caden specify exactly what he was promising in return for his cooperation.

Alfred gave a mental shrug. He was tired. Just lying there and having Caden rub him all over didn't sound like too bad an idea, especially not when it seemed likely to at least end with some sort of orgasm.

Squirming around, he lay down on his stomach, keeping his legs pointedly together, just in case Caden hadn't realised who was going to be topping whom afterwards. It was damn near impossible for him to find a position where his cock wasn't trying to drill a hole in the mattress underneath him.

The blankets moved slightly beneath him as Caden rearranged himself behind Alfred. Holding his breath, he waited impatiently for the other guy to get on with it so they could move on to more interesting business.

"I've wanted to get my hands on you ever since I first set eyes on you," Caden whispered, as he finally placed warm, oiled palms on Alfred's shoulders.

Unsure what to say, Alfred made a non-committal sound in the back of his throat. There was no way in hell he was going to admit he'd wanted to screw Caden for just as long.

"You carry so much tension in the muscles," Caden murmured.

Alfred only just resisted the temptation to roll his eyes. The guy was on about his bloody massages again. If the other man's hands hadn't felt quite so amazing, as they quickly found the first of a great many sore spots across Alfred's shoulders, he was quite sure he'd have shaken the other gamma off, pulled himself off the bed and stormed out of the room.

As it was, Alfred was quite prepared to put off his grand exit until after the other man had finished what he was doing, and until after Caden had let him screw him. Hell, he was pretty sure he could even put it off until after they'd both had a nice little nap, too. Even as the thought made its way sluggishly through his brain, Alfred's eyes slowly drifted closed.

So much tension...

Caden worked his fingers carefully into the muscles along Alfred's shoulders again and again, quietly cherishing each caress he was permitted to offer the other wolf. He hadn't been lying about seeing all that stress lodged in his body. His only falsehood had been one of omission. He'd completely failed to mention how difficult it had been for him to hold back and not try to ease Alfred's pain before.

Caden shook his head. His lover was as hard as a rock, and not just in those places he should be while getting naked with his future mate for the first time.

As he gradually coaxed the younger wolf to relax under his touch, Caden felt himself relax, too. The world was a better place when he was allowed to ease Alfred's way in it. Dipping his head, he pressed a gentle kiss between the other man's shoulder blades.

"What're you doing?" Alfred immediately demanded, peering over his shoulder at him.

"I couldn't resist," Caden admitted softly. There was no hint of an honest apology in his words and he didn't try to fake one. "You're perfect."

Alfred tensed all over again, undoing every scrap of good Caden's massage had done over the previous hour. He obviously thought Caden was making fun of him. Caden's heart broke a little as he realised Alfred had good reason to feel that way.

No doubt there had been far too few comments and compliments offered in his direction over the years — heavens knew there hadn't been a single one Caden could remember hearing since he'd joined the pack.

Not for the first time, Caden struggled to push down the almost overpowering urge to throttle the whole damn lot of them, and their buggered-up hierarchy, too.

Pouring a little more oil onto his palms, Caden forced himself to relax his hands and let them glide across Alfred's skin with faultless technique. Very slowly, taking care not to miss a single knot of muscle, he made his way down the other man's back, across his arse and along his legs.

So much tension, so much pain, and if only the other wolves had enough sense to really look at the man in front of them, it could all have been avoided so easily...

A bitter taste filled the back of Caden's mouth. He had to clear his throat before he could even attempt to speak.

"If you'll roll over, I'll do your front now," he said, very softly.

Alfred sluggishly did as he was told. His movements were already starting to become slow and sleepy as the massage seeped into his frame and maybe even, Caden barely dared to hope, because the kind touches from another wolf were beginning to soothe his soul a little.

Caden sat back on his heels with his hands clenched into fists at his sides as he watched the other man struggle to move a body exhausted by work far harder that it was used to doing. Alfred wasn't ready to see any effort to help him as anything other than an accusation of weakness yet. But soon, Caden promised himself, soon Alfred wouldn't be able to look at him and see anything other than love — Caden would see to that.

His gaze roved over Alfred's body, taking in every detail until, finally, they came to rest on the other wolf's erection. The younger wolf's cock was harder than ever, his shaft curving back towards his stomach. Unless Caden was very much mistaken, there would be a wet patch on the blanket beneath him when he rose, where his pre-cum had seeped into the fabric.

"Let's get one thing straight," Alfred suddenly said, sitting up with obvious effort.

"You prefer to top?" Caden guessed, pulling his gaze away from the other wolf's cock with some difficulty. His mouth was watering just from the sight of it. It would be so easy to just lean over, wrap his lips around the tip and lap up another taste of him.

"Yes," Alfred said. "And—"

"Good."

Alfred frowned. "What?"

"I'm glad," Caden said. "Everything always runs so much more smoothly when there's one wolf who much prefers to top and another that much prefers to be topped."

Alfred blinked at Caden as if he couldn't actually believe that any man in the world was capable of calmly stating such a preference.

"Most of your previous lovers preferred to top too?" Caden asked as he placed a hand on Alfred's chest and gently pushed him back until his head rested once more upon the pillow.

Alfred shrugged.

Caden looked up and met his eyes. "I can understand why."

"Tops don't always look like Gunnar, or like Marsdon and Bennett," Alfred snapped.

"True—you've got a much better arse than any of them, for one thing," Caden said, with a smile.

Alfred glared at him. "Yeah, well, just you remember that you're not going to get a piece of it and we'll get along fine."

Caden murmured contentedly as he stroked his palms down the other wolf's chest. As his hands slid over Alfred's stomach, he shuffled backwards and nudged his lover's thighs until he was able to kneel between the other man's spread legs in the perfect position for stage two of his plan for the night.

Leaning forward, he pressed a light, almost chaste, kiss to the base of Alfred's shaft, then another slightly lower down over his ball sac.

"But, I thought..." Alfred protested. He lifted his head. His hand left the mattress and moved halfway to Caden's shoulder, but the other wolf seemed too relaxed, too sleepy, to even complete the gesture. He might have thought he was going to get to mate with him properly, but he didn't seem to be in any condition to push the issue right then.

"Let me make you feel better?" Caden asked once more.

The simple fact that he had the sense to know Alfred would react far more kindly towards a request than an order or a demand seemed to be enough to swing the other wolf's decision in his favour. Alfred nodded once and let his head fall back onto the deep, fluffy pillow.

Keeping his movements slow and almost as lethargic as Alfred's, Caden bowed his head over the other man's cock and gently took the shaft between his lips.

The taste of him immediately filled Caden's mouth and there was no way he could hide his pleasure at that. He murmured around Alfred's cock as his eyes dropped closed to better savour the taste. It was just as glorious as it had been out by the woodpile, salty and more-ish. He was already addicted.

For several long moments Caden forgot all about his carefully laid-out plans. There wasn't a single part of him capable of remembering the blow job was supposed to be praise for working hard and acting like a good wolf all day. All Caden knew as he lowered his head and took more and more of Alfred's hard shaft into his mouth was that he was going down on the wolf he loved. He didn't need an excuse to want to do that.

Alfred let out a little growl as he rocked his hips up, trying to get more. Caden didn't even hesitate. It wasn't in him to deny his future mate anything in that moment. The desire to submit sang out inside him so loudly he couldn't even hear his pounding heartbeat past it. Pleasing his lover was the only thought inside his head.

Suckling tenderly around him, Caden finally managed to remember he was experienced enough to have developed a bloody good technique over the years. Dipping his head over the other man's crotch again, he took him all the way to the base and made good use of his throat as well as his mouth. Caressing the length with his tongue on each descent and lapping at the tip each time he pulled back, he began to put all his experience to good use.

A frustrated moan escaped from the back of Alfred's throat as Caden pushed him to the edge and held him there, but the younger wolf didn't say anything. He didn't try to reach out and force Caden into hurrying up, either.

Alfred merely lay back and accepted what Caden was offering as if he instinctively understood that when someone gave another wolf permission to please him, he gave up a certain amount of control over what would happen next.

Caden glanced up at his lover through his lashes. Alfred was relaxed back in perfect comfort, the way any dominant wolf might once he'd realised that the man who loved him would never be happier than when he was serving and servicing his mate.

A flurry of success rushed through Caden. Somehow, most of it decided his cock was a suitable final destination. His self-control wasn't quite sufficient to stop his hips rocking forward as he instinctively sought for something to hump against. There was nothing within reach. Caden's frustration doubled over and over again, but he was helpless to relieve it.

Of course, he could have wrapped his hand around his cock, but the idea of doing that without his lover's permission sent a shiver of uncertainty down his spine. He sucked harder around the other wolf's cock in response.

Alfred's hands suddenly clenched in the blankets on either side of his body. That was Caden's only warning before, with a jerky little thrust of the hips, Alfred spilled into his mouth.

Swallowing rapidly, Caden took everything the other wolf had to give him, unwilling to risk missing a single drop.

Barely a second later, Alfred reached for his shoulder. Caden tensed, sure that there would be a vivid bruise on that patch of skin the next day, but against all his expectations, the grip the other man took on him was gentle. It felt more like a request to stay there than an order to do so.

Caden knew it was stupid to think Alfred really could have learnt so much in so short a time, but as he moved to rest his forehead against his lover's hip bone, the tip of Alfred's cock still nestled between his lips, it was almost impossible for him to believe it wasn't true.

Alfred was learning. All the potential Caden saw in him really was that close to the surface. The man he loved was soon going to be the wolf Caden knew he could be with just a little bit of encouragement.

Perhaps it wouldn't actually take as long as Caden feared it might to undo the damage the pack had done to him. Perhaps they could think about—

Alfred's hand slid over Caden's neck. Fingers twined in his hair and tugged him up the other wolf's body. Going with it, Caden let Alfred's cock slip from between his lips as his lover guided him up the bed and brought their lips together for the first time.

The kiss was so sweet, so sleepy, it was almost impossible for Caden to remember that Alfred was actually licking the taste of his own cum out of his mouth as one tender little kiss drifted on into another, then another.

Tilting his head to the side, Caden wasn't capable of doing anything other than offering up his lips for the other man to do with as he pleased. He'd done what he'd set out to do, and it was all going so well and, and he'd been watching Alfred from much too far away for so long, and...

Fabric brushed against Caden's back. He jerked in surprise. He tried to look over his shoulder, but that was impossible, because suddenly his shoulders and his back were both flat against the mattress and somehow, while he'd been paying far more attention to the kiss than his surroundings, their positions had reversed and Alfred was looming over him while Caden lay pinned to the bed.

Reaching up, he put his hands against Alfred's shoulders, but he didn't have the strength of will to actually push him away. His fingers merely stroked over the slight sheen the massage oil had left on the other wolf's skin, caressing rather than truly resisting.

Candle light flickered across Alfred's face as he stared down at Caden, lending a warm glow to the other man's expression, making him look far more affectionate and pleased with the world than Caden had ever known him to be before.

"We should slow down," Caden managed to whisper.

Candlelight be damned, a frown instantly flashed across Alfred's forehead. Tension rushed back into his body. "Who died and made you king of the bed?" he demanded, a touch of a growl in his voice.

Caden managed to push a little at the other gamma's shoulders as he sought mental space. Alfred's hand quickly wrapped around his wrist and pinned it to the mattress.

Too quick! Even as some annoyingly sensible part of Caden screamed that fact at him, the rest of him was more than happy to simply sigh in complete contentment.

That was exactly how things should be between them. It was what they both wanted. It was what both their natures needed to find in their mate. And…and it was still too soon for either of them to have what they wanted.

It almost tore something deep inside Caden's soul, but somehow he forced himself to shake his head. "We need to slow down," he repeated.

All his years of flirtation served him well. His tone of voice was exactly what he wanted it to be. None of his inner anguish crept through.

"You're saying you've never…" Alfred hesitated. As he pulled back, his hand left Caden's wrist.

Caden blinked at him, trying to work out what the other wolf was talking about.

"I thought you'd have had dozens of guys," Alfred said, with a somewhat suspicious frown.

Caden sat up as he realised what Alfred thought. "I have. That's not why I want to go slow." Looking up through his lashes, he met the other man's gaze and held it. "But they weren't important. You are."

Alfred looked away. "There's no need to make silly excuses. If you don't want—"

"I want," Caden cut in. He wanted it so badly he could barely take a deep breath, but his usual flirtations obviously weren't going to be enough to convince the other wolf of that. Not knowing what else to do, he grabbed Alfred's hand and clumsily wrapped the other man's fingers around his erection.

Alfred's anger faltered and gradually faded away, until only confusion was left.

"I want everything you do," Caden promised. "But, I don't want us to get ahead of ourselves. You, this, *us*—it's too important to screw up by rushing into things."

Alfred held his gaze for several long seconds. It took every scrap of strength Caden had to keep his eyes up and locked with Alfred's rather than lowering them in submission.

Very slowly, Alfred began to move his hand, stroking Caden's cock with a slow, purposeful rhythm. Caden gasped. His eyes fell closed. "I..." His throat went dry. He was too close. He couldn't get another word out. Caden covered Alfred's hand with his own, in a request for him to stop.

"If you're going to try to tell me that that you really believe it's too soon for me to even jack you off, I'm going to call you a liar."

Caden whimpered. For the first time he could remember, there was a touch of real confidence rather than mere bravado in Alfred's voice. He deserved a reward for that. Caden was half tempted to believe that he deserved a reward too. Hell, he was pretty willing to believe anything in the world if it kept Alfred's hand moving around his shaft.

"Your hand must be sore after—"

"I'll be the judge of what I do with my own hands," Alfred cut in.

Helpless to do anything else, Caden gave in and nodded his willingness to alter his carefully laid-out plans.

"No. Not until you move your hand out of the way."

Caden blinked open his eyes. He looked down at where his hand still covered Alfred's. It would be a stupid thing to do. If he gave over too much control now, it would be so much harder for him to take back the reins when he needed to, and he knew he would need to at some point.

But, in that moment, it didn't really matter how much of a fool it made him, his hand fell to the blanket at his side and there was no way in hell he could stop it.

Alfred grinned as he seemed to sense that he really was the king of the bed right then. If there was any hierarchy on the mattress, it was all going one way. He began to move his hand once more, very slowly, rubbing his thumb against the head of Caden's cock, spreading the pre-cum over the sensitive tip.

Caden moaned. His hips thrust up off the bed.

He was a tease himself. He knew that. He was pretty willing to consider it one of his major life skills, but suddenly, Caden realised he had a competitor for the title of biggest tease in the bedroom, too.

The light in Alfred's eyes told him everything he needed to know. The other wolf had him in the palm of his hand, figuratively as well as literally, and he wasn't going to give that up until he was bloody well ready.

"Please?" Caden whispered, with his best-ever puppy-dog eyes.

Alfred chuckled. The slow, infuriating rhythm didn't change one bit. Caden bit down on his bottom lip. Obviously Marsdon had been right when he'd said that Alfred could be a sadistic little bastard when a man caught him in the wrong mood — or in the *right* mood. Caden's jury was still out on that.

Within minutes, teasing had turned to torment, as more and more bliss was forced into Caden's body and he was refused any form of release. Alfred's only response was to hum contentedly under his breath while he watched Caden squirm against the sheets. Bound more firmly by his own long-standing desire to submit to the other wolf than he could ever be by any leather or metal, Caden was helpless to do anything but take it.

Pleasure built up inside him like an increasingly perilous tower. There was no way it could stand forever, no matter how hard he tried to strengthen it. Even as Caden realised that, a gust of breeze caught at the fragile ramparts and the whole thing came crashing down to earth. Pure ecstasy exploded inside Caden as it fell. Every cell in his body smashed into a million pieces, then somehow snapped back together.

And through it all, Alfred's hand never stopped moving. Caden's fingers fisted into the blankets. His body arched off the bed, thrusting uncontrollably into his lover's stationary grip. Then, as rapidly as it had picked him up and run with him, the bliss passed. Caden collapsed onto the mattress. Very slowly, he blinked open his eyes.

Alfred was leaning on one elbow, staring down at him, his eyes full of fascination. He stroked his palm over Caden's cock once more, pulling a whimper from him. Alfred must have known it was too soon for his touch to be anything other than painful, but he didn't stop and Caden couldn't scrape up the will to ask him to.

A dozen or more strokes later, Alfred finally took his hand away of his own volition and Caden managed to take his first full breath since he had come. Relaxing back against the pillow, he had to force his eyes to stay open. Afterglow always made him sleepy, but he couldn't allow that to make any difference right then.

He had to stay awake, stay in control…

Caden glanced at the other wolf. Alfred had rearranged himself with his head resting on his own pillow. The younger wolf wasn't ready to take over control of them both yet, Caden knew that. Alfred still needed time to heal. He still had to find a better place in the pack, and Caden had no choice but to remain his equal while he did that.

Tomorrow, Caden promised himself. Tomorrow, he'd get everything back on track and put his plan back on schedule and everything would be fine.

For now, just while Alfred was watching over him, he'd close his eyes, just for a few moments…

Chapter Three

"What the hell happened?"

Alfred tensed as he heard the alpha's angry voice fill the air. He froze in his task, knowing all hell was about to rain down around him, knowing he had displeased the leader of his pack. Fight or flight instincts bounced around inside him fast enough to make him dizzy, but neither seemed able to win out. All he did was freeze in place like a bloody rabbit caught in the headlights.

"Damn thing flooded," Steffan called out from further down the field, where he was frantically working to stop more of the water rushing into the half-formed trench.

His words freed Alfred to snap back to the task at hand. Keeping his head down, he worked just as hard as all the other wolves, ignoring the ache in his joints and the protests from his muscles as he pushed himself to keep going long past the point of exhaustion, in the vain hope of preventing any more damage being done.

He didn't even have time to worry about what would happen when the frenetic activity levels subsided and Marsdon had a chance to ask all those questions that Alfred was dreading having to answer. Then, without any warning, the last of the temporary repairs were put in place and the moment was already on top of him.

"Who was supposed to be keeping a watch on the dam?" Marsdon demanded the moment he tossed down his shovel. As he glared around the group of wolves before him, the alpha tried to push his hair back from his face. He used the back of his wrist, but mud was still smeared across his forehead in the process.

Alfred looked around the group. There was barely a patch on any of them that wasn't coated in the stuff. No one said anything.

The only sound Alfred heard was the frantic hammering of his own heart. There was a big rock half-covered in mud a yard or two to his left. Alfred moved his gaze to it and kept it firmly fixed there, doing his damnedest to look as inconspicuous as possible.

A minute passed. A low growl escaped from the back of Marsdon's throat. "Alfred?"

"Why assume it was me?" Alfred snapped, tearing his eyes away from the rock and glaring back at his alpha with all the venom he could muster.

"Because if it was anyone else, they'd have had the balls to own up and take responsibility by now!" Marsdon bit out as he turned to face him. "Get back to the house."

Alfred shook his head as guilt stabbed him in the gut and twisted the knife. His eyes ran over the mess all around him and, for the first time in so many years, he found himself looking for a way he could make things right rather than for a way to get out of being ordered to do that. "No, I can—"

The alpha didn't even wait to hear his offer. "Back to the house. Now!"

Marsdon didn't add that he didn't want to set eyes on Alfred for the rest of the day. He didn't have to. Alfred knew all that, and more, just from the tone of the older man's voice. All the others had to know it too.

He looked at the other gammas. They all stood in a ragged line with him, facing their alpha, leaning on their shovels as they tried to regain their breath. Not one of them was willing to meet his eyes. Their complete attention remained on Marsdon.

There was no help to be found. Maybe Alfred had never given them reason to want to help him, but as they all seemed to turn their backs on him with perfect synchronicity, he'd never felt more alone in his life.

He took a step back, more from the feeling of being without a pack than anything else. Finally, one of the gammas moved. Steffan's head began to turn towards him.

No! He couldn't let the big oaf see any hint of fear in his eyes, any suspicion of weakness in his stance. Far better to be considered a thoughtless bastard than a coward. Spinning away from them all, Alfred cast his shovel aside as he turned tail and ran.

He raced back towards the house, mud clinging to every inch of him. There was only so far he could run before his feet slowed to little more than a stiff-limbed shuffle.

He trudged on, but the cold and the damp seemed to seep into his body even further with every step. He wrapped his arms around his torso, although it did little to keep out a chill that seemed to come from inside him as much as from outside.

"What happened?"

Alfred slowly lifted his gaze from the ground. Francis was rushing towards him, his eyes open wide with worry.

"The area we dammed up before we started working on the river diversion collapsed," Alfred informed him, knowing he wouldn't get a moment's peace from the stupid little fool until he answered all his damn questions.

"Is anyone hurt?" the other wolf asked, the colour already draining from his face.

"Steffan's fine," Alfred snapped, knowing that was the question the other wolf really wanted to ask. Francis just wasn't honest enough to admit he cared more for his mate than for any other member of the pack.

Storming into the house and slamming the door behind him, Alfred couldn't help but think that if he was half as good as Francis was at telling all those appropriate little lies, the rest of the pack might like him just as much as they liked Francis.

Stripping off his mud-soaked clothes, Alfred tossed them in the vague direction of the already-overflowing laundry hamper in the corner of his bedroom and scrambled into the shower.

Hot water poured down over him. He scrubbed at his skin, leaving scratches and scrapes in his wake as he frantically tried to wash away both the mud and his mistakes at the same time. Soaping his hands, he lathered his skin, but the bubbles didn't make him feel the least bit cleaner or any less like the pack's resident screw-up.

He'd only looked away for one stupid little minute! One bloody minute when his thoughts of Caden had got the better of his focus on that stupid dam, and now...

Alfred shook his head, sending muddy water droplets splashing off his hair and running down the sides of the shower cubicle.

And now, reality was back. Forget about being Alfred the potential mate, Alfred the wolf that Caden might actually think was worth his interest. He was Alfred the screw-up, Alfred who couldn't be trusted to do a single damn thing right in his entire life.

Dropping his head forward, he let his temple rest against the cold tiles. One tiny little lapse of concentration and everything was back to normal. If only he hadn't been stupid enough to ever hope things could be different.

Alfred turned off the water and rubbed half-heartedly at his skin with a rough towel. Somehow, he gathered the energy to retrace his steps into his bedroom and pull on a fresh set of clothes, but his limbs felt like lead. Every movement took more effort than anything could ever be worth.

He was still sitting on the edge of his bed staring at nothing when he heard the rest of the pack arrive back at the house.

Taking advantage of those moments when they would no doubt be tucked away in their own rooms and cleaning themselves up, Alfred hauled himself to his feet. Within seconds, he'd sneaked unseen out of his bedroom, down the stairs and out of the house.

If Marsdon didn't want to set eyes on him, fine. If the other wolves in the pack didn't want to treat him like he was one of them, then that was bloody well fine too. Alfred didn't need any of them. He scurried around the side of the building and quickly hid himself away in his favourite secluded little spot. No one was likely to come looking for him there. He sat down heavily on the overgrown grass and let out a sigh of relief.

The wall had been warmed by the sun. He was out of the fresh spring wind. And, most importantly, he was out of range of the rest of the pack's annoyance. Right then,

Alfred was pretty sure that was the most he could hope for from life. Closing his eyes, he rested his elbows on his knees and cradled his head in his hands.

It wasn't that he cared what any of them thought of him, Alfred reminded himself. He didn't, not even a little bit. They could all go to hell and—

"Why?"

Alfred jerked his head up, a growl building in his throat. This was his one safe refuge, and—

There was no one there. Frowning, Alfred looked all around him again. Leaning forward, he risked a peek around the edge of the building, too. Nobody. Finally he looked up. He'd never noticed that the alpha's bedroom window was almost directly above his little hiding place before. Tucked away in the shadows at the base of the house, they wouldn't see him if they looked out, but he'd heard Bennett's voice, loud and clear.

"Why what?" And that was Marsdon—obviously still pissed off as hell.

"Why wasn't he watching the water levels?" Bennett asked, patiently. "He must have known how important it was. If he took his eyes off it, then he must have had a good—"

"He stopped watching it because he doesn't give a damn about anyone but himself," Marsdon cut in.

Alfred leant back against the wall just below their window and wrapped his arms a little more tightly around his knees. Words washed over him. They weren't anything he hadn't heard before. They weren't lies, either. And he *didn't* care about any of them, he reminded himself. Why should he?

"What the hell are we going to do with him?" Marsdon finally asked, a few minutes later. The alpha's anger seemed to have drained away somewhat, or perhaps he had just run out of things to call Alfred. Even though Alfred hadn't heard Bennett leave, Marsdon seemed to be talking more to himself than to his mate.

A frown grew between Alfred's eyebrows as he stared at the ground right in front of his feet. The sadness in the alpha's voice cut so much deeper than his anger.

Suddenly, Alfred heard Marsdon give a harsh little laugh. "I know that I'd like to throttle the little sod. But, since I'm pretty sure you're not going to agree to just stand back and let me do that, tell me, pup—what are we going to do with him?"

Pup, Alfred thought, as he tipped his head back and let it connect heavily with wall behind him. Because, somehow, Bennett could act in ways an alpha wasn't supposed to and yet still keep his place in the pack. Somehow everyone still saw him as an alpha, while Alfred was stuck being a—

"Alfred?"

Alfred looked up, half expecting to see one of the alphas leaning half-way out of the window and glaring down at him. No one. Alfred turned his head. Caden stood just a few feet away. He was downwind. There'd been no sound as he'd approached. Alfred had no way of knowing how long the other wolf had been there, spying on him, eavesdropping on a conversation he had no right to be privy to.

Caden held out a hand towards him, inviting him to stand up and close the gap between them. In no mood to play nicely, or approach him only to see another wolf turn away from him in disgust, Alfred stayed exactly where he was.

Eventually, Caden stepped forward, his hand still extended towards Alfred. "Are you okay?"

Alfred shrugged. His grip on his own hands turned white-knuckled as he pointedly ignored whatever trap Caden was trying to lay for him. "Why wouldn't I be? Same shit, different day, that's all."

"Francis told me what happened out at the dam," Caden admitted.

Alfred said nothing. Pointedly staring past him, he refused to even glace at Caden's face, let alone reach out and put his hand in his. When gentle fingertips stroked along his jaw line, Alfred ignored that, too.

A chaste little kiss pressed to his opposite cheek was far harder to dismiss as entirely unimportant. Caden sat down next to him. His arm slipped around Alfred's waist, determinedly wriggling its way between his spine and the rough stone wall until Alfred gave in and arched his back to make it easier for him.

The other gamma's head came to rest on Alfred's left shoulder as he curled in close to his side, and Caden let out a soft little sigh, as if he was finally exactly where he belonged. "I'm sorry you had such a bad day. I know you wouldn't let something like that happen on purpose."

The gently spoken words made it damn near impossible to ignore the other man's presence. Not quite sure what to do with the sudden display of affection, Alfred looped his arm around Caden's torso and clumsily welcomed him against his body, patting him vaguely on the shoulder with his right hand.

His left hand, without even bothering to check with his brain for permission, slid straight down to rest on Caden's backside. Damn, but he had a glorious arse. Alfred's fingers slid into the back pocket of Caden's jeans and palmed the firm, round muscle.

His cock immediately began to harden behind his fly. All at once, Alfred knew exactly what he needed to distract him from his latest screw-up. And, since Caden seemed to be offering it up to him on a platter, it would hardly be polite to say no!

Alfred glanced down between their bodies. His wasn't the only erection straining against a pair of tight blue jeans. Moving his right hand into Caden's hair, he tugged at the pretty blond strands.

Caden tilted his head back and offered his lips up to be kissed without the slightest protest. With success pounding through his veins, Alfred dipped his head and brought their mouths together. The other wolf's lips were soft and sweet against his.

Alfred lapped against them, eager to get more of that taste. Caden parted his lips willingly enough and mewed his approval into the kiss as their tongues slid against each other in an intimate little dance.

Hands roving more and more frantically over the other wolf's body by the moment, he tugged at Caden's clothes, desperate to yank them out of the way and get at the skin beneath. Caden's hands slid between their bodies and pressed against Alfred's T-shirt, but he didn't seem to have a clue what he was doing. His touch was hindering rather than helping.

Alfred growled his frustration into the kiss, nipping at Caden's lips as he sought for a way to remind the other man exactly who was in charge.

Caden mumbled something against his mouth. He pushed harder at Alfred's chest. Quickly losing all patience with him, Alfred twisted their bodies around so Caden was pinned down against the sun-warmed grass right alongside the foot of the house.

That should have settled everything. In Alfred's mind it certainly made everything very simple, made the whole world seem very right. But Caden merely wriggled all the more, as if trying to squirm away from him. That was a bloody stupid thing to do. There was no logical reason on Earth why anyone would want to put even the smallest amount of empty air between two bodies that felt so marvellous when pressed tightly together.

He caught hold of Caden's wrist and pinned it to the grass. That felt so good. He did exactly the same with his other hand, trapping the slightly smaller man with his entire body as he tried to deepen the kiss.

Pleasure built quickly inside Alfred, pushing away the accusing looks from the other wolves and Marsdon's harsh words. None of that mattered when he was there with Caden, and —

Suddenly the other wolf wrenched his head to one side, breaking the kiss. For the first time, Alfred noticed that Caden was struggling to pull his hands out of his grip.

That was wrong. "What the hell?" Every instinct in Alfred's soul suddenly went into reverse. Letting go of the other man's wrists, Alfred moved both his hands to Caden's face and stilled his head. Tightening his grip as Caden railed against it, Alfred made Caden look up at him, determined to meet his gaze and find out what the hell was going on, why his lover wasn't submitting to him the way they both knew he should.

"We can't," Caden whispered. He closed his eyes for a moment, but not before Alfred saw the touch of pain in them.

Newfound impulses screamed at him to find out what was wrong with his mate's world and fix it. "What are you talking about? We can't what? Why?"

Caden cleared his throat. When he opened his eyes, he looked up at the sky as if fighting very hard to concentrate on what he needed to say. "We can't do this."

"Why not?" Alfred repeated, impatience creeping into his voice.

Caden took a deep breath. "Today, at the works by the river—"

Alfred frowned. "You said you..." He snatched his hand away from Caden's face and scrambled away from him until there were several feet of empty air between them. Anger rushed through him, searing hot and desperate to burst out through the most vicious words he could frame, but he barely had time to open his mouth before Caden was speaking again.

"I said I knew you wouldn't let that happen on purpose. I know you're better than that. I know that you're a good wolf, a strong wolf," Caden said, as he sat up. "But, until I can trust that *you* know that—we can't do this, not...not like this."

Alfred looked down at the way Caden had wrapped his own fingers around his wrist as he fought for the right words. Alfred had held him like that, and it had felt so right, so perfect, and... He closed his eyes as he turned his face away from the other wolf.

He could hide from the sight of him, but there was no way to hide from Caden's scent. It howled the other wolf's desire for him. Alfred was almost willing to swear he could smell his desire to submit hanging in the air around them.

But that wasn't the only thing. Confusion. Uncertainty. Regret. There were so many other emotions—things that had no place being in either of their minds when they mated for the first time.

"Every wolf is born belonging to a pack," Caden suddenly said.

"Don't you think I know that—?" Alfred began.

"But he's also born belonging to himself," Caden went on, as if he hadn't even heard the interruption. When Alfred turned his head, the other wolf met his eyes without hesitation. "And some wolves keep possession of themselves for their whole lives, and they are happy that way."

Alfred didn't try to speak up again when Caden paused. His throat had closed up so tightly, Alfred could barely push air, let alone words through it. The idea of giving up ownership of himself made him want to leap up and tear the throat out of the whole world. But the idea of taking another wolf under his protection and making that wolf his...

Caden seemed to think for a long time before he finally went on, and Alfred had no choice but to wait. "There are other wolves that can't be happy that way. They have to give away part of themselves and they have to hand over control of themselves to another wolf. I'm not happy belonging to myself, Alfred. But I won't put myself in your hands until I can be sure that you know what a good wolf you are."

The thought of Caden belonging to him that way, of him not just being his mate but of being *his*...

Alfred tightened his hands into fists, pulling blades of grass up by the roots as he fought against the urge to reach out, pounce on Caden and hold him so tightly no one would ever be able to tear them apart. A wolf like Caden could have anyone, and...

"You mean until I can convince the pack that—" Alfred stopped short as Caden moved closer.

The other wolf didn't bother to rise to his feet. He simply crawled forward until he was kneeling right in front of Alfred, almost touching him.

"Will the pack realise you're a good wolf once you realise it?" Caden mused. "Yes, I think they will. But it's not their opinion of you I care about."

Alfred could only stare into the very serious blue eyes in response. Caden's eyes were full of so many emotions it was as impossible for Alfred to decipher them there as it had been in Caden's scent. He had no idea what the other wolf might see in his own gaze—all he knew was that he needed to make sure there was never any pain, never any sadness in Caden's eyes, ever again.

That was his job now. And if the only way he could convince Caden to allow him close enough to be able to do his job properly was to play nicely with the rest of the pack, then...

"That's really what you want?" he checked.

Caden nodded, holding his gaze. His eyes and his scent both screamed he was telling the truth.

"What do I need to do to convince you?" Alfred asked. Whatever it was, he'd do it. In that moment, Alfred had no doubt about his ability to do that. Screwing this up wasn't an option.

Caden hesitated. He dropped his gaze back down to where he grasped his own wrist with his opposite hand.

Alfred shook his head at himself. Suddenly, it was obvious he shouldn't even be asking Caden questions like that. He should be the one making the decisions. Proving he could do what he was told wouldn't mean anything. He had to prove he could make the right decisions for them both, that he could be the one telling Caden the right things to do.

What would a good wolf, a good mate, do now...?

"Maybe," Caden began.

"No," Alfred cut in. "It's fine." He pulled himself up to his feet. "I know what I'm doing. I can sort it all out. You don't need to worry about it."

Caden blinked up at him as Alfred stood over him, but it wasn't the usual flirtatious flutter of lashes. Very slowly, the other gamma nodded, as if he was more than willing to simply accept that pronouncement.

Success rushed through Alfred. He half turned away. Then, he hesitated. Unable to leave Caden's side without doing *something*, and knowing full well he couldn't do what he really wanted, Alfred crouched down and pressed a brief, chaste kiss against Caden's temple.

"Everything will be fine," he whispered.

As he straightened up and turned away from his future mate, Alfred repeated those words inside his head. *Everything will be fine.*

They'd sounded a lot more confident when they were spoken outside his head than inside it, but he couldn't let that matter right then. The only thing he could think about was what a good mate would do, what a wolf who knew he was a good wolf would do.

* * * *

"You always have had bloody awful taste in men, but I think even you outdid yourself this time."

Caden stopped relaxing back next to the stream running through the forest and sat up straight. Leaning forward, he peered past the foliage just in time to see his brother step out from behind the bushes.

There was a growl in Gunnar's voice. Maybe it was from his recent shift, maybe he was just randomly pissed off. Caden didn't give the matter too much thought. Reclining comfortably back against the old tree trunk once more, he simply concentrated on the way the last of the evening sun caressed his bare skin and the pure wonderfulness of the world.

All he had to do was stay away from the farmhouse a little longer, give Alfred a little bit more time and space to decide on his next move, and he'd be able to make his way home to his future mate's side, all sleepy and snuggly.

"Don't you have anything to say?" Gunnar asked as he walked past him, his naked skin splattered with mud from his run.

"Alfred's a good wolf," Caden offered. It was almost impossible for him not to grin like a loon as he said it. Who could ever have guessed that he'd come on so quickly—that just the mildest hints would have him leaping up and *sprinting* in the right direction?

True, pushing him away had been the hardest thing Caden had done in his life, but—

"You mean he will be a good wolf when you've finished screwing him into submission?" Gunnar demanded. Crouching down at the river's edge he dipped his hand into the water and scooped up a few mouthfuls with his palm.

Caden's eyes narrowed as he glared at his brother's back, but by the time Gunnar had turned back to him he had once more schooled his features into something passive and more suitable for dealing with the beta. "What makes you so sure he's the one who'll be submitting to me?"

Gunnar let out a harsh burst of laughter. "Even you've got more sense than to let him play the dominant with you. The man's a fool. No, worse than that—he's a sadistic little bastard towards anyone weaker than him whenever he thinks he can get away with it."

"Strange, then," Caden mused, "that I've never known him to take a cheap shot at Talbot."

"He wouldn't dare," Gunnar growled, immediately rising to his full height to loom over anyone who would even mention such a possibility.

"Not even before Talbot came under your direct protection?" Caden asked, not in the least bit daunted by the other wolf's blustering.

"What?" Gunnar demanded.

"I'm pretty sure Alfred had no idea you were even remotely interested in our omega until you two were formally mated," Caden said. "But I've still never heard him snap at Talbot the way he does at everyone else. Don't you think it strange that out of all the wolves in the pack, it's the one that everyone agrees he should outrank who's never had anything to worry about where Alfred is concerned?"

"I think he's strange in far more ways than that," Gunnar said.

As Caden stared mildly up at him, the beta's hackles slowly seemed to go down.

"Why him?" Gunnar finally asked, as he crouched and brought them closer to the same height.

"I could ask you the same thing," Caden said, idly running his fingers through the moss at his side. "Talbot's no more my type than Alfred's yours."

"Even mentioning their names in the same breath is a bloody insult," Gunnar snapped, as he threw himself onto the ground next to Caden and glared up at the sky as if the pretty little patch of blue and the warmth of the sunlight had both been created specifically to annoy him.

"Alfred's a far better wolf than any of our pack realises," Caden told the clearing, the riverbank and anything else within earshot. They were all more likely to take any notice of his words than Gunnar was.

Right on cue, Caden's brother huffed his disbelief.

"I see more than you ever will when you look at him," Caden said, resting his head back against the tree and forcing his words to remain calm no matter how much he wanted to howl them loud enough for everyone he'd ever met to hear.

"And what would you see if you looked at the mess down by the river? It was a simple job, Caden."

"Far too simple for a wolf with Alfred's potential," Caden pointed out. "But as for what I see..." He thought about that for a while. "I just see what any wolf would be able see if they cared enough to look. I see a faltering step on a young shifter's path towards becoming a good wolf."

"A damn spinning top would take a more direct route," Gunnar muttered. With a half sigh, he pushed himself off the ground. He'd barely reached his full height when he started to morph back into his lupine form.

Caden held his brother's eyes as the more overtly wolfen side of the other man dropped onto all fours before him.

Gunnar turned away, obviously bored with the topic and intending to resume his run now he'd apparently confirmed to his own satisfaction his little brother wasn't going to do as he was told without one hell of a fight.

Caden waited until his older brother was at the tree line before he called out to him. "Gun?"

The wolf stopped and looked back towards him.

"You know the interesting thing about spinning tops?"

The wolf's gaze remained steady.

"They never set themselves spinning out of control. It's other people who do that. The thing itself doesn't actually have any choice in the matter, does it?"

Caden took Gunnar's pissed-off growl as a signal that his words had been heard, even if he was sure their actual meaning had gone straight over Gunnar's head.

Pulling his knees up in front of him, Caden drew a line on the bare skin along one of his thighs. His fingertip went around and around in a complex little pattern. His eyes followed its every movement. Just like a spinning top, there was no real way for him to work out in advance where the pattern would go next, all he could do was watch carefully and pray.

Finally, Caden caught hold of the fingertip with his other hand and held it still, unable to watch its progress for another second. His eyes dropped closed. His grip on his own finger gradually turned painful. His eyes crinkled at the corners as he closed them tighter.

Perhaps it wasn't entirely impossible to give the top a little push in the right direction—if a wolf were careful and subtle and…

Caden opened his eyes. He'd been away from Alfred's side for quite long enough. Rising gracefully to his feet, he quickly completed his own shift and set off in the opposite direction to his brother.

Within minutes the farmhouse was within sight. He let his paws carry him straight through the kitchen door without bothering to turn back into his human form. Voices floated out from the main hall as he passed the kitchen table. Tilting his head slightly to one side as he forced his lupine senses to pay attention and make sense of the human words, he made his way forward.

"…Alfred…"

That one name came through to him loud and clear. He shifted in the doorway, steadying himself on the frame as he swayed. "Pardon?"

Marsdon and Bennett both turned to look at him. "What?"

Caden pushed his hair back off of his face as he cleared his throat. "You were talking about Alfred," he said, with a respectful little dip of the eyes.

"He's gone. Disappeared without telling anyone where the hell he's going," Marsdon said, anger clinging to each syllable.

A shiver ran down Caden's spine. He practically felt the blood drain from his face, too.

"We hoped he'd joined you on your run and forgotten to tell anyone. Hell knows what kind of mischief he's got himself into now," the alpha went on.

Caden turned away from them both without a word. He was back on four paws by the time he reached the door leading to the courtyard. His claws scrabbled against the cobblestones as he tried to rush across them faster than lupine legs could carry him. He vaguely heard someone call out to him, but he couldn't stop.

The yells changed to barks and growls. A moment later, Caden felt the unmistakeable sensation of running as part of a pack. Marsdon and Bennett were larger wolves than him, with longer legs. They easily caught up with him. Caden saw them out of the corners of his eyes as they flanked him, running at either side of him as he rushed towards the river works.

That's where Alfred would be, Caden had no doubt about that. The only thing he was less sure about was what sort of condition the other man would be in when they found him. A wolf would have to be a fool to try to tackle that sort of work on his own. If he was less than up to his neck in river mud or ice cold water it would be a bloody miracle.

Caden knew he could make sure Alfred became a good wolf. He could make sure the man he loved found his rightful place in the pack, too. But he couldn't bring a wolf back from the dead.

There were some things even pretty blond hair or a charming smile couldn't achieve.

Chapter Four

Caden's paws slipped and slithered beneath him. He clawed at the mud, but there was no way he could gain any sort of purchase. On either side of him, he saw brief flashes of fur and dirt as the alphas skidded to undignified stops alongside him.

His own momentum pushed him on farther, until he finally stopped just short of tumbling into the deep trench. Perched right on the edge of the scar being cut across the field, Caden found himself completely unable to move. All he could do was stare.

Alfred!

The younger wolf was plastered in mud from tip to toe, but that barely registered in Caden's mind. He'd never seen anything more glorious in his life. The man he loved was unharmed. That was all that mattered.

Panting for breath, he ran his eyes over Alfred's form. One or two parts of him decided they were willing to believe there were other things that always mattered, beside the fact he was healthy and well, hard at work repairing the damage his lapse had caused earlier in the day. For one, Alfred's sodden clothes were clinging to his skin in a very interesting way.

As Caden dragged his attention back to the other gamma's face, Alfred's eyes went from him to each of the alphas and back again, obviously trying to work out what the hell was going on.

While Caden remained trapped in his lupine form, unable to pull himself together enough to complete a shift, the alphas deftly transformed into their human shapes on either side of him.

"So this is where you disappeared to," Marsdon said, pushing muddy blond hair out of his eyes.

"You were right," Alfred said, his gaze now fixed firmly on the shovel in his hands. "It was my fault it overflowed. I should have been paying more attention. So it's only right that I should be the one who fixes the damage."

"In the middle of the night?" Marsdon demanded. "Without telling any of your pack where you were going?"

As Caden watched through lupine eyes, Alfred opened his mouth to respond — and no doubt to point out that it was far from the middle of the night, it was barely dusk. Or perhaps to inform the other man it wasn't exactly uncommon for wolves to leave the house without their alphas' permission. At the last second, Alfred turned his attention back to Caden.

Their eyes met. Caden held his breath. Alfred lowered his gaze for a second. He seemed to think very carefully before he finally spoke up.

"I'm sorry," he said, without even the slightest hint of his usual recalcitrant attitude in his voice. "I should have thought about that before I came out here. I didn't intend to worry anyone. Next time I'll..." He hesitated for a moment as if he really had to think about what he should have done differently. "Tell someone where I'm going?" he hazarded.

To his left, Caden was vaguely aware of Marsdon opening and closing his mouth a few times. The entirely appropriate response was obviously the last thing he expected to hear falling from his cousin's lips.

Bennett quickly stepped forward on Caden's right, to fill in for his baffled mate. "That would be a very good idea. This kind of work can be dangerous to do on your own. It's always best to have another wolf working alongside you, just in case."

Alfred slowly nodded his understanding, his eyes politely lowered in due respect for a more senior-ranking wolf. "I won't make the same mistake again."

Still sitting in the mud on the edge of the bank, Caden barely held back a whimper as he fought against the desire to leap forward, pounce on Alfred and lick him all over like an excitable little puppy. His tail wagged back and forth in the mud as his enthusiasm got the better of him.

Bennett smiled his approval as he stepped forward again. He ruffled Alfred's hair as he moved past him to inspect his work. "You've done a lot already."

Alfred said nothing. He didn't even seem to know how to react to that sort of praise. Caden whimpered very quietly. No one seemed to hear him.

"Did you intend to do more tonight, or are you ready to come home?" Bennett asked.

"I want—" Alfred cut himself short. He didn't look towards Caden right then, but Caden could almost feel the other wolf's consideration wrapping around him while he debated his next move—while he tried to figure out what a good wolf would say in that situation.

"With your permission, I'd prefer to finish this section this evening?" Alfred eventually suggested.

Bennett nodded his approval. "I'll send someone out to work on it with you."

Alfred opened his mouth as if to protest, but Bennett held up a hand.

"That's not up for debate," he said, with more gentleness in his voice than dominance. "I wouldn't be acting like a good alpha if I left any wolf from my pack out here on his own. Someone will come out and help you. Until they get here, I want you to take a break."

Caden barked excitedly. All three shifters turned to face him. Mentally reciting all the curses he could think of, Caden clumsily morphed back into his human shape. Scrambling backwards, he just about stopped himself from falling into the ditch.

Clearing his throat, he tried to speak again. "I'll stay and help!" There was still more than a hint of excited yap in his voice, but at least he had made himself understood.

Bennett seemed to think about that suggestion carefully, but when Caden looked towards Marsdon, the other alpha's brow was creased into a deep frown. He obviously wasn't thinking about anything of the kind. After the way Alfred had welcomed Bennett to the pack, he was probably still far more interested in trying to work out what mischief Alfred was plotting.

Caden bit his tongue hard enough to draw blood. The bitter metallic taste filled his mouth, but it did little to temper his desire to howl that if he just gave Alfred a chance, Marsdon might see just how wrong he was about the gamma.

"Fine," Marsdon finally sighed, after some silent message passed between him and his mate. "Try to keep your minds on the work and not get each other killed. If you're not back within the next two hours, we'll send someone to find you."

Alfred nodded. "Thank you."

Marsdon gave them both one more suspicious look before turning away. Caden was only vaguely aware of the alphas leaving them alone alongside the river works. He couldn't take his eyes off Alfred for long enough to actually watch them leave.

Alfred turned away first. His gaze went back to the shovel in his hands. That finally freed Caden to snap out of his day-dream. Stepping forward, he clumsily reached for one of the other shovels with hands that were still half sure they were paws.

"No."

Caden's fingers had barely brushed against the handle before the word made him snatch them back and hide them guiltily behind him.

"Don't," Alfred said, just a fraction more gently. "If our alphas want someone else to stay here in case I fall in the damn river, I'll accept that. But I don't want your help. I broke it, and I'll fix it."

Caden let his hand fall back to his side. Stepping forward, he closed the gap between them until he stood directly in front of Alfred.

"You're a good wolf," he said softly, and pressed a little kiss against his somewhat muddy cheek.

Alfred coughed and cleared his throat. Caden was pretty sure that, beneath all that mud, the other wolf was blushing very prettily.

"You can sit over there until I'm finished," Alfred informed him, apparently not willing to give in to the temptation of an enjoyable distraction right then.

The confidence and dominance that flooded into his voice in response to another wolf's gentle praise made

Caden smile as he quickly obeyed his lover's command. Moving back to the same patch of muddy ground where he'd first sat staring at Alfred, completely unharmed and hard at work, Caden rested his elbows on his drawn up knees and resumed his observations.

Alfred had obviously walked out there in his human form. He was still wearing his jeans and his T-shirt, although all they seemed to be doing right then was soaking up more and more mud and water and making it ever harder for him to complete the task he'd assigned for himself.

His wet jeans had moulded themselves to his arse perfectly, and it didn't matter how much Caden preferred to bottom, every single time Alfred bent over, there was nothing he wanted more than to pounce on his future mate. If Alfred would quickly roll them over and reverse their positions, and if Caden himself would be the one who'd end up pinned against the muddy floor while the other wolf pounded into him with increasingly harsh and frantic thrusts, then that would be just so much the better.

Caden licked his lips at the very possibility. It was all he could do not to slip his hand down and wrap his fingers around his erection. It would feel so wonderful, with his hand all slicked with river mud, and he needed to come so badly he could barely hold back a howl of frustration. But he didn't have permission.

Looking down his body, at both the streaks of mud and at his rising shaft, Caden didn't move a hand to deal with either. Right there, right then, he belonged to Alfred — it felt safe and right that he should belong to Alfred. And, while that was the case, it wasn't his place to lay a hand on his own body, for any reason.

His more dominant mate would decide what was to be done with him, all Caden would have to do was obey and enjoy. And until Alfred was ready to turn his attention to him, all Caden could do was squirm in the mud.

His breaths sped up as he realised he might actually be able to hand over just a little bit more control to the other wolf in good conscience. A strange little mew of anticipation escaped from the back of his throat.

Alfred immediately turned to face him. "What's wrong?"

Caden swallowed rapidly. "I'm fine."

Alfred frowned. "Are you cold?"

Caden shook his head. He was pretty sure if he got any hotter his blood would start to bubble and boil inside him. If anything, he was so feverish with desire he was in danger of drying out the mud he sat in, but he couldn't say that.

Sex was his one bargaining chip—and it would stay that way until it was completely safe for him to give it up forever. It was far too soon for him to admit he was just as desperate to get screwed as Alfred was to screw him. Once they were mates, then maybe the truth could come out, but until then...

Caden looked down his body once more. His gaze settled on his erection. Of course, it was just possible that the other man would notice how turned on he was without either of them saying a word.

"I like watching you work," Caden offered.

Alfred gave him a strange look.

Dipping his gaze, Caden smiled up at the other wolf through his lashes in practiced flirtation. "It makes you look more dominant than ever..."

Alfred turned away from him, a slight frown marring his brow as he returned his attention to his task. It was only a few minutes before he stopped again and glanced at Caden once more.

"This section is finished. I'll leave the rest until tomorrow when there's better light. I don't want you sitting out in the cold any longer than you have to." He walked across and set his shovel neatly with the others leaning against an old tree stump.

"There are other ways you could warm me up, if you wanted to," Caden offered, doing his best to keep a complete over-abundance of enthusiasm out of his voice.

Alfred was standing almost directly over him. From that angle he was huge and powerful and completely faultless in the more submissive wolf's eyes.

"Such as?" Alfred asked.

"I've heard that combining body heat can be a lot of fun," Caden suggested.

"Oh?"

Caden nodded coyly, as if it didn't really make that much difference to him if Alfred took him up on his invitation or not.

Crouching next to him, Alfred pushed Caden's hair back from his face. His hands were coated with mud. Caden felt dirt smear across his temple. Alfred stilled for a moment, as if something so insignificant could actually be considered a problem, but Caden quickly leaned in to his touch, desperate to make it clear he didn't mind getting a little bit messy in both a very good and potentially very erotic cause.

A touch to his other wrist caught Caden's attention. Glancing down, he saw Alfred's fingers trace a line over his skin, leaving a ring of mud around the joint. Lifting his hand, Caden offered his entire arm to Alfred and nodded his acceptance.

The other wolf quickly took hold of him. His other hand immediately copied the action around Caden's other wrist. Success radiated from Alfred's eyes in the darkness as he leant forward and brought their lips together.

Their balance was precarious to start with. The moment Alfred dipped his head to deepen the kiss, they toppled, their bodies skidding in the wet mud. Caden gasped as his back hit the ground, Alfred landing on top of him and pressing him down into the soft earth.

Clothes made rough and cold with mud rasped against Caden's body, but that didn't matter. All that mattered was the friction they provided against his cock. Moaning his complete approval into the kiss, Caden parted his lips and hurriedly gave the other man whatever access he wanted.

Caden tried to reach out and pull the other man down harder against his body, but Alfred wouldn't allow it. His hands tightened around Caden's wrists, demanding they stay exactly where he wanted them to be.

Temporarily freed from any responsibility to pretend that was anything other than exactly what he wanted, Caden bucked his hips and rubbed their bodies together. Alfred's erection pressed back against him through the other wolf's clothes, but it wasn't enough. He wanted skin against skin.

Alfred growled as he thrust against him. The kiss turned fierce. The younger wolf nipped at Caden's lips and took total possession of his mouth. Shoes kicked against his bare feet as they both sought for any kind of leverage they could find in their slippery surroundings.

"Please?" Caden gasped the plea into the kiss.

Alfred only growled in response.

There was no way he could really be denying him anything in that moment. Even Caden himself didn't know what he was actually begging the other man for. Even so, the plea merely made the other wolf hold him tighter and made his movements rougher and more perfect. There was no flirting, no prettiness, just raw sex, harsh need and dominance. Caden revelled in it.

Alfred's denim-clad leg slid between Caden's as he broke the kiss. Tossing back his head, Alfred howled his pleasure as he came inside his jeans. The slight change in angle was all Caden needed to fall into his own personal spiral of bliss. He was vaguely aware of his cum spilling between them and mixing with the mud, but the sensation was damn near drowned out by the way Alfred filled his senses and his world.

The other wolf's scent, his touch, the sight and the sound of him, all blended together and somehow managed to make Caden's pleasure deeper than anything he had ever known. Any desire he had to retain control and keep himself safe died in that moment.

As they fell still, Alfred remained on top of him, pinning him to the ground with his weight as well as his strength as they both fought for breath. Caden made no complaint.

Eventually, as his body recovered, Caden was able to lift his head a fraction. He lapped gently at Alfred's neck—the only part of his lover he was able to reach. The fact that the little patch of skin was just as muddy as the rest of him wasn't important. He could still taste the wolf beneath it all.

Alfred murmured his approval before slowly dragging himself upright. Reaching down, he helped Caden up, too. Of all the stupid things in the world, Caden found himself feeling silly and shy in front of the other wolf.

There was no need for that. It wasn't as if the other man could really know how little control Caden had over himself—how much control he'd given away to Alfred in that brief encounter.

Swallowing rapidly, Caden pushed a hand through his hair. His fingers got stuck halfway. The mud was drying and matting the blond strands together. Caden winced and wrinkled his nose as he imagined how he must have looked right then. It was a wonder Alfred had even bothered with him while he was in that state.

"You're beautiful."

Caden met Alfred's eyes for a moment. It was hardly the first compliment he'd ever received, but as they stood there on the half-formed river bank, it hit Caden harder than any flowery-worded statement ever had. A blush made its way to his cheeks, although he doubted it was visible under all the dirt.

"You're not so bad yourself," he managed to whisper in return.

Alfred put his arm around his shoulders in a protective little gesture as he turned them towards the house without ever asking his lover's opinion on the idea. Caden merely smiled and accepted that as the other man's right that night.

* * * *

"Did you see Alfred and Caden when they got home last night?"

Alfred stopped at the top of the stairs. The door leading into the alphas' bedroom was open just the tiniest crack. No doubt both men had been 'resting' there, the way they often did in the middle of quiet days. Or at least days that were quiet until Marsdon and Bennett's howls of pleasure filled the air. They'd probably been in far too much of a rush to make sure the door was sealed behind them.

Marsdon laughed, a deep relaxed sound that indicated all was well in his world. "Yeah, I saw. They looked like they'd crawled out of the bottom of the river, there was that much mud on them!"

"And?" Bennett prompted.

"And who'd have thought that pretty little Caden could succeed where our big strong beta failed?" Marsdon asked, his tone still rich with humour and satisfaction.

Alfred frowned as he crept closer, careful that his shadow shouldn't be seen by any wolf on the other side of the door.

"They do seem to be well suited," Bennett said, his voice soft and sleepy — like a wolf who had *really* enjoyed his rest.

"More to the point, Caden seems to have brought the little brat to heel better than I ever hoped for."

"Marsdon..." There was just a touch of chiding in Bennett's tone.

"Well, someone has to. We couldn't have let him run riot forever, pup. We can't bring a mating pair into the pack until everything is stable, and we can't put that off much longer, can we? Little baby wolves have to come from somewhere, you know."

"I know, sir. I just..."

"You just want every wolf in your pack to be happy and content no matter what it takes?" Marsdon finished for him.

"Like you don't," Bennett replied.

Alfred could practically hear the smile in the other wolf's voice, but he couldn't bring a smile to his own lips in response. His frown deepened instead. He stared at the door until the sound of rustling clothing warned him that he'd be risking certain discovery if he lingered there any longer.

He'd already heard enough anyway. Turning away, Alfred quickly strode down the stairs, but the sound of his footsteps completely failed to drown out the echoes of the alphas' words.

It almost sounded like it was all their idea—like they had been as much behind Caden approaching him as they had been instrumental in bringing Gunnar and Caden to the pack in the first place.

Alfred shook his head as his steps sped up. It wasn't like that between him and Caden. With Gunnar it had been obvious he wasn't really interested in being his mate, that he was just ticking the boxes of appropriate behaviour.

But Caden was different. He was only doing what he wanted to do. He wasn't simply playing along and going through the motions because his alphas ordered him to. He couldn't be.

Even as he wrote it off, a bitter taste filled the back of Alfred's mouth at the possibility. The idea of Caden feeling like he had to trade his mouth and his arse to a mate he had no real desire for, just to please his alphas...

Alfred's hand tightened into a fist at his side. It wasn't like that...was it?

Memories scrolled through his brain far too quickly for him to make any sense of them. Caden had certainly seemed enthusiastic. He'd really seemed to want Alfred as much as Alfred had wanted him last night. And he'd said he loved him and...

And he'd been very serious about the whole going slow thing. He'd been incredibly quick to make excuses for them not to have sex straight away...

And what kind of idiot could really believe that a wolf as perfect as Caden could actually want anything to do with a screw-up like me? a little voice from the back of Alfred's psyche piped up.

Striding quickly through the kitchen, Alfred peered around the courtyard, searching for any sign of Caden.

The vague memory of someone saying they were going to work in the barn had him striding quickly across to the huge wooden doors, but, once again, he found himself slowing as he reached a small opening, just big enough to allow a conversation between other wolves to reach him as he stood on the outside peering in.

"It won't actually make any difference to you if I point out you're acting like a whore, will it?" Gunnar's growl was instantly recognisable.

"Do you think that's what Talbot is doing when you mate with him?" Caden's softer lilt asked in return.

"Not the same thing!" Gunnar barked.

Alfred peeked cautiously through the crack between the door and the old oak frame of the barn, hoping he wouldn't be spotted. Gunnar was pacing back and forth across the big dusty space, the same way he always did when he was pissed off with the world.

He kept disappearing and reappearing in the thin slice of the other wolves' world that Alfred was able to glimpse. Further back into the barn, Caden seemed to have given up trying to keep track of his brother and was resting back in the hay, staring up at the barn roof.

He was as gorgeous as ever, with the sunlight from a high window shining on his hair and his legs sprawled out in the hay. His whole body was an invitation for another wolf to pounce on him. If only Gunnar would stop walking about and blocking the damn view, it might have been a perfect sight.

"Not the same thing at all," Gunnar repeated.

"It's exactly the same thing," Caden said, twirling a piece of hay between his fingers as he smiled at his brother's obvious discomfort.

"Are you telling me that you're not trading sex for good behaviour from him?" Gunnar demanded, stopping to loom over his little brother.

Alfred's hand tightened into a fist as the urge to leap between them and protect Caden suddenly made itself known inside him, but the muscles lost all their strength as the beta's words sank in.

It couldn't be true. Alfred waited for Caden to speak up and tell the beta that, but Caden merely shrugged, his smile never faltering.

The breath caught in Alfred's throat as his faith in the unfairness of the accusation faltered, but even after everything he'd heard both there and at the alphas' bedroom door, some little part of him refused to believe it could actually be true.

"We all have our strengths," Caden told his brother, mildly. "Yours may be growling orders and bossing everyone around. Mine are…"

"Bending over for brats?" Gunnar suggested.

"Ever heard the phrase: you'll catch more flies with honey than vinegar?" Caden asked. "I can vouch for its accuracy."

"Unbelievable," Gunnar muttered, shaking his head as he returned to his pacing.

Caden sat up and brushed a few loose ends of straw from his shirt. "Where's the harm?" he asked. "If Alfred needs a little extra motivation to take a step in the right direction and become the sort of wolf his pack wants him to be, then is it really so terrible for me to use some less-than-innocent methods to nudge him in the right direction?"

Alfred didn't wait to hear Gunnar's answer. He couldn't listen to another word, couldn't stay there a moment longer.

Caden had… He and Caden had…

Alfred's feet carried him one step back, then another. His hand came up to cover his mouth as he fought back the conflicting desires to either howl, scream or throw up.

Spinning around, he rushed away as fast as his feet could carry him. Stumbling whenever he forgot to take due notice of the ground passing rapidly beneath his shoes, he broke into a clumsy run.

His feet covered the grass more and more quickly as he headed instinctively for the tree line, but speed didn't help. It was impossible to outrun the words — they were already in his head and the wind whipping against his clothes and snatching at his hair didn't blow a single one of them from his mind.

Out by the wood pile, in Caden's bed, even out by the river — it had all been a game to Caden, some sick little game the alphas had arranged for the other gamma to play with him. On the edge of the woods, Alfred slowed down. Collapsing against one of the trees, he struggled for breath as his lungs burned and his muscles cried out in pain.

Stupid! He'd been such a fool to believe Caden had any real interest in him. Alfred swung his arm, lashing out at the world in general. His fingertips brushed against one of the tree's branches. Before he'd even thought about what he was doing, he'd caught hold of it.

It was a thin branch. It came away from the trunk easily enough. Desperate to share some of the pain inside him and make everyone else hurt too, he swung the branch at the tree trunk again and again, sending leaves and bark flying around him.

He keep swinging the branch until his lungs whimpered their lack of oxygen and his heart raced so fast he was sure it would leap straight out through his rib cage.

Finally exhausted, he slumped onto his knees and let his head drop forward to rest against the battered bark. He closed his eyes, but it was impossible for him to hide from the anger coursing through him. He'd barely caught his breath before he turned back towards the house, fury burning in his eyes.

Chapter Five

"Alfred?"

Alfred heard Marsdon calling out to him just as he reached the kitchen door, but he was in no mood to heed his alpha. He wasn't capable of listening to anyone and even if he tried, he knew they would just lie to him, try to make him believe things that weren't true and —

"Alfred!" There was an added snap to Marsdon's voice that time.

Every lupine instinct Alfred possessed yelled that he should listen to the leader of his pack, but he pushed all that aside. Marsdon was the one who'd ordered Caden to…

Alfred growled beneath his breath. Marsdon had made the wolf he loved into a whore, and he deserved no hint of respect from anyone.

A rough hand landed on Alfred's shoulder and span him around as he reached the centre of the kitchen. The larger wolf tightened his hold on him when he tried to squirm away. There was no escape. Jerking his head back, Alfred glared up at Marsdon. "What?"

"Why didn't you stop when I called you?"

"What the hell made you think I would?" Alfred shot back.

"Alfred…" The word was a clear warning. The growl in Marsdon's voice wasn't the least bit playful or paternal.

"Since when are you surprised I don't listen to a word you say?" Alfred threw at him.

The image of Caden on his knees before him, and the way that beautiful picture was tainted by the knowledge that Caden hadn't really wanted to be there, that he was just whoring himself out on an alpha's orders, made it impossible for him to hold back anything.

He pushed at the alpha's hands, struggling to get away from him, but Marsdon merely shoved him back against the kitchen cabinets and held him there as if he had a right to do that, as if his rank gave him the right to do whatever the hell he wanted with any wolf in his pack, no matter who got hurt in the process.

Writhing against the hard edge of the cabinet, Alfred kicked out, shoving against Marsdon's body with all his might, and achieving no movement whatsoever.

That just made Alfred angrier than ever. Helplessness rushed through him, whipping up the storm inside him into something stronger than he'd ever felt in his life. The fight to get Marsdon's hands off his shoulders morphed into a fight for survival inside his head.

Lupine claws crept out of his fingers. Marsdon's shirt tore. There was no way his actions could be anything other than a challenge, but Alfred was past caring.

The alpha's hands suddenly moved to his wrists in a sickening mockery of the way he'd taken hold of Caden, back when some stupid part of him had actually believed the other gamma could enjoy being held that way. The alpha's fingers wrapped tightly around Alfred's skin and span him around so his back was to Marsdon's chest.

He was trapped then, his hands useless, his struggles futile.

"If you have any intention of remaining a member of this pack, you'd best learn to control that temper. There's only so much any alpha will accept."

"Maybe I don't want to be part of your bloody pack," Alfred screamed. "Maybe I don't want to be part of any pack!"

Not if that was the price Caden had to pay for him to be accepted, not if —

"Alfred?"

Marsdon spun them both around to face the softly spoken word.

Caden and Gunnar stood in the doorway leading in from the courtyard. A frown spread across Caden's brow as Alfred's eyes met his, as if he couldn't quite believe what he was seeing.

"What?" Alfred demanded. "You really thought a few blow jobs would make me into a brain-dead little zombie, prepared to jump at every higher ranking wolf's command?"

Caden stepped forward. Alfred desperately tried to back away, but there was no getting past Marsdon while the alpha's grip on his wrists kept him trapped and helpless.

Very slowly, the other gamma settled his palm on Alfred's cheek. He tried to jerk his head away. All he succeeded in doing was head-butting the alpha's shoulder.

"Tell me what's wrong?" Caden asked, gently. There was so much emotion in his eyes, and it looked so much like real concern, like how another wolf might look if he really did love him.

Alfred closed his eyes as he turned his face away from all the lies. "Get your hands off me."

"Alfred," Caden began.

"It's over."

"Over?" Caden repeated, blankly.

"Yes, over!" Alfred yelled, unable to keep the words back. "I have no interest in being your mate — no intention of being blackmailed and bribed with the possibility that you just might let me screw a fine piece of arse at some point. What is it that you don't understand about that?"

"Alfred!" Marsdon snapped.

For just the briefest moment, the alpha's grip on him eased. Jerking away from him, Alfred wrenched himself out of his hold and lurched away from the other man. He stumbled forward until he found his way blocked by the long kitchen table.

"That's all you are," Alfred growled at Caden as he span back to face him. He didn't know if he was trying to convince Caden or himself, but the words tumbled out faster and faster regardless. "You're just a pretty piece of arse. Well, I have no interest in being mated to some silly little slut who'll cheerfully whore himself out whenever he wants to get his own way. Understand?"

The blood seemed to drain from Caden's face. There was no hint of the pride or smugness that Alfred had overheard in the barn anymore. "I... You..." He dropped his gaze as he trailed off into silence.

"That's enough." Suddenly Gunnar was standing in front of Caden, big and stupid and worse even than all the others in the pack.

A growl built in the back of Alfred's throat. For a moment, his muscles tensed. His body screamed its desire to leap forward and claw each inch of flesh from the other man's face. At the last moment, the tiny little part of Alfred that still remembered what it was to be part of a pack won out. He threw himself towards the door rather than the other wolves.

Bennett was in the courtyard, making his way towards the house, just as Alfred emerged through the doorway. He said something, but Alfred didn't really hear it. The world before him was flooded with tears, but that didn't matter. He didn't care where he was going, as long as it was as far away from Caden as he could get.

* * * *

"Would anyone like to tell me what the hell that was all about?" Marsdon demanded as a stunned silence settled over the kitchen.

Caden barely even registered the question. All he could do was stare at the door Alfred had run through, unable to bring a single word to his lips in order to frame an answer.

"Caden?" Gunnar's voice tugged at the edge of his consciousness, but even that failed to rouse him from his stupor right then.

Alfred thought that he was nothing more than a —?

Big, strong hands landed on Caden's shoulders. He was turned forcibly away from the kitchen door and made to face his brother.

Gunnar glared down at him. His expression was angry, but he was nowhere near as furious as Alfred had been. And Caden knew his brother well enough to be able to see that beneath all of Gunnar's anger was a hell of a lot of concern. He hadn't seen any hint of that in Alfred's eyes — all he'd sensed in Alfred's scent was hatred.

"I…" Caden couldn't think of any other words to add to that one, lonely little syllable.

Alfred had all the potential in the world to be a good wolf, to be the kind of man any shifter would be proud to call his mate. But it had never occurred to Caden that a wolf with so much potential wouldn't want to be mated to someone whose main talent lay in fluttering his eyelashes.

He swallowed rapidly, trying to make his throat work, even if his brain wouldn't. Looking up, he saw everyone staring at him. "He didn't mean it," he whispered. Alfred couldn't have meant it. Could he?

Lifting a hand, Caden shook off his brother's touch and pushed his fingers through his hair. There was no mud to stop them now. If Alfred had wanted him when he looked like a muddy little mongrel, it stood to reason that he must still want him when he was all clean and pretty. "He's probably just having a bad day and—"

"Don't stand up for the little bastard!" Gunnar growled.

Caden quickly lifted his gaze and met the beta's eyes. "It's not all his fault."

"Then whose fault is it?" someone asked, very calmly, from behind them.

Caden turned towards his alphas. Bennett was at Marsdon's side now. His words sounded like an honest question, but the answer was far too dangerous to say out loud.

Even with panic swirling through his veins and the possibility of Alfred not wanting to be mated to anyone who only had a pretty face to recommend them hanging over his head, Caden knew it was something that simply wasn't said. Not by wolves. Not within a pack.

"Yours."

And the word was out, hanging in the air between them. It was too late for Caden to snatch it back, and as a damn near deafening silence settled over them, he found he didn't want to. Who cared how dangerous anything was when the worst had already happened?

"What did you say?" Marsdon snapped, stepping forward and blocking Caden's view of the other alpha.

"Not Bennett in particular," Caden corrected, as he realised what Marsdon thought. "All of you — all of *us*. The entire pack is to blame for the way Alfred acts."

Marsdon folded his arms across his chest as he squared his stance. "Gunnar's right — trying to make excuses for him and blaming everyone except him every time he screws up isn't going to do — "

"Don't you mean *if*?" Caden asked, his voice perfectly calm and controlled now that there was no going back. He hadn't meant to have the conversation like this. Hell, he'd hoped he could have got away with never needing to have it at all. But, if it was happening, he knew he had to make sure it happened right — he had to give Alfred that much of a fighting chance.

Whatever was destined to happen between them, whatever Alfred really thought of him, he owed any wolf he loved that much.

Marsdon frowned. "What?"

"Don't you mean if he screws up rather than when?" Caden asked again. "Is it really fair on him that you always assume he's going to screw up right from the start? Doesn't that just tempt fate and make it all the more likely he'll do something wrong?"

Bennett stepped forward before Marsdon could say anything, and laid his hand gently on his mate's arm. "I think we'd best sit down. This sounds like it'll take a while." He moved forward and pointedly took a seat at one end of the long pine table. Marsdon silently claimed the seat next to him.

Feeling very much like he was crossing quicksand, Caden sat next to his brother, opposite the alphas. Folding his hands neatly on the table, Caden stared down at them for a long time, trying to find the best possible words.

"Have you ever wondered why Alfred has never settled into your pack very well?" he finally asked.

"Because he's a selfish little brat who couldn't care less about anyone but himself," Marsdon suggested. "Because he'd rather stir up trouble than be a useful member of anyone's pack." The alpha was sitting back in his chair, his arms folded across his chest, and didn't appear to be the least interested in hearing anything that contradicted that view.

"Could any wolf really be happy living that way?" Caden asked, forcing himself to keep every word polite and softly spoken, making sure his body language screamed out that he wasn't trying to challenge anyone. "Would any wolf really want that?"

"No, no wolf would want that," Bennett said. "But if no one tells us anything else, that's the only thing we can believe." He leant forward, all his attention on the conversation. At least one of the alphas seemed willing to listen.

Caden took a deep breath and let it out slowly. "I know it's usually obvious what rank a wolf is most suited to from the time he's a little pup."

"Oh?" Marsdon said.

"But what if someone made a mistake? Or what if there are occasions when something happens to make the alphas of a pack wonder if someone's first impressions of a pup weren't entirely right?" Caden said to his neatly clasped hands. His knuckles were slowly turning white as he struggled to push forward. He was pretty sure he'd cut off all the circulation to the fingers on his left hand. They were starting to feel numb.

"If you have something to say, say it," Marsdon snapped. "But I'm telling you now, if you've acquired Alfred's habit for trying to stir up trouble then—"

"I think you've assigned Alfred the wrong rank among the gammas in your pack," Caden blurted out.

The challenge should have made Marsdon launch himself to his feet in fury. Caden was braced for it, willing to receive the full force of the other wolf's anger, even while nerves made him sure he was going to throw up long before the end of the conversation.

There was no furious howl. The other wolf merely tilted his head to the side and considered him in silence for several moments.

Caden risked a brief glance up and met Marsdon's eyes. From there, he turned to Bennett. When he saw the complete lack of emotion in his other alpha's gaze, Caden suddenly realised what they had both thought he was going to say.

"I know you're a good alpha," Caden said to Bennett. "I've never doubted that. You're both good alphas, good wolves. But if someone forced you to live in another rank, maybe you wouldn't be such good wolves. Perhaps, if there was something that made you doubt you were living out your right role, you'd be more like Alfred. Maybe you'd find there was something that screamed inside you, making you desperate to rock the boat hard enough that you might find yourself in a different place when everything settled after the storm."

"You think that's what Alfred has been trying to do?" Bennett asked.

"I think he's spent his whole life feeling as if he's out of place, as if he can't settle into his pack, or even into his own skin, because every wolf around him has been pushing him to be something he's not. Everyone assumes he's not that different to our omega — that he should be treated much the same as Talbot."

"He's nothing like Talbot !" Gunnar snapped to Caden's left.

"You're right, he's nothing like our omega," Caden said, and barely missed a beat before he pushed on. "He's much more like our beta."

"What?"

Caden hadn't heard his brother's voice reach that pitch since it had first broken and descended into its habitual deep growl. The beta launched himself to his feet. His chair tumbled back and clattered onto the tiles behind him.

"If Talbot was pushed into a different role, he'd worry and fret and struggle to please the people around him, even though it hurt him in a million different ways," Caden said, shoving back his own chair and squaring off against his brother without the slightest hesitation. "But if *you* were forced into a lower place in the hierarchy, we all know you'd give the whole world hell until you got moved to where you wanted to be. Tell me, who do you think Alfred is more like?"

"Sit down, both of you."

Caden glanced towards Marsdon out of the corner of his eye.

"If I have to get to my feet in order to make you both sit down and stop acting like silly little children…" the alpha warned.

Caden slowly did as he was told. The conversation was far too important to derail just because his brother was a jerk. Gunnar would still be there, and no doubt he'd still be a jerk, tomorrow. He could be dealt with then.

Gunnar picked up his chair and sat back down with a huff.

"You believe that Alfred might flourish if he was moved up the ranks among the gammas?" Bennett asked.

Caden nodded.

"Even without any...bribery taking place?" the alpha asked, quite gently.

"Alfred was angry—he lashed out." Caden wasn't entirely sure who he was trying to convince. Right then, a pretty face and a good technique didn't seem to count for a lot.

"And you still wish to be mated to a wolf who is inclined to lash out that way?"

Caden's lips twisted into a slight smile. "When he realises that he outranks me, he'll stop." He made sure all the other wolves saw his confidence in that fact, even if it wasn't built on an entirely solid foundation.

"And if he doesn't?" Marsdon cut in.

"Then..."

Caden's gaze dropped to Marsdon's forearm and the mark cut into the skin there. It was a huge risk to take. But if it was the only way to make his point, then...

"As things stand, I don't trust him to reach out and touch the back of my neck. I know that will change when our respective ranks change, but if for some reason it doesn't, then we'll have to...find a way to live our lives just with me reaching out for his forearm?" he suggested.

For several minutes the whole world seemed to wait and watch the alphas, to see what their reaction would be. Caden could hear his own heart pounding so loudly in his ears he was sure everyone else in the room had to be able to hear it too, but no one mentioned the racket.

It wasn't as if every wolf in the pack didn't know what it meant when Bennett reached out and touched the scar on his mate's arm, or what Bennett was offering Marsdon when he did that. Everyone knew there would soon be howls of pleasure emanating from the barn or the alphas' bedroom.

And when Marsdon touched the scar on the back of Bennett's neck, Caden had no doubt that he was asking his mate to submit to him, to hand over control to him for a little while, that Marsdon was telling his mate what he needed from him when he offered him that particular caress.

"That has nothing to do with a wolf's place in the pack," Marsdon said, each word enunciated very carefully.

Caden ignored him in favour of meeting Bennett's eyes and holding them. "Would you let Marsdon reach for the back of your neck if he wasn't secure in his place in the pack?"

"That's not the same—"

Marsdon stopped short when Bennett held up a hand. "No," he admitted. "I wouldn't."

Caden held his breath.

"I think I understand what you're trying to say."

"But—" Marsdon began.

"He's not insulting me," Bennett cut in, before the other alpha had time to build up any sort of momentum. "He's not insulting anyone." Still holding Caden's eyes, he nodded slowly. "I think it's time someone went to fetch Alfred."

Gunnar immediately pushed back his chair. "I'll get him."

"Don't get into an argument with him, but don't take no for an answer when you tell him he's to come home either," Bennett commanded, as Gunnar made his way to the kitchen door.

The beta nodded his understanding. Unless Caden was very much mistaken, his brother was supremely glad the mushy stuff had now been taken care of and he could get back to doing the kind of thing he did best.

As the door closed behind the beta, Caden was left alone with the alphas, the sole focus of their attention.

"You're very observant," Bennett said.

Caden made no reply.

"And now," Bennett went on, "I think both your alphas would like to know exactly what you've observed."

Quickly looking from Bennett to Marsdon and back again, Caden weighed up his options. "I've noticed the scars mean a lot to you," he offered as an opening bid.

"Yes," Bennett allowed, and nodded for him to continue.

"I think, when you touch the scar on Marsdon's arm, you're asking him to take control for a while, telling him that you'd like to follow his lead the next time you mate."

Neither alpha moved nor spoke.

"And when he touches the scar on your neck, he's asking for you to let him take control that way."

The room remained still and silent.

"I don't know what signals you use when you want to take control of Marsdon or he wants to give up control to you," Caden said. The moments the words hit the air, he knew he had stumbled on exactly the right thing to say, and it wasn't exactly a lie, there was no need to add he was pretty sure such a gesture had never been used.

Bennett smiled slightly. "I think we all know those signals don't exist."

"Bennett!" Marsdon wasn't smiling at all.

"It's not a problem," Bennett told his mate. "Caden's never had any intention of questioning my ability to lead this pack, have you?"

Caden shook his head. "I have no doubt you're an alpha. But...I think you're an alpha who knows how much it can hurt when something makes you doubt where you belong in a pack."

Bennett looked down. "If you're right about this, Alfred deserves all our sympathy."

"Yes," Caden agreed.

"And if you're wrong?" Marsdon asked.

Caden dropped his gaze. The answer was obvious, although he found it impossible to admit it out loud. If he was wrong, he was going to be screwed—and not in the way he'd been hoping for.

* * * *

"Put me down, you bastard!" Alfred did his best to shout the words, but it wasn't easy while Gunnar's shoulder seemed to be determined to knock the air out of his lungs every time the beta took a step.

"Careful, brat, those are Caden's parents you're questioning the morals of, too," Gunnar warned as he marched on.

Every step bounced Alfred on his shoulder. For someone who seemed to be covered in muscle, he was incredibly bony. The other wolf's grip on him wasn't painful as such, but it was immovable as hell. His biceps stayed locked over the back of Alfred's legs no matter what he did.

Alfred hit against Gunnar's back and kicked out as hard as he could. Nothing made the damnedest bit of difference.

Looking around as best he could while hoisted over the other wolf's shoulder, he realised they were making their way back to the farmhouse. "Let me go!"

Gunnar simply ignored him and held more tightly to his legs, preventing Alfred's kicks landing hard enough to do any real damage.

Alfred's upside-down view of the courtyard, then the kitchen, suddenly span. He was deposited unceremoniously onto the cold tiles in the middle of the kitchen floor. Glaring up at Gunnar, Alfred opened his mouth to hurl another insult at him.

His eyes fell on Caden instead. Every thought, every word, fled from Alfred's head. He closed his mouth and ground his teeth together as fresh anger flooded through him.

"Good of you to join us," Marsdon said.

Alfred scrambled to his feet and turned to face the alpha.

"Save it for the challenge ring," the older wolf advised, before Alfred could even part his lips.

"What?" The single word hung in the air, small and lonely as Alfred's mind reeled.

"No! This isn't what—" Caden rushed out.

Alfred glanced in his direction just in time to see Marsdon silence him with a look.

"But," Caden tried again.

"You were right," Marsdon informed the other gamma, before turning back to Alfred. "It's time you found your rightful place in the pack—whatever that might be."

For once, Alfred failed to see the usual anger spinning in the other wolf's eyes. Marsdon looked almost...curious? But that wasn't important.

"You're throwing me out of the pack..." Alfred took a step back, cursing himself for his stupidity in being surprised, in letting his shock creep into his words.

He'd known from the start that he didn't really belong there, that he didn't fit into Marsdon and Bennett's pack the way all the other wolves did. He should have expected this. He should have been ready for it.

Perhaps if he had anticipated it, his heart wouldn't have broken a little at the sudden realisation he was about to find himself all alone in the world, without a pack. Even a pack who felt nothing but contempt for him was better than that. And Caden was—

Ice solidified in his veins. Alfred jerked his gaze up to meet his alpha's. "Only me?" he demanded. "I'm the only one being sent into the challenge ring?"

"Is there anyone you believe should join you there?" Bennett asked.

"No!" Alfred rushed out. "Only me." He nodded then, purposely not looking at Caden. There was no way the other gamma could go into the ring. Caden had to be kept safe. He couldn't be punished because even he couldn't make Alfred worthy of a place in the pack.

"Only me." Alfred managed another nod.

Marsdon's eyes narrowed a fraction. He looked to Caden, but when he turned his attention back to Alfred, all he said was, "Collect up the others and get to work. We all know you know how to make a ring."

Alfred obeyed the command more quickly than he had followed any order the alpha had ever given him. He rushed out of the kitchen before he dragged Caden down with him. It didn't take long to find the others. They had all congregated well within shouting distance of the kitchen, every one of them needing to know what was going on in their pack before they had any chance of resting easy in their own skins.

They trailed behind Alfred as he stormed down to a patch of grass that they'd all visited once before, what felt like several lifetimes ago.

The sun shone. A gentle breeze caressed Alfred's skin. There were even bloody birds singing in the trees. It wasn't quite what he'd thought hell would look like, but he had no doubt that was exactly where he was. And he quickly set about making it into something capable of casting him down into even hotter flames.

By the time the alphas, Caden and Gunnar joined them, the circle was complete, the grass within it trampled down to make a spacious fighting area. Unable to trust himself if he looked towards Caden, Alfred's attention focused on Bennett. The alpha seemed so right in his role it was impossible to believe he had ever been accused of being anything but exactly what he was, that Alfred himself had been the one to send him into the ring.

"Into the circle, Alfred," Marsdon ordered. "Everyone else, move across to the other side."

The wolves all obediently took up their positions, all except Caden. When Alfred glanced over his shoulder, the other gamma seemed rooted to the spot. He stayed right there until Bennett retrieved him and led him to stand with the rest of the pack. Unable to risk looking higher, Alfred watched Caden's shoes move to stand right the middle of the pack, surrounded by wolves that would look after him.

That was good. Alfred took a deep breath. Caden was safe. That was the most important thing. That was the *only* thing.

"You are now in limbo," Marsdon announced. "Each wolf in our pack will pass through the challenge circle, and you will each have the chance to find out where your natural place will be within our hierarchy if you remain in this pack. When the matter is settled to both your satisfaction, that wolf will pass through to the other side of the circle. Any questions?"

Alfred shook his head.

Marsdon turned away. A look passed between him and Bennett. Each wolf nodded his acceptance of whatever plan they'd silently come up with.

"Francis—you're up first."

Alfred quickly turned his attention to Francis. The other gamma wasn't much bigger than him. Any fight between them would be a close call on the best of days. Alfred pushed his hand through his hair. There was so much adrenaline rushing through his body he was practically shaking, and no one had even landed a single blow.

Very slowly, Francis began to circle him. Alfred matched him move for move as they gradually closed in on each other, their feet passing easily over the trampled-down grass. "What the hell's going on?" Francis hissed, ducking his head to keep the words just between them.

Alfred shrugged.

"Tell me," Francis commanded. "You're not the only one this will affect!"

"You have no right to issue orders to me," Alfred spat.

Anger flashed in Francis' eyes. He lunged forward. Alfred reacted just in time, stepping to the side and neatly dodging the attack. Twisting around, he caught hold of Francis' arm and used the other wolf's own momentum to send him crashing to the ground. Pouncing on him, Alfred pinned him down against the flatted grass.

"I'm not Steffan!" Alfred growled into his ear, his brain unable to keep any of his instincts in check for a moment longer. "He might like taking orders from you, but I don't!"

Francis bucked. The world span. Alfred landed heavily on his back. His head thudded against the earth. Before he could focus, Francis was gripping his shoulders. "Maybe if you acted like you could make a good decision on your own, I wouldn't have to —"

"When have I had the chance?" Alfred bit out, twisting and almost managing to throw the other man off.

"What?"

"I can't make a good decision if I'm never given the chance, can I?" Alfred growled.

Francis stared down at him as if he really didn't have a clue what was going on. "You want to move up the hierarchy. This is all just because you want to outrank me?"

Alfred swallowed, but the answer that bubbled up inside him came from a part of his brain that was too ancient to understand words. He nodded, careful not to tilt his head back too far and display any sort of submission.

Francis' guard seemed to falter. The same instinctive part of Alfred's mind that had told him to nod prompted him into immediate action. The world tumbled around them. Their positions were once more reversed.

Alfred's hands quickly found Francis' wrists and pinned him to the ground. The other wolf tensed, completely unable to hide how much he hated being held down. A frown passed across Francis' brow as he seemed to fight against his revulsion in an effort to think more clearly. He was always thinking, always studying the world around him, weighing up the evidence.

Against all logic, Alfred somehow found himself pulling back from a certain victory. Releasing the other wolf's wrists, he merely loomed over the prone wolf, casting a shadow over Francis' body as the sun beat down on the back of his neck.

If he was to have any chance of convincing Francis he deserved to outrank him, he needed to gain his respect.

There would be no triumph in being accepted simply because doing that would be the quickest way for Francis to get out of a position he loathed.

Francis stared up at Alfred, studying him for what felt like an eternity with no hint of submission in his eyes. Alfred could damn near see the wheels in the other wolf's head turning.

Finally Francis nodded. "I have no objection to seeing what you could do with a higher rank," he allowed. Even though he chose his words with obvious caution, his tone practically screamed that he really didn't care one way or another where he actually stood in the hierarchy between the gammas.

For several seconds, Alfred was speechless.

"But that doesn't mean I won't make your life a living hell if you hurt Steffan—in this ring or out of it," Francis added.

That was what he really cared about. His mate. For the first time in his life, Alfred didn't think the other man a fool for that.

Francis dropped his eyes, just once and just for a moment, but it was enough. Success rushed through Alfred, unlike anything he'd ever known. As he pulled himself to his feet, he found himself instinctively offering to help the other wolf up, too.

A hint of surprise made it into Francis' eyes, but he didn't say anything. He merely nodded to him before turning away and making his way to the opposite side of the challenge circle.

Alfred turned back to the wolves on the other side of the ring. Their expressions varied tremendously, but the most common ones by far were shock and curiosity. Alfred's guard was down as he looked across the line. He forgot why he wasn't supposed to risk looking one particular wolf in the eye.

Caden was so pale, it seemed as if it was only Bennett's arm around his shoulders that was keeping Caden on his feet. His eyes seemed very big, even bluer than ever. As Alfred watched, Caden swallowed rapidly, as if he was barely keeping his emotions in check. Alfred took a step forward, his hand already rising from his side as he instinctively reached out to Caden.

"Steffan," Bennett suddenly said.

Alfred blinked. He turned his attention back to the rest of the pack just in time to see the big wolf move forward to take his turn.

Stepping into the circle, Steffan squared up against Alfred, just as tradition suggested he should, but Alfred couldn't seem to make his muscles work. He remained exactly where he was. Turning his head, he looked from the pack, to Francis, and back to the other wolves once more.

No one there wanted to see the gentle giant hurt, not even Alfred himself. If it were Caden in there, then... The very idea of it sent a wave of horror through him, turning his stomach. He'd want to kill anyone who raised a hand to his mate. He could hardly blame another man for feeling the same way.

Without making even the vaguest attempt at a fighting stance, Alfred stepped forward and closed the gap between himself and the larger wolf.

Steffan hesitated. He looked to Francis for guidance, his eyes flicking quickly from his mate back to Alfred, as if he wasn't sure if he was about to be caught in some sort of trap or not.

"We all know you're stronger than me," Alfred said. As hard as the words were to utter, he knew there was no avoiding them. "Every wolf in the pack knows who would win any fight against you, if that was all the challenge circle was about."

And, for so many years, every wolf in the pack had automatically assumed Steffan should outrank him because of it. Pushing down that knowledge, Alfred kept his chin tilted up and his eyes on Steffan's face. The longer he stood in the circle, the more clearly his thoughts seemed to settle into his head. Size and strength meant less than nothing.

Steffan remained silent. Their eyes were locked. The other gamma didn't lower his gaze, but Alfred could almost feel his desire to do so filling the circle.

"Do you care what your rank in the pack is?" Alfred asked. "Or how many gamma wolves outrank you?"

Steffan looked across at Francis for a brief moment, then back to Alfred again.

"Francis isn't going to love you any more or less if you keep trying to give me orders or if I start issuing them to you," Alfred pointed out.

Steffan's lips curved into a slight smile. "I know."

All Alfred could do then was wait. Steffan knew what Alfred was asking him to do. He had to realise it was all in his hands, whether he wanted it or not. It seemed to take a lifetime for the huge wolf to make a decision, but finally, Steffan's gaze dropped to the trampled-down grass.

Alfred could have kissed him for that tiny little sign of submission. He resisted the temptation. There was no need to make Francis charge back into the circle in a fit of jealousy—no need at all to piss off either of the two wolves who suddenly seemed willing to give him the chance he'd been waiting for his whole life.

Steffan took a step towards the other side of the circle to join his mate, carefully walking around Alfred.

"Wait there."

Alfred's attention snapped towards Marsdon. Steffan turned to face the alpha too, a guilty look creeping into his eyes, as if they'd been caught doing something dirty.

"Tradition states that wolves have to lay a hand on each other while they are in the circle."

Alfred turned back to face Steffan once more. The other gamma was obviously waiting for him to decide what their next move should be. Alfred hesitated. He already outranked the other wolf. The idea of lashing out at a man below him in the hierarchy filled his mouth with a bitter taste.

Without even tapping into the part of his mind that understood anything above instinct, he found himself holding his hand out towards Steffan. A much larger hand engulfed his palm as they politely shook hands.

Alfred glanced towards Marsdon. One nod confirmed that the letter of the law had been satisfied. As Steffan moved towards Francis, Alfred looked to the others.

For reasons best known to themselves, Marsdon and Bennett seemed to have given him the easiest challenges first. Steffan and Francis had always had less interest in rank than any other wolves he'd known. No other member of the pack would be so easy going.

"Gunnar—you're up next."

Alfred didn't curse. He kept his lips tightly shut and avoided uttering a single word to make sure that would be the case.

So, this was where it really started. He felt the atmosphere change and realised that everyone else knew it too. They were all well aware of how much Gunnar hated him—and how much he had wound up and pissed off the beta during their time there.

Talbot touched Gunnar's arm, stopping the beta before he could actually step into the circle. Dipping his head, Gunnar whispered something into the little wolf's ear before pressing a kiss to his temple and resuming his progress towards Alfred.

Pure confidence swirled around the beta like a tornado ready to destroy anything in its path. There was no doubt that he cared enough to make up for Francis and Steffan's near-ambivalence about rank. There would be no token challenge.

Alfred took a deep breath. If he didn't square up against the beta it would just hurt all the worse when the other man charged at him. Gunnar took a fighting stance and raised an eyebrow at Alfred, as if warning him that no one would be playing bloody silly games this time around.

Alfred took the hint and took up a suitable posture. He tried to take yet another deep breath, but all the air rushed out of his lungs as he hit the ground hard enough to make his teeth rattle in his head.

When he opened his eyes, Gunnar was right there, his nose an inch from Alfred's face, a deep growl emanating from the back of his throat.

Chapter Six

Alfred dipped his gaze without wasting time on a first, let alone a second, thought. Instincts were flying through him now, freed of all the anger that had bubbled inside him for as long as he could remember.

Gunnar was a beta and Alfred knew right then, in a way he never really had before, that it was the rank Gunnar belonged in. He hadn't been given the rank because he looked like a beta, he'd been given it because he was a beta right down to the core.

Even as Alfred turned his head and stared down at the battered grass to his left, he began to understand what it was to want to belong to a pack where there were wolves that outranked him, not because life was unfair, but because they should outrank him. In one blinding flash it felt both right and safe to know that there were wolves in the pack that were above him, watching over him and the other gammas.

"Now?" Gunnar demanded, still barely an inch away from his nose. "*Now* you decide you want to stop acting like a brat?"

Alfred risked a glance up. The other man was so close he was blurry.

"No," he whispered. "I just realised that I don't want to be a beta."

"And that makes everything okay?" Gunnar growled. "It makes what you said to Caden a few minutes ago okay?"

Alfred swallowed rapidly. The other man might as well have thrust his fist straight into his chest and squeezed his fingers around his heart, stopping it from ever taking another beat.

Everything he had said to Caden played back in his head, and there was no way to escape it. "I was wrong to say that," Alfred whispered.

"Yes," Gunnar bit out. "You were."

"I love him." Alfred had had no intention of saying those words to anyone, and to Gunnar least of all, but suddenly they had already been spoken and it was too late to change that. Each syllable hung in the middle of the challenge circle, all pink and fluffy with pretty little hearts and sparkles decorating the air around them.

The beta growled again, but there seemed to be more frustration than anger in his grumbling now.

Alfred watched Gunnar carefully as the beta pulled back. Every muscle in the more dominant wolf's body was bunched up so tightly, it was almost impossible to believe he wasn't going to explode and lunge at him at any moment.

Gunnar wasn't looking at him in return. His attention was on the wolves still waiting to cross the challenge circle. He growled again as he turned back to Alfred.

"Just because I've no interest in seeing someone my brother is stupid enough to care about being thrown out of the pack, that doesn't mean I like you or that I forgive you for *anything*," he bit out.

The beta was still crouched down, as if ready to attack, but Alfred somehow managed to gather up every scrap of courage at his disposal and sit up.

"If you ever hurt Talbot or Caden, I'll make you wish I'd killed you in this circle," Gunnar warned.

Alfred slowly nodded his understanding.

Gunnar jerked himself abruptly to his feet and strode over to the far side of the circle without a word, leaving Alfred sitting all alone in the centre of the flattened grass.

The next wolves to pass through the circle were the other gammas. They'd all seen what had passed between him and the first three visitors to the circle. A little bit of rough and tumble was a small price to pay for seeing four more wolves move past him to the other side of the circle.

A couple of sneaky blows from men he had taken his own fair share of digs at over the years weren't so entirely unexpected. He took them with all the grace he could muster, knowing he probably had them coming. But it was only when he failed to return them that the other wolves retreated in apparent confusion.

As he watched the last of his fellow gammas leave the ring, Alfred wiped the blood away from his split lip with the back of his hand. His ribs burned from a well-aimed kick. His head span from a harsh blow. He knew that by morning, there would be a dozen other parts of his body that would be calling him a fool for not hitting back, but it was hard to believe that any of that mattered.

Success pounded through him like the heartbeat of the universe. Gunnar was the only wolf who had refused to yield his place in the hierarchy to him. Alfred stood in the middle of the challenge ring, the highest ranking gamma in the pack.

Except he wasn't actually part of the pack right then. Wolves still stood ready to challenge his newfound desire to belong and be a piece of something larger than himself. If the alphas refused to accept him into the fold, it wouldn't make a damn bit of difference what the gammas all thought.

"Talbot."

Alfred's eyes snapped towards the little omega. He'd been slowly gaining confidence since he'd been mated to Gunnar, but right then, he seemed to be back to where he had been several months ago, a bundle of nerves and anxiety barely held together by his fragile frame.

A memory presented itself in Alfred's mind of when Bennett had been in the circle. He'd let Talbot pass through with barely a word. Alfred dropped his gaze to the grass in front of him. Suddenly, he understood why.

"You're a good omega," Alfred said, as he looked up.

Talbot lifted his gaze, his expression all shock and no challenge. He stood on the edge of the ring as if he was more than ready to jump back out of it at the first sign of anger from his opponent.

Alfred stepped carefully forward, keeping all his movements calm, making sure there wasn't even the slightest hint of a threat in them. Finally, he reached the omega.

"You'd be wasted as a gamma."

Talbot said nothing.

"We need someone to balance out Gunnar and the alphas," Alfred went on. "You do that perfectly. I couldn't, neither could anyone else in the pack."

A little touch of colour rose to Talbot's cheeks. "I don't want to challenge you," he admitted.

Alfred swallowed and cleared his throat. "Do you want me to be part of your pack?" Heaven knew he hadn't actually given the omega any reason to want him within miles of him over the years.

Talbot nodded. He smiled slightly. He really seemed to mean it.

"Why?" Alfred blurted out.

"Because omegas aren't the only wolves a pack needs," Talbot said very softly. "And because Gunnar might never have noticed me if he hadn't been pointed towards a wolf who was the exact opposite of what he needed in a mate."

"Shake on it?" Alfred suggested, trying to hide his relief as best he could in order to appear strong and reassuring in the other wolf's eyes.

Talbot held out one small hand.

Alfred shook it. At the same time, he ruffled the omega's hair with his other hand. It was a clumsy attempt to copy a gesture he'd seen the other wolves bestow on Talbot so many times over the years, but Talbot seemed to sense he was doing his best. The little guy didn't even flinch at his raised hand.

Dipping his head, Alfred dropped his voice to a whisper. "You'd better go to your mate, before Gunnar has a fit waiting for you to get out of the circle."

Another smile reached Talbot's lips as he quickly did as Alfred commanded.

The omega had barely left the circle when Bennett stepped forward. He strode into the centre with complete confidence and Alfred's mind immediately raced back to the last time he'd faced Bennett there.

There'd been no quiet little conversations with wolves he'd known his whole life for Bennett. The challenges to an alpha's place in the pack were never that simple.

"I'm sorry," Alfred said.

Bennett didn't say anything for a long time.

"I didn't know," Alfred whispered.

"Yes, you did," the alpha corrected. "You knew exactly what you were doing when you challenged me, and you know exactly what would happen once you sowed doubts in the other wolves' heads."

Alfred swallowed. When he met Bennett's eyes for a moment, he knew there was no way in hell he'd be allowed to hide behind even half-lies right then. "Yes," he admitted. "I knew."

"So tell me why," Bennett ordered, slowly starting to circle Alfred.

Unable to turn and keep his attention on the other wolf without risking making himself so dizzy he'd be unable to keep his footing, Alfred stayed very still.

"Because they all respected you. Because they accepted the fact you should outrank them without a thought. Because..." Alfred closed his eyes for a moment, but when he opened them, he forced himself to meet the other man's eyes. "Because if I had acted that way with a lover, they'd have taken it as a sign that I really belonged at the bottom of the pack. It wasn't fair that you should be able to do that and keep your place while I..."

"While you were forced to live in a rank your nature isn't suited to," Bennett finished for him.

"I just knew I was angry," Alfred said, with a frown. "I don't think I even really knew why until..." He waved a hand at the circle beneath their feet, unable to find the right words to go on.

Bennett nodded as if that made perfect sense. His hair fell forward into his eyes, but he made no attempt to push it away. "That's what a challenge circle should be used for."

Alfred stared at the trampled-down grass. The scent of it filled his lungs as he took a deep breath.

"To make a pack stronger, not weaker," Bennett went on.

Alfred nodded. His eyes fell closed.

"To allow a wolf to find his rightful place in the pack."

Another jerky little nod was all Alfred could manage.

"Do you have any hesitation in accepting me as your alpha today?"

"No!" Alfred had never been more certain of an answer in his life.

"Then from this moment on, you're part of my pack." And Bennett turned to leave the circle as easily as that.

"Wait!" Alfred rushed forward and caught hold of his sleeve. "That's it?"

The alpha smiled slightly. "You mean don't I want revenge for what happened last time we stood in this circle?" Bennett shook his head. "That's not what being an alpha is about."

The thin cotton slipped from Alfred's fingers as the alpha turned and walked away. He stared after the other wolf, trying to think of something to say. He knew he deserved to be hammered black, blue and any other colour Bennett fancied for putting the alpha in the circle all those months ago. He was equally sure that a good wolf would take his punishment and maybe he'd be able to move on after it, but if Bennett wouldn't go along with that idea then—

Without any warning, Alfred's legs were swept out from beneath him. He landed heavily on the grass. His fingers clawed at the blades as he stared up at Marsdon.

The older wolf crouched in front of him, resting his forearms on his knees, the gentle breeze catching at his hair. "When you step out of this circle, you'll be given a completely fresh start, an entirely clean slate. Nothing that happened before that moment will count against you. So, this is your last chance. If you want to take a swing at a member of your pack, do it now."

"I didn't hurt them," Alfred blurted out, with a glance towards the other members of the pack.

"I know. I didn't think you had it in you, but you acted exactly as the top-ranking gamma should. But, if you need to fight *now*, you can. I'll fight you. I'll see that you don't get too badly hurt in the process, and I'll see that you don't hurt me too badly, either."

Alfred stared up at him. That was another part of being an alpha, he saw that now too — it was just the opposite side of the same coin that Bennett had offered him. Alfred closed his eyes to hide a wince. Right then, the other wolf's kindness hurt far more than any blow from him ever could.

Several minutes passed before he was able to force himself to meet the alpha's eyes. The anger he'd seen there last time the challenge ring had been formed wasn't there now, but as Alfred thought back to that day, he understood why Marsdon had hated him so much ever since.

"I'm sorry," he whispered for what felt like the millionth time that day.

"For anything in particular?" Marsdon asked, still crouched next to him.

"For making you watch Bennett in the ring." Alfred looked down. "I didn't know how hard it would have been, to watch a wolf you loved... I just..."

"Well, kiddo, I think you're about to find out exactly what it's like. I'm not the last wolf you have to convince to accept you back into the pack." Marsdon stood up. He walked away.

Alfred didn't watch him go. His attention was all on the lone wolf still standing on the other side of the ring. Caden's pretty blond hair was blowing in the breeze, his lips were as pink and kissable as ever, but his normally stunning eyes were full of tears.

The blood drained out of Alfred's face at the sight.

Caden's feet stepped forward and carried him across the grass. He wasn't sure what was controlling them, but he knew it couldn't be his brain. His mind had shut down completely the moment he had seen Alfred step into that ring.

Reaching the centre of the circle, Caden lowered himself to his knees next to Alfred but he couldn't bring himself to believe he had the right to reach out to the other wolf. Not after he'd screwed up so badly. Not after he'd put the man he loved in limbo. If he'd only had the sense to stick to fluttering his eyelashes and left the more serious matters to other men. If he'd just kept his mouth shut, then…

Caden closed his eyes very tightly and felt fresh tears run down his cheeks. The only thing he could hope for now was that the circle would help Alfred find his true place in the pack. Wasting hope on himself and trying to believe they still had a future together would have been unforgiveable.

"Caden?"

He didn't look up at the sound of his own name. When Caden opened his eyes, he kept them fixed firmly on the blurry little patch of ground between them.

A hand appeared in his field of view and moved cautiously towards his cheek and wiped away a few of the tears.

"There's nothing to be afraid of. You know I'd never want to hurt you, right?" Alfred whispered as he pulled himself up off the ground and knelt right in front of Caden, their knees touching.

Caden still kept his gaze lowered. Alfred's jeans were dusty and grass-stained after his scuffles. That was his fault, too. It was all his fault—everything in the whole damn world was his fault. "I'm sorry."

"Isn't that my line?" Alfred asked.

Caden frowned at their knees.

"What are you sorry for?" Alfred's hand on his cheek dropped down to his throat. Slipping it under his chin, he gently forced Caden's head back.

He had no choice but to meet Alfred's eyes then. "I never meant for them to put you in limbo. I just wanted them to give you a chance to find where you really belonged in the pack." Caden swallowed rapidly. He'd never heard his own voice sound so weak, been so unsure of his ability to talk another man into liking him.

Alfred stared at him in silence for a long time. Even while their eyes were locked, it was impossible for Caden to know what he was thinking.

"Thank you."

Caden blinked. More tears fell.

Alfred wiped them away. "Even if you didn't do it on purpose, whatever you said to our alphas put me here. It was where I needed to be." He stroked Caden's cheek again. There wasn't the slightest hint of anger in his voice or his eyes. His scent confirmed it all.

Finally, Caden remembered how to breathe. Closing his eyes, he tried to bow his head as pure relief made him dizzy

"No, don't."

It was more a request than an order, but Caden couldn't refuse the other wolf any more than he could disobey him.

"I love you."

Caden blinked in confusion at the words, but Alfred didn't. His eyes remained open. He held Caden's gaze as if both their lives depended on it.

"After what I said to you earlier," Alfred said, the tiniest hint of uncertainty creeping into his voice. "I know I've no right to hope that—"

"Always," Caden cut in. He offered the other man a hopeful little smile.

Alfred grinned back, but Caden's view of that expression only lasted for a fraction of a second because within a moment their lips were together and his eyes were dropping closed to better concentrate on the wonder of the kiss.

Without needing to engage his brain, Caden found his hands sliding into Alfred's hair. He tumbled back, but Alfred somehow managed to brace their fall. The grass was soft beneath them, the scent of the crushed blades hung in the air, and it was soon joined by the scent of their rising desire.

Desperate to deepen the kiss, Caden leaned up so far that they rolled over. Alfred let out a playful little growl and kept them tumbling over until Caden was once more on his back, his lover pinning him to the ground.

Feeling the cut on Alfred's lip made Caden whimper. He tried to hold Alfred's head still so he could lap at the wound and kiss it better.

Strong, determined hands wrapped around his wrists and pushed them to the ground. Alfred seemed to still then, as if concentrating very hard on Caden's reactions, needing to be sure he noticed even the tiniest signal his lover was trying to send him.

Caden mewed his pleasure into the kiss. Lifting his hips off the grass, he rubbed a flourishing erection against

Alfred through their clothes as he quickly sought to prove how much he loved it all.

A rumbling little growl of pleasure from Alfred was filled with more triumph than Caden ever remembered hearing before, even in the loudest howl from any other wolf.

Whimpering gently, Caden tipped his head back, eager to display any sign of submission he could before the wolf he loved. Alfred immediately pressed a kiss against his neck and —

"I think that more than fulfils the touching requirement."

Caden jerked his head around to face Marsdon as the alpha's words forced their way into his senses. He and Bennett were still standing on the edge of the challenge circle. So were all the other wolves.

"That's not quite the kind of rolling around you're supposed to do in there," Bennett added.

Caden looked warily up at Alfred. Whatever anger and annoyance he expected to see on his face was entirely absent. The only thing in his eyes was pride and possession. He liked that they had all seen them together. He liked that they all knew who Caden was going to belong to soon.

"Yes, we all get the point," Marsdon said. "You suit very well. We don't need a complete demonstration. But, if you'll put each other down for two minutes we can make it official. Then you can go continue in private."

Alfred sprang up from the ground so quickly, dragging Caden up onto his feet with him, Caden's head spun.

"I — ?" was all Caden managed to say, because suddenly Alfred was pulling him forward.

A moment later, just as Caden was starting to catch up, Alfred stopped abruptly. Still trying to make an arousal-addled mind work properly, Caden looked down. The edge of the challenge ring barred Alfred's path.

"You're both very welcome in our pack," Bennett said, all frivolity suddenly leaving his voice.

Marsdon nodded his agreement, his expression just as serious as his mate's.

Alfred took a step forward, crossing the line in the grass. A little cheer went up from the other wolves. Caden glanced at his lover out of the corner of his eye. From the look on Alfred's face and the slight blush on his cheeks, it was the first time anyone had ever cheered for him in his life.

Alfred's grip on Caden's wrist tightened, as if his sudden change of fortune had taken away all his bearings and Caden was now his only solid point of reference. Leaning into the other wolf's body, Caden encouraged his soon-to-be mate to slip an arm around his shoulders and allow him to wrap an arm around his waist in return.

A smile that didn't seem to be entirely as confident as it purported to be hung on Alfred's lips as they all made their way to the spot where all the other mating ceremonies in the pack had been conducted.

It took all Caden's strength of will to step away from the other wolf for long enough to be formally mated to him, but it was he who made the decision to separate their bodies. Unless Caden was very much mistaken, it would be the last decision he needed to make on that score for quite some time. Alfred had more than proved he was ready to step forward and take care of them both.

Even when he allowed Caden to step away, Alfred kept hold of his hand. As they faced each other, his grip on Caden remained as tight as ever. The alpha's hands covered theirs, sealing them together, offering them their complete blessing and their unwavering approval.

Caden held Alfred's gaze. He saw every flicker of emotion, saw what the alphas' actions meant to him. Alfred's grip tightened around his hand even further, completely cutting off the circulation to three of his fingers, as if he was scared Caden might try to pull his hand away.

"Alpha to gamma, wolf to wolf, we offer you the chance to form a new life, a new bond, a new pairing within our pack," the alphas recited.

"An unmated wolf takes a mate and forms a bond with another unmated wolf from your pack," Alfred said, each word full of triumph and confidence. "A bond that can never be broken."

Caden lifted his gaze. His own brand of strength flowed into his words as he repeated them back to his lover. There was no flirtation, no pretence in there—just honesty, just love.

The alphas barely had time to release their hands before Alfred jerked Caden into his arms. The grip he took on him was almost painful, almost—there was just a touch of control mixed in with the strength, more than a hint of reassurance woven through the possessive gesture.

Other wolves patted Caden on the shoulder and ruffled his hair, but there was little else they could do while Alfred held him like that. He heard congratulations flowing around them, but couldn't lift his head to meet anyone's gaze.

"Don't make me break you up by force," Marsdon eventually said, laughter dancing in his voice.

When Alfred let him go with obvious reluctance, Caden forced himself to turn away from his mate and accept congratulations from the pack properly.

"If you can keep each other from getting into too much trouble, I guess it's a good thing," Gunnar muttered as he stepped forward.

"Yeah, I love you too," Caden told his brother, letting his smile grow into a grin.

Gunnar humphed and turned away, leaving Caden momentarily alone. Instinctively seeking out his new mate in the crowd, Caden spotted Alfred on the other side of the pack, listening very carefully to what the alphas were saying to him.

He tried to track the way Marsdon and Bennett's lips moved and work out the words, but it was impossible, and he had to give up any attempt at it when Talbot stepped forward to shyly offer up his own congratulations.

Caden wrapped his arms around the little wolf and gave him a brotherly hug.

"I'm glad you're both so happy," Talbot whispered. "So is Gunnar. He's really pleased you've found a mate. He's just..."

Caden laughed. "He's just Gunnar. You're the only wolf he'll ever admit he gives a damn about."

Talbot blushed, but it was hard to focus on the pretty pink hue in the younger wolf's cheeks, because there was a low, jealous growl coming from right behind Caden's back. Turning around, he found himself once more face to face with his mate.

Before even a fraction of a second had passed, Alfred's hand was wrapped around his wrist. Caden grinned over his shoulder and waved goodbye to the rest of the pack as he found himself being dragged hastily back to the house to solidify his bond with his mate.

The other wolves laughed, obviously as amused as hell at the show of jealousy, but no one tried to stop them.

The ceremonial spot had obviously been chosen for its prettiness rather than its closeness to the house. By the time Alfred's bedroom door slammed behind them, Caden was more than a little out of breath after keeping up with his mate's frantic pace over that distance.

Collapsing cheerfully across the other man's bed, he smiled up at the ceiling as if it was the most beautiful thing he had ever seen in his life. The view was improved even further when Alfred joined him on the mattress, leaning over him and filling his field of vision.

"My mate," Alfred said, with surprising tenderness.

"Yes." There was as much triumph in Caden's voice as he said it, as he'd ever heard in Alfred's.

The other wolf's moved his hand to Caden's wrist and stroked his fingers softly over the skin there. Caden's arms had fallen to either side of his head as he tumbled onto the bed. It was damn near an invitation to pin him down, but Alfred didn't immediately accept it.

"Whatever you want," Caden whispered.

Alfred's eyes left his wrist. He held Caden's gaze for several long seconds. Caden tilted back his chin, baring his neck and offering up his complete submission.

Dipping his head, Alfred pressed a kiss to his throat. He nipped softly at the tender skin. The touch of teeth sent a wave of adrenaline rushing straight to Caden's cock.

His hips rocked up. He already felt as if he'd been hard for several lifetimes. Now that he was finally free to let his instincts take control, it was impossible for him to hold anything back. A needy little whimper escaped from his throat. "Please?"

"Tell me what you want."

Caden shook his head.

Alfred frowned slightly, obviously not the least impressed with his mate saying no to him in that particular matter.

Caden smiled slightly. There really was more dominance in him than any of the other wolves in the pack realised. Gunnar was going to be kept on his toes by the wolf just below him in the hierarchy.

"If you're hurt after fighting the other wolves, then —"

Alfred's frown deepened. "I'm going to hurt like hell tomorrow, but nothing is going to stop us being together tonight."

"Then I just want you to do whatever you want with me. That's what feels right," he said.

Alfred's frown slowly faded away. A smile twisted his lips. It obviously felt right to him, too. When their mouths came together it was even better. Caden parted his lips and offered complete access to his lover without any hesitation.

Clothes fell away. Caden wasn't entirely sure who took them off. One minute they were there. The next moment, the world was full of beautifully bare skin. Caden ran his hands over Alfred's body, glorying in finally being in the other wolf's bed and being able to truly be himself with his mate.

"Perfect," he whispered.

Alfred shook his head, but Caden caught his face in both his hands and made him stop.

"You're perfect," he repeated, holding his mate's eyes as he said it, needing him to know he meant it with his whole heart.

Alfred caught hold of his wrists and held them easily against the bed. "You're the perfect one. You're gorgeous."

Caden didn't deny it.

Alfred chuckled as he seemed to realise that Caden had been told it often enough to believe it. "And all mine," he added.

That made Caden blush in pleasure. It was something he hadn't heard before—or at least never believed to be the truth when another man said it.

As they kissed, their bodies rubbed together, and their hard cocks were quickly teased to the edge of orgasm between them. It was all so simple, all so perfect. Until Alfred suddenly pulled back.

Caden let out a whimpering little protest.

"No. Not this time." Alfred said, in a very determined tone. "This time we're both going to last long enough to actually have sex."

Caden wasn't about to argue with that plan. "Do you have lube?"

Alfred hastily retrieved it from his bedside drawer.

"Shall I?" Caden asked, holding out his hand for it. "Or do you want to?"

Alfred's fingers curled around the tube as if he was horrified by the possibility that Caden would try to steal it and the right to take care of his mate away from him.

Dominant down to the core…

With his lips curving into an easy smile, Caden rolled over onto his stomach, happy to offer his arse to his lover to do with as he pleased. Alfred seemed to lose any sort of inclination to rush, then. He stroked his palm over the full, round muscles, gently squeezing them as he caressed.

Caden looked over his shoulder and blatantly wiggled his backside in invitation. The move made Alfred smile, but it didn't make him hurry the hell up. Pulling one of the pillows forward, Caden bunched it up and rested his head on it, looping his arms around the softness as he finally let all his attempts to control the situation slowly fade away. With his cheek resting on the soft cotton, he had the perfect vantage point from which to observe his new mate over his shoulder.

He really was glorious. Even as Caden watched, he seemed to settle more easily into his newfound role in their relationship. He was in charge and he was thriving on it.

"I didn't try to be a better wolf because you're gorgeous," Alfred suddenly informed him.

Caden peered over his shoulder at Alfred.

The other wolf was still staring at his arse as he caressed him. "I did it because you believed in me."

Caden squirmed under the other man's hand, not sure what to say.

"A pretty face and a fantastic arse aren't your real strong points," Alfred said as he looked up and their eyes met. "It wasn't your flirting that made me want you, it was those times when you forgot to flirt and I saw the honesty in your eyes."

Caden turned his head, half hiding his face in the pillow. In that moment he had the strangest feeling that he looked exactly the same way Alfred looked when he heard words no one had ever bothered to say to him before.

Finally, as the silence stretched out, Alfred slicked his fingers and slid them between Caden's cheeks. His touch was so gentle, so careful, and Caden loved him for taking care with him — even if there was really no need for him to treat him like a scared little virgin.

He tried to be patient and let the other wolf tease and play with him for however long he wanted, he did his best to simply let Alfred's dominance reign, but eventually he had to reach out and put his hand on Alfred's arm.

"I'm as ready as I'll ever be, love." He was careful to just offer the information. There was no demand, no suggestion regarding what the other man might want to do with that knowledge. And there was no attempt to flirt his way into getting what he wanted either.

His restraint was immediately rewarded. Alfred's hands went to Caden's hips and pulled him up so his knees were underneath him. The moment his arse was offered up high in the air, Alfred had the tip of his slicked shaft against Caden's hole.

There was no hesitation. One jerky thrust had Alfred inside him. Caden tensed at the sudden stretch and he felt the atmosphere change as he let out a little gasp.

"I'm sorry," Alfred blurted out. "I..."

"It's fine. I'm fine. And I like it a bit rough," Caden admitted, twisting around and managing to glimpse his mate over his shoulder.

Alfred didn't look convinced.

"With a wolf who I can trust, with a mate who I know would never really want to hurt me more than I enjoy, I like it a bit rough," Caden repeated. Keeping any attempt at manipulation out of his words was damn near the hardest thing he had ever done.

Alfred nodded, very slowly.

Caden dropped his head back to the pillow. As his body relaxed and accepted the other wolf, he nodded, letting Alfred know he was ready for anything his mate wanted to throw at him.

The next thrust made him gasp again. His mate had taken him at his word on his preferences. The following thrust took his breath away completely. He clutched at the pillow as wave after wave of sensation rushed through him, almost too quickly for him to process. His back arched as he closed his eyes and automatically pushed out his arse for more.

Alfred's grip on his hips tightened as his cock pounded deeper into Caden's hole again and again, laying claim to him over and over in the most basic way another man ever could.

Caden's eyes fell closed. All that existed then was pleasure—it existed only when Alfred wanted to provide it, and it was all the more blissful because of that. Caden pushed back into every thrust, desperate to come, and even more desperate to make his mate come deep inside him.

He clenched his hole around the other wolf's shaft, trying to milk the orgasm out of him as best he could. When Alfred reached around Caden and took his cock in a firm grip, he knew neither of them would last much longer.

It barely took a few strokes for Alfred to have Caden howling and clawing at the pillow as he came on his lover's command. Alfred's howl soon blended in with his. The habitual discordant note was completely absent from the other wolf's howl now. The realisation seemed to keep pleasure swirling through Caden's veins for far longer than he had thought possible.

Wave after wave of bliss stormed the shoreline of his psyche, almost breaking it down and washing it away, before he collapsed, exhausted, onto the mattress.

The world was slow and sleepy then. Unable to summon up any desire to move of his own volition, Caden merely allowed Alfred to arrange them as he pleased when the other gamma finally separated their bodies. He soon found himself lying with his head on the other wolf's chest, the world around him gently rising and falling according to a rhythm of Alfred's choosing.

No one spoke for a long time—not until a memory picked that moment to jump up and down in the back of

Caden's mind and demand his attention, regardless of the lethargy in both his body and his brain.

"What did the alphas say to you after the ceremony?" Caden whispered, his voice softer, sleepier and less flirtatious than he ever remembered it being.

Alfred made a vague noise in the back of his throat as he encouraged Caden to curl in more comfortably to his side.

"Just before you got all jealous over me and Talbot," Caden reminded him.

Alfred growled at the memory.

That made Caden smile against his lover's chest, but it didn't completely distract him. "What did they say?" he asked again, being careful to make it a request rather than a demand for information.

"That it's amazing what the love of a mate can do for a wolf," Alfred admitted.

Caden lifted his head. There was just the tiniest touch of uncertainty still in Alfred's eyes.

"They were right, you know. I do love you."

Alfred smiled slightly, but the uncertainty stubbornly stayed put.

"I'm going to keep telling you that every day until you believe me," Caden promised.

"I love you, too," Alfred whispered back, with just the hint of a blush on his cheeks.

"I believe you already," Caden said. "But that doesn't mean I don't want you to tell me every day anyway." There was no flirtation in his voice then. For the first time that he could remember, there didn't seem to be any need for it.

Alfred chuckled as he pulled him down for a kiss. Caden smiled as their lips met. It was just possible that their mating would prove to be the making of them both.

About the Author

Kim Dare is a twenty-seven year old full time writer from Wales (UK). First published in December 2008, Kim has since released over thirty BDSM erotic romances.

While the stories range over male/male, male/female and all kinds of ménage relationships and have included vampires, time travellers, shape-shifters and fairytale re-tellings, they all have three things in common—kink, love and a happy ending.

Kim Dare loves to hear from readers. You can find her contact information, website details and author profile page at http://www.total-e-bound.com

Total-E-Bound Publishing

www.total-e-bound.com

Take a look at our exciting range of literagasmic™
erotic romance titles and discover pure quality
at Total-E-Bound.